Where the Innocent Die

MJ LEE

WHERE THE INNOCENT DIE

CANELO

First published in the United Kingdom in 2020 by Canelo

This edition published in the United Kingdom in 2020 by

Canelo Digital Publishing Limited
Third Floor, 20 Mortimer Street
London W1T 3JW
United Kingdom

A CIP catalogue record for this book is available from the British Library.

Print ISBN 978 1 78863 802 9
Ebook ISBN 978 1 78863 744 2

Look for more great books at www.canelo.co

Printed and bound in Great Britain by Clays Ltd, Elcograf S.p.A.

4.06 A.M

TUESDAY

AUGUST 20

Chapter 1

At four in the morning, Joe Cummings hated the sound of his footsteps on the stairs.

He'd tried wearing different shoes but still the squeak of sole on lino echoed in the dim stairwell.

He reached the second floor and stood next to the heavy door, underneath the welcoming light of the single bulb above it. The keys rattled on the end of the chain hanging from his belt as he brought the largest one up to unlock the door in front of him, checking through the reinforced glass before he did.

You could never be too sure these days. Hadn't Ronnie from the day shift found a woman lurking behind one with a pot of hot water, waiting to throw it on him?

He stepped through, locking it behind him, hearing the click of the key turn in the mechanism. The large sign on the back of the door reminded him constantly of his job.

CHECK IT. LOCK IT.

He stopped for a few seconds to listen.

It was quiet tonight. But if he were honest, it was quiet every night.

In the room on the right, the Iraqi man was coughing continuously. He was claiming a Section 35, but it didn't matter, he was on the list for tomorrow.

In a weird way, Joe would miss him. His continuous coughing always meant there was life behind the closed doors on the second-floor corridor.

He checked his watch.

4.06 a.m.

Just two hours left and he could go home. Back to the warm bed just vacated by the missus. But not before he made the kids their cornflakes and put on a pot of coffee for Andrea. His partner wasn't human until she had her coffee in the morning. If she could, she would take it as a drip attached to the back of her hand. As it was, one pot wasn't enough for her.

Joe looked up at the camera pointing down at him. He considered giving Tony a little wave but by this time in the morning he would be nodding off. They were short-handed again, with Dave calling in sick once more. Tony had volunteered to come in on his day off. When he could have been at home, he was here staring at a bank of cameras. Who could blame him if he dozed off for a second or two?

Absentmindedly, Joe reached up to press his card against the reader on the wall, but stopped just before he did.

These days with these machines, he had to do his rounds religiously. Before if he missed an inspection nobody was none the wiser, but now his boss, known unaffectionately as Tiny Tim, would call him at home demanding to know why the card reader was not displaying a readout and why he had not followed standard operating procedure as laid down in the manual.

Fuck the manual. He was a human not a machine.

He considered missing this one just to wind up Tiny Tim, but decided it wasn't worth the hassle. He didn't need any more demerit points on his record.

He tapped the card against the reader, hearing the electronic beep to show he had registered.

'And bloody beep to you too, mate,' he said out loud, walking down the corridor.

Eight doors on either side meant there were sixteen beds on this floor. He always thought of them as beds rather than as people sleeping on those beds. He wasn't heartless but it was the only way to do the job when the day came for them to leave.

And the day always came.

This place had been called a detention centre until the government in 2014 decided to change the name to Immigration Removal Centre. As they said, to 'give a true indication of the role and function.'

But Joe knew it was just bollocks. He had worked in Strangeways too, and they were the same.

They might call them rooms instead of cells. The inmates might be called detainees not cons. They might be deported instead of released.

But here and Strangeways were the same.

The whole point was to keep people locked up. The only difference as far he could see was this place was far more modern and Strangeways was the arsehole of the world.

Joe stopped.

What was that?

In the subdued lighting of the corridor, he stared hard at number 7.

Was the door open?

The door shouldn't be open. The detainees were locked and secured with lights out at 9.15. Nothing was opened until the morning shift came on at six and went round to let them out after 7.30 a.m.

Why was the door open?

He glanced over his shoulder. A shiver stomped down his spine. It should be locked. Had one of the inmates got out?

He rattled his keys, finding the sound reassuring in the silence on the corridor.

Should he call Tony on his walkie talkie or check it out for himself?

The old bugger was probably sound asleep by now and he would spend the rest of the shift whining if Joe woke him for no reason. The man could moan for Britain at the Olympics. God, he went on and on and on.

Joe took two steps forward.

He was sure the door was open; a dark, black line stood out where there should have been nothing but the door meeting the eau-de-Nil paint of the wall.

He hesitated for a moment and said, 'Is anybody there?' hearing his own voice croak in the middle of the sentence.

No answer.

He tried the light switch on the wall, expecting the neon lights in the room to flicker as they always did, and flash on.

Nothing.

He toggled the switch two or three times, hearing it click, click, click in the silence.

Still nothing.

'Please come out if you are inside.' He heard his voice, firmer now, more commanding.

No answer.

Had someone managed to get out? But the door at the end of the corridor had been locked. He gazed back at it. Yeah, definitely, he had just unlocked it himself.

He pushed the door open slightly, saying out loud, 'Please come out or I will have to come in and get you and you don't want me to do that.'

He took the rubber cosh out of his pocket. They weren't supposed to have these, against standard operating procedure, but all the DCOs carried them. I mean, if you had to face a violent detainee all on your own you had to have some sort of protection, didn't you?

He pushed the door open wider. The dim light from the corridor crept slowly into the room. 'Anybody there?' he asked again, raising the cosh over his head, ready to strike down if anybody rushed him.

There was a strange metallic smell coming from the room. What was it?

He took one step inside the door and stopped.

The light haloed the bloodstained body lying on the bed against the far wall, a deep gash on her throat, red and dripping with blood.

Joe Cummings took one look and turned to retch onto the grey lino of the corridor.

27 DAYS LATER

MONDAY

SEPTEMBER 16

Chapter 2

Detective Inspector Thomas Ridpath was feeling nervous.

He'd just dropped his 10-year-old daughter, or nearly 11 as she never ceased to remind him, outside Altrincham Grammar and watched as she had been swallowed up into the bowels of the school, clutching her BTS pencil case in one hand and her email confirmation in the other.

Before she left, she had waved, saying, 'Bye Dad, take care of yourself,' and then turned and strode away, her ponytail swinging in the early morning light.

There were other parents in the car park too, all equally nervous. After all, it was the day of the entrance exams. The day when the school judged his young daughter to see if she had the right qualities to enter their esteemed establishment.

For the next two hours she would take the verbal, non-verbal and numerical reasoning tests to decide on her admission. They would get the results to see if she was accepted in October.

A test for her, but torture for him.

They had completed all the forms, been to the open day, practised the previous exams at home and now it was all down to Eve and her trusty pencil case.

If it were up to him, he wouldn't have taken it all so seriously, but Eve had insisted. She wanted to go to this school and no other.

Seeing her confidently stride into the building with all the other candidates, he flashed back to her as a baby, giggling happily as she shoved her big toe in her mouth, sucking on it with a smile plastered across her round face.

Where had the time gone? And what had happened to that young child?

He started the engine of the car and gripped the steering wheel. He mustn't get too emotional about these things. Children grow up as they had always done and always would do. He just wished he could have the time back again, just for a moment, when she enjoyed the pleasure of sucking her big toe.

He reversed out of the parking space and headed for the M60 to take him back to the Coroner's Office in East Manchester.

Polly's mum would pick up Eve later and take her back to her primary school where she would be grilled on every question by his wife. He always thought his daughter handled having a mother who was a teacher at her school well. He would have hated it. Not that he was a particularly good pupil. He barely passed his 11+ exam and spent the rest of his time at school playing football, hanging around with the deadbeats and working just hard enough to avoid finishing bottom in the class. His mother exhorted him constantly to do better. 'Don't be like your sister, ending up in jail. She's a bad 'un and you could turn out the same, young man.'

But he hadn't. Instead, after a short time in an insurance office, he had joined the police, working his way through the ranks until he was promoted to be a probationary Detective Inspector and member of the Major Investigation Team of Greater Manchester Police.

And then the cancer had struck.

Bastard myeloma.

A year of worry, drugs, chemo, more drugs, more worry and sitting and watching Alan fucking Titchmarsh day after day, until he was finally pronounced free of cancer just over a year ago.

'But you are never totally free,' a little man in his head would always be whispering. 'It's going to come back. Do you feel tired now? Is your body throbbing? Are your bones aching?'

Always there, always whispering.

He still went every month to have his blood checked and, if he caught a cold or flu in winter, he was supposed to be rushed into Christie's Hospital to spend a few days under observation.

It had nearly cost him his job at Greater Manchester Police. When he was finally in remission, instead of accepting him back into the Major Investigation Team, they had offered him a job as a coroner's officer; same rank, same salary but less stress, they explained. Just temporary, until they could be sure of his recovery.

Why did people always pretend they were doing things for his good and not their own?

He could have just sat back and done nothing, taking the money and getting away with the bare minimum, but that wasn't him. There were still cases to investigate, people to protect, challenges to be faced. And they didn't know about Mrs Challinor, a coroner who believed in what was she was doing and more importantly, believed in him.

He signalled left and accelerated around the round-about, turning immediately left to park next to the Coroner's Court.

He checked his watch.

He was late for the work-in-progress meeting yet again.

Chapter 3

'Ah, you've decided to join us, Ridpath.' Mrs Challinor sat at the head of the table, a pile of case files in front of her.

The office manager, Jenny Oldfield, sat next to her wearing a bright red gingham dress with matching lipstick and eye shadow. On the opposite side of the table sat the senior coroner, Carol Oates, and a locum coroner from Derbyshire, David Smail. Closest to Ridpath was his assistant, Sophia Rahman, who handed him the case list and a latte.

'Sorry, Coroner, it's Eve's school entrance exam this morning. I left you a note about it.'

'I remember those,' Sophia piped up. 'Mum forced me to take four in Manchester before they found a school stupid enough to take me.'

Carol Oates sniffed. 'Can we start, Mrs Challinor? I have to prepare for an inquest tomorrow.'

'Good idea. Let's talk about the Williams inquest, shall we?'

'Eighty-seven-year old man, died in a nursing home in Reddish. No doctor was present so we've decided to hold an inquest.' A slight pause as Carol Oates turned the page in her file. 'The family has accepted the death was from natural causes. The man was suffering from Alzheimer's and prone to outbursts of violence.'

'He wasn't in a secure unit?'

'The family didn't want him there.'

'What do you think, Ridpath?'

'I've not been involved, Mrs Challinor.'

'I didn't believe it warranted an investigation from Ridpath, Coroner. There have been no other deaths in this nursing home. It has a good reputation and there's a long waiting list to get in. A doctor has certified the death as old age exacerbated by the effects of senile dementia.'

'It's your call, Carol, but I'd re-check the data on the deaths. You're ready for the inquest?'

'I will be just as soon as I can review my notes.'

'Good. David, you're handling the Connor case.'

'I am. Not going so well I'm afraid. The family feels the hospital was negligent in their duty of care towards their three-year-old daughter...'

'This is the sepsis case?'

'Yes, Coroner. It was the weekend, and the doctors in A & E missed it and sent her home with some aspirin. She became worse and on Monday the parents took her to their local GP who immediately rushed her to emergency again. Unfortunately, she died two hours after being admitted.'

'The jury is empanelled, Jenny?'

'It is, Coroner. The inquest will take place in court no. 2 tomorrow.'

'Be careful on this one, David, the press is all over it like a cheap suit. I'm certain there will be civil litigation after the inquest. Remember our job is to find why, how and when she died, not to apportion blame. But if you feel the hospital was negligent in any way, we must act to prevent any similar cases occurring again.'

'Yes, Margaret.'

They studied the other extant cases. In any one given week, there were over 150 deaths in the coroner's district of East Manchester. She had to decide which would be further investigated, which would have post-mortems and which necessitated full inquests. It was a non-stop circle of work which the coroner seemed to revel in.

'And finally, there is one of my inquests. I believe I am in court no. 1 on Thursday morning, is that correct, Jenny?'

'You are, Coroner.'

'The jury is ready?'

'It is.'

'Good. I've been reviewing this case and it troubles me. It concerns the death at Wilmslow Immigration Removal Centre of a detainee, Wendy Tang.'

'Immigration Removal Centre?' asked David Smail.

'It's a jail where they house people who have committed no crime other than being in this country,' Sophia spoke before the coroner could reply.

'I hate to tell you, Sophia, but overstaying a visa or being here illegally is a crime in this country,' snapped Carol Oates.

'Like the Windrush Generation? What crime did they commit?'

The coroner held up her hands. 'Ladies, we will not argue these points here. Our only concern is to examine the facts in the case and, as the death occurred while the inmate was in the government's jurisdiction, an inquest is mandated.' She pointed to the file. 'However, the report from the Removal Centre and the subsequent investigation into the death of this woman leaves a lot to be desired. It's as if nobody could be bothered or cared.'

She closed her notebook. 'We have a busy week ahead. Please ensure we do our jobs to the best of our ability and leave our differences…' She stared at both Carol Oates and Sophia, '…at the entrance to this building. Is that clear?'

There was steel, and a threat, hidden in the last question. It produced a mumbled, 'Yes, Coroner' from the two women.

'Ridpath…'

'Yes, Coroner.'

'I'd like you to stay behind for a moment after this meeting if you would.'

Chapter 4

As the others filed out of the room, Ridpath was left in his seat wondering what he had done wrong. Had Mrs Challinor finally had enough of his lateness? Was she going to let him go? Was there a problem he knew nothing about?

Her first question immediately worried him.

'How are you feeling, Ridpath?'

'Feeling? Fine, Margaret. The hospital wants me to go back tomorrow morning for some more tests. Apparently they want to re-check my last blood work.'

Mrs Challinor smiled. 'No, I meant about working here.'

'Still enjoying it. Sophia is working well, handling the bureaucracy and I'm getting better at dealing with the issues of the families. As you know I was never great at breaking bad news. Mr Blunt they used to call me in MIT.'

'Sometimes, it's best to tell people the truth. They always handle honesty better than dissembling or equivocation.' She sat back in her chair. 'Good, I'm glad you're still enjoying the job. And what about the family?'

Ridpath glanced at the clock on the wall. 11.30. Eve would have finished her exam by now. 'Eve's growing up too quickly but Polly is the same as ever, happy I'm managing my work and life balance better and spending more time with her. All in all, life's good at the moment.'

'I'm glad to hear it.' She ran her fingers through her hair. 'And how's the workload?'

Ridpath thought for a moment. Where was this going? 'The workload's fine. Since Sophia has taken over the bureaucracy, form filling and keeping files in order, it's freed me to actually spend more time on cases and with families.'

'No, I meant your workload right now.'

'Not bad. There's the Routledge case to follow up for David. Carol Oates asked me to look into the circumstances of the death of a painter who fell from his ladder, a Mr Robinson. I have my usual weekly meeting with MIT tomorrow morning and I need to find time to go to the hospital, but I suppose I can postpone it until later.'

'No, you need to go if they've asked you. I promised Polly I would never compromise your health. I want you to keep my promise, Ridpath.'

Once again Ridpath felt the women in his life were ganging up against him. First Eve and now Mrs Challinor. 'I will find the time, Coroner.'

'But no work is urgent, right?'

'Nothing I have to get onto this minute.'

'Good.' She pulled out a green file from her desk drawer. 'You heard me talking about the case of Wendy Tang.'

'The woman who committed suicide in the Immigration Removal Centre?'

'That is what everybody is assuming.'

'What?'

'I spent all last night reviewing the case. It's a catalogue of mistakes, compounded by errors and incompetence.'

Ridpath raised his eyebrows.

'The Removal Centre management was more concerned with avoiding blame than anything else, the forensic work perfunctory, the police investigation incompetent at best, while the post-mortem was rushed and unsatisfactory.'

'Pretty damning, Coroner.'

'Even worse, the files for the case only arrived on Saturday, and none of them are conclusive, even though we have had an inquest scheduled for Thursday and the incident occurred nearly one month ago. There are so many holes in the investigation you could drive a Manchester bus through it.'

'It's a detention facility. Security must be tight.'

'One would think so.'

'But if it wasn't suicide, what could it be?'

'I don't know, but after Shipman, I'm not letting assumptions about a death pass on my watch without a proper investigation.'

It was Mrs Challinor's particular nightmare; the coronial system had failed to spot the nearly 300 murders committed by Dr Shipman in Manchester during the 1990s. Even though she was only peripherally involved, Ridpath knew she was determined no such mistakes would ever happen again on her watch.

She paused for a moment, running her fingers through her long grey curls. 'Look, it probably was suicide, but we have a duty to investigate all deaths occurring in government custody.'

There was a silence in the room.

Outside the picture window the wind was blowing through the trees, in the distance the traffic rumbled along the M60, and nearer an ice cream van was playing *Oranges and Lemons* to tempt children to try its cold charms.

Inside, Ridpath finally spoke. 'But you said the inquest was starting on Thursday. It's only three days away.'

'Correct.'

'Can you postpone it?'

Mrs Challinor slowly shook her head. 'I've been in touch with the family. They're looking for answers and closure and flying in from China. We can't waste any more time. It's been over a month already since her death.'

'We haven't released the body to them?'

'It's still in the mortuary. I've asked Dr Schofield to re-look at the post-mortem. He was reluctant at first – you know how doctors are when reviewing the work of one of their colleagues.'

'But he agreed to do it?' Ridpath wasn't surprised given the persuasive powers of the coroner.

Mrs Challinor smiled. 'So while he is re-looking at the medical side, I want you to check the investigation.'

'A wide brief, Coroner.'

'I know.'

'And only a short time to get the work done.'

'I know. But there's more, Ridpath.'

He stayed silent as she stared down at her desk and reached out her long, elegantly manicured fingers to brush a piece of lint which had fallen on her white blotter. 'How many people do you think have died through contact with the police in the last twenty years?'

'I don't know.'

'Guess?'

Ridpath shrugged his shoulders. '25.'

'Since 1990, there have been 1717 deaths following contact with the police; 1102 in custody, 403 in pursuit, 141 in road traffic injuries and 71 by shooting. How many officers do you think have been found guilty of misconduct or negligence?'

'I don't know.'

She formed a big O with her thumb and forefinger. 'Zero. One officer was found guilty of unlawful murder by a coroner's jury in 2011 but he was subsequently cleared during a criminal trial.' She paused for a moment. 'How many people have died at Immigration Removal Centres since the year 2000?'

Ridpath shook his head.

'36. How many of the officers or the companies running these centres have been found guilty of negligence? I'll tell you the answer. Zero, once again.'

'What's the point, Mrs Challinor?'

The coroner pushed her fingers through her hair. 'The point is, Ridpath, it's extremely difficult to discover the truth in these deaths The whole system is designed to prevent it from coming out. From the Home Office, through the Ministry of Justice, to the companies running these Centres and the police investigating deaths.'

'You seem to be suggesting some vast conspiracy, Coroner.'

'No, it's institutional. The system is built to protect itself, not the victims of its actions.'

'Like the Catholic Church and its protection of paedophile priests.'

'Exactly. And closer to home, the people murdered by Harold Shipman.'

'So you're saying we should be careful.'

'We should always be careful, Ridpath. Neither of us are particularly liked by the powers that be. You're too much of a maverick and I'm… well, I'm too involved in my cases for the cold fish at the Ministry.' She ran her fingers through her unruly nest of grey curls again. 'You know I had an email from the family in China asking me what was happening. It was in English but obviously written by a teenager studying the language.' She looked up at him. 'What could I tell them?'

Ridpath didn't answer.

'We don't really look at deaths in custody? We don't care about those who die in Removal Centres? We can't be bothered about these sorts of people because they are classed as illegal immigrants and therefore their lives have no worth? Of course I didn't. I wrote back in the usual bland language we use for these occasions.' She picked up a printout of the email, reading it aloud. '"The UK Coroner Service is committed to finding the truth of any death, particularly when the death occurs while the victim is under the jurisdiction of the British government." I think I later even used the phrase "we will leave no stone unturned". God, I hope the teenager who translates the emails understands the idiom.'

'It's the only thing you could write, Mrs Challinor.'

'And now I've written it, I want it to be true, Ridpath. I want to find the truth of this death, to leave no stone unturned, to find out what actually happened.'

'Even if it leads to the conclusion this woman committed suicide?'

'Of course. For once I want to be able to tell the truth to this family.' She sighed. 'They tell us our job as coroners is to protect people. "An advocate for the dead to safeguard the living," in the current management-speak job description. Well, I am going to do the job despite the objections of those in authority who would try to obstruct me. It's going to be difficult, Ridpath, are you ready to join me?'

Ridpath thought for a moment. 'When and where do we start?'

She passed two thin files across her desk. 'Now, and with these.'

Chapter 5

Ridpath returned to his office carrying the files. In the corridor he was accosted by Carol Oates. He had a feeling she had been waiting for him.

'What was all that about? Very cloak and dagger asking you to stay behind and closing the door.'

'Nothing much, just updating me on a case.'

Carol Oates tucked a stray blonde hair, which had escaped from her immaculate chignon, behind her ear. 'Oh, which case was that?'

'One of the coroner's.' He attempted to pass her in the narrow corridor, but she stepped in front of him.

She continued to play with her hair. 'You know we've been working together for the last year, but we've hardly ever talked. Perhaps we should go for a drink after work, get to know each other better.'

Ridpath stepped around her. 'A great idea. We should bring Sophia along too. You both need to work on working together.'

The smile vanished. 'Your assistant needs to learn how to take instructions, Ridpath, not question my decisions. And a word in your ear.' She leant in closer and lowered her voice, 'The coroner isn't flavour of the month with the Ministry or the Chief Constable. Too awkward, too confrontational, too...'

'Too good at her job?'

'…Too difficult. She needs to be careful and so do you.'

With those parting words, the woman turned and flounced back to her room. Ridpath stood there for a moment before returning to his office where Sophia was waiting for him.

'What did she want? I wouldn't trust that one as far as I could throw up on her.'

'Nothing, but you need to work with her better, Sophia. She's a senior coroner and you're—'

'Just a skivvy.'

'I was about to say an important member of my office whose job it is to work as part of a team.'

'Ok, I get the message, but I still don't like her.'

'You don't have to like her, you just have to work with her.'

She made a moue with her mouth but he knew she understood. In the six months Sophia Rahman had worked for him, she had been brilliant, displaying an intelligence and capacity for work matching Ridpath's own. As a maverick, he recognised the same character in her and felt a bit of a fraud for lecturing her on the strengths of teamwork. But there was a time for individuality in an investigation and now wasn't it.

She handed him a sheaf of papers. 'These are the cases from the weekend. The coroner has already been through them and marked the ones she wants to follow up. I separated them into two piles for you to go over and we can decide what needs to be done.'

'Thanks, can we do them later? I want to read these first.' He pointed to the files.

'Looks like homework from the coroner.'

'It is. The Wendy Tang case and the inquest is starting on Thursday.'

'Not much time.'

He pulled out the chair and opened the first file. 'Give me half an hour.'

She held up her Starbucks mug. 'You want another coffee? I'm going on a caffeine run.'

He shook his head. 'Nah, I'm already wired from the last one. What was in it, rocket fuel?'

'I gave you a triple shot. I figured you needed waking.'

'Thanks. Now can I need a bottle of Valium to calm me down.' He held out his hand, which was trembling slightly. Was that the coffee or something else?

'You've had enough. I'll see if anybody else wants one.'

'Don't forget to ask Carol Oates.'

'I won't, but they don't do poison at Starbucks.'

She closed the door in the office, leaving Ridpath alone with the file.

He scanned the Greater Manchester Police logo at the top of the page and the rest of the document. It was the usual pro forma opened for every case. The investigating officer was a DS Ronald Barnes. The name was vaguely familiar. Had they been on a course together?

Ridpath read the report. The usual bumf about the Police and Criminal Justice Act 1967 was followed by a report disclaimer. 'This statement consisting of (four pages signed by me) is true to the best of my knowledge and belief and I have made it knowing, if it is tendered in evidence, I shall be liable to prosecution if I have knowingly stated in it anything I know to be false or do not believe to be true.'

Ridpath had read a million of these in his time. This one was blunt and to the point, lacking any sort of description or hyperbole.

> Statement of Ronald Barnes
>
> Occupation: Detective Sergeant, A Division, Greater Manchester Police
>
> Number: 43675
>
> Date: 25 August 2019

Interesting, the report was written five days after the event. Was this a particularly slack copper? Usually, these things were written within a day. 'So your memory is still fresh' had been drilled into them again and again at the Training College.

He carried on reading.

> On August 20 at 06:10 hours 1995, I was dispatched to an incident at the Wilmslow Immigration Removal Centre, Old Hall Road, arriving at 06.25 a.m.
>
> On arrival and entrance to the Centre, I was escorted to room 7 on the second floor. Inside was the deceased body of an Oriental woman lying face upwards on a bed. Her throat appeared to have been cut and there was blood all over the bed and floor.
>
> Beside the bed, I saw a knife with a seven-inch blade and bloodstains all along the edge and on the tang.

I immediately called for a forensics team and a pathologist to attend the scene.

Subsequent enquiries revealed this woman to be a detainee at the centre, Wendy TANG (DOB 23.06.93.) The first attending officer on the scene, Constable Martin LAMBIE (PC 7869) had arrived at 4.25 a.m. to find the woman already dead.

The death had been reported by a Detainee Custody Officer, Antony OSBORNE in a phone call to the Response Centre at 4.10 a.m.

The body had been discovered by another DCO, Joseph CUMMINGS at 4.06 a.m.

The duty pathologist, DR AHMED, was called and a scene of crime team arrived at 07:02 hours. Prior to their arrival the room had been closed since the incident and the rest of the inmates detained in their cells.

The following statements were taken and are appended to this document:

Mr Joseph CUMMINGS (DOB 14.6.87) – DCO
Mr Antony OSBORNE (DOB 12.02.73) – DCO
Mr David CARLTON (DOB 08.11.79) – Centre Manager

The pathologist pronounced Ms Tang dead at 07:32 hours. The body was removed to the mortuary for a post-mortem at 08:15 hours.

Room 7 was sealed and remained closed while the scene of crime officers examined the premises for evidence.

Signed and dated. Ronald Barnes (DS, Rowley Station)

Three witness statements, typed and signed, were attached to the case file. Ridpath read them through quickly. They all seemed to confirm the story: the body of a woman was found with her throat slashed and a knife nearby. The police were called. Standard operating procedures for Wilmslow Immigration Removal Centre were followed at all times.

Sometimes the same words were used in the statements, always a giveaway to Ridpath – either the witnesses had been coached what to say or the investigating officer had helped them with the statements.

There were just three other attachments, all written by Ronald Barnes, and one was dated a week later.

Comparison of the fingerprints of the woman whose death was recorded at the Wilmslow Immigration Removal Centre, Ms Wendy TANG, to those of another woman on IDENT1, reveals the woman was previously known as Wendy CHEN aka CHEN Hong Xi (surname in capitals), a native of Shanghai, China.

This information has been added to the databases and the Police National Computer.

Not so uncommon, the dead person having another name. But Ridpath was surprised there was no other information recorded. Why was the woman's name on the PNC?

The second additional page was a summary of the forensic findings.

> The room had many different fingerprints and skin epithelials, not surprising in an institution where inmates come and go into rooms at their leisure. No fingerprints or outside DNA found on the body of Wendy Tang aka Wendy Chen aka Chen Hong Xi. On the knife, only her fingerprints were present.

Ridpath turned to the last page in the file. It was another note from DS Barnes.

> In view of the pathologist's report of suicide, and in the absence of any evidence or witness statements to the contrary, I am able to conclude Ms Wendy Tang aka Wendy Chen aka Chen Hong Xi, a detainee at the Wilmslow Immigration Removal Centre, took her own life in the early hours of August 20th.

> This case file will be now passed to the coroner.

And that was it.

No pathologist's report included. No other witnesses interviewed. No follow-up on who the victim was or why she was living under a different name.

Mrs Challinor was right to have had her suspicions. It appeared DS Barnes was just going through the motions.

Why hadn't he investigated this death properly?

Ridpath reached for the second file and opened it. Here was the pathologist's report. He scanned it briefly. Through the jargon, Latin and medical descriptions, one message stood out loud and clear. In the pathologist's opinion, taking into account the reports of the Centre's staff, Wendy Chen had committed suicide.

The report was two pages long. There was no toxicology, no description of the body save for the wounds she had on her throat, and a perfunctory examination of the vital organs.

Even a layman like Ridpath could see the report wasn't thorough or comprehensive.

It was almost as if both departments, the police and the pathologist, were simply going through the motions.

Was it because they were certain she had committed suicide?

Chapter 6

As Ridpath was thinking about the case, Sophia came back into the office.

'I bought you something healthy from the caff: a bacon and egg sarnie.' She plonked two large doorsteps of white bread with something sandwiched between.

'Which bit of it is healthy?'

'I got you a salad too.' A plastic box of some limp lettuce leaves, a floppy slice of cucumber and a stray tomato appeared next to the bread. 'You should eat it when it's warm, or at least lukewarm.'

'While I make a call, can you take a look at this pathologist's report?' Sophia had studied Biomedical Sciences at university. It was one of the reasons he had employed her. 'We can go over the other cases afterwards.'

'You're gonna give me heartburn, Ridpath.'

He checked the file Mrs Challinor had given him for the Wilmslow Immigration Removal Centre's number. His call was answered after the third ring. 'I'd like to speak to Mr David Carlton, please.'

'He's not here.'

The voice was brusque and offhand. 'Who's in charge at the moment?'

'Pete is.'

'Can I speak to Pete?'

'He's busy doing the rounds.'

'Right. This is the Coroner's Office. I'd like to come and see the Centre this afternoon. It's regarding the inquest on Wendy Tang also known as Wendy Chen.'

'You have to complete the form and book an appointment two weeks in advance.'

'No, I want to come this afternoon.'

'No form, no entry, them's the rules.'

Ridpath took a deep breath. 'And this is the law. You are required to allow the representatives of the coroner onto any government premises for the purpose of their investigations. Any contravention of this law is an offence under paragraph 3 of Schedule 5 of the Coroners and Justice Act 2009, and is classified in common law as obstruction. Do I make myself clear?'

There was a long pause on the other end of the phone.

'Do I make myself clear?'

'I'll have to talk to Pete.'

'Go ahead. I'll be there at three o'clock this afternoon. Goodbye.'

Ridpath placed the phone back on the cradle.

'God, you scared me Ridpath.' Sophia was staring up at him, her mouth open wide.

'Let's hope I scared him more. So what do you think?'

'Of this?' She held up the pathologist's report. 'It's a bit shallow isn't it. Almost as if the man couldn't care. It feels like he reached his conclusions before he even started cutting up the body.'

Chapter 7

Wilmslow Immigration Removal Centre was at the end of a short street close to Manchester Airport. It was housed in one of those four storey government blocks which seemed to proliferate in the 1960s like mushrooms after rain.

Ridpath drove up to the metal gate topped with barbed wire and stopped. A CCTV camera swivelled round to look at his car as he pressed the intercom. 'DI Thomas Ridpath of the Coroner's Office.'

A voice crackled through a tinny speaker. 'We've been expecting you, DI Ridpath. Please park your car in the Visitor parking spot and press the intercom next to the grey door.'

The gates swung open, revealing a large sign with the words *Wilmslow Immigration Removal Centre*, and beneath it in equally large letters, *Managed by the New Hampshire Detention Services, a division of Gentian Worldwide.*

Ridpath drove through and parked his car. The place looked forlorn and empty and sad. There were no windows facing the car park, just a stark grey wall, with a metal shutter guarding the entrance to a loading bay and next to it, a small grey door. The whole place was surrounded by a chain linked metal fence topped with barbed wire.

He walked to the door and pressed the intercom. As he did so, another CCTV camera swivelled round to greet him. 'DI Ridpath again.'

'Please hold your ID up to the intercom camera.'

Ridpath did as he was told using his coroner's ID instead of the one he still had from MIT.

'Thank you, an officer will be down to escort you through the facility shortly.' The voice went dead. Ridpath looked around. The place appeared more like a warehouse than a place where human beings were kept. The only difference was most warehouses weren't surrounded by barbed wire.

The door swung open behind him. 'DI Ridpath?'

He was surprised to hear a woman's voice. For some reason, he had expected all the guards to be male.

'Can I see your ID again?' she asked.

He handed it over and she stared at it and then at him, checking the picture matched.

'Please come in.' She stood aside to allow him to enter and closed the door, locking it with a large set of keys.

A large sign on the back of the door said LOCK IT, CHECK IT in stark capital letters.

'If you could sign in, leaving all your valuables with the reception desk. Please include your mobile phone. We don't allow any photography or video recording in the facility.'

The woman spoke in a monotone but the accent wasn't from Manchester, but somewhere else, somewhere nondescript.

He approached the desk where a burly man wearing a white shirt and tattoos sat behind glass with a row of televisions on his left.

Ridpath stared at them, seeing little pictures of each of the areas in the removal centre. In the centre of the console was a large red button with ALARM written above it.

'If you could walk through the metal detector.'

Ridpath did as he was told, looking upwards and waiting to hear the loud beep indicating metal had been detected.

No sound came.

'I'm afraid the Centre Manager isn't available but he'll try to join us later. I can answer your questions regarding the facility.'

'And your name is...?'

'Lucy Bagnall. I'm the PR manager for New Hampshire Detention Services.' She didn't offer to shake his hand or give him her card. 'How can I help you today?' she said in a tone suggesting help was the last thing she was looking to provide.

'As you know, I represent the coroner investigating the death of one of your inmates...'

'We prefer to call them detainees.'

'...The death of one of your detainees, Wendy Tang also known as Wendy Chen Hong Xi.'

'A most regrettable incident. New Hampshire takes its responsibilities incredibly seriously concerning the welfare, safety and security of our detainees. We ensure each and every person housed in one of our facilities receives the care and attention they need and deserve.'

Ridpath had read the website before he went to the place. The words were exactly the same.

'Can you tell me about the Centre?'

'Of course, come this way.' She opened another door with a large set of keys and Ridpath was in an entrance room with a tiny table in the middle, a television mounted on the wall and industrial grey chairs lined against the far side.

'This Removal Centre has 32 rooms and is classed as a Short-Term Holding Facility, meaning our detainees spend less than one week with us. In fact, most spend less than 48 hours.'

'How long had Ms Chen been in the centre before her death?'

The woman opened a folder she was carrying as if checking the information. 'Miss Chen, or Miss Tang as we knew her, had been with us for two days. She arrived on August 19th and was processed immediately. She had been picked up by UK Immigration Enforcement during a raid in Stockport. She was fast-tracked for deportation and was due to be removed the day of her suicide.'

'Removed to where?'

The woman checked the file again. 'Back to China. Shanghai, I believe.'

'Can we backtrack for a second? You said she had been fast-tracked for deportation. Why?'

'I'm afraid we don't keep that sort of information, Mr...?'

'Ridpath.'

'You'll have to ask Immigration Enforcement.'

Ridpath wrote in his notebook. 'I will. And you also said she had been processed on entry. Can I have a copy of your processing document?'

'Why?'

'I'd like a copy for my files.'

'One was already given to the police.'

It wasn't in the report written by Detective Sergeant Barnes. He would have to find out why. 'I know, but we are a different department. You know how it is.' He was playing his 'I'm just another bureaucrat' card. He hoped it worked.

'I'm afraid I will have to check with my superiors. We are always conscious of our duties under the Data Protection Act regarding confidential information about our detainees. I'm sure you understand.'

He'd had enough of the foreplay. 'I don't actually. I am an officer of the court investigating the death of a young woman while under the protection of the British government. All information that would help in my investigation should be made available to me. I could subpoena the documents. I'm sure your director and his management in America would not enjoy being accused of withholding information. And particularly when the story appears in the British newspapers.'

Ridpath smiled as he watched the woman's eyes flicker left and right as she processed this information. Which was better, to continue to stonewall him and risk the wrath of her bosses or keep to her story about Data Protection Laws?

Self-interest finally won out.

'As we have already provided this information to the police and you are an officer of the court, I will try to make a copy before you leave today.'

'Thank you. And now can I see the place in which the woman died.'

'Of course, come this way.'

She unlocked the door and Ridpath was faced with a flight of stairs leading upwards. 'This is the ground floor.

Our detainee rooms are on floors two and three. The ground floor also contains the Control Centre, the visitor's room which you have just seen...'

'Do you get many visitors?'

'No, most detainees are not here long enough to receive visitors.'

'And you do have a two week notice period for visits.'

'The regulation only applies for official visits,' she replied with an unconvincing smile. 'Requests from relatives of detainees are processed much faster in accordance with the Short-Term Holding Facility Statutory Rules of 2018, number 409. I am sure you are aware of this legislation?'

Ridpath nodded his head, writing a mental note to himself to check the rules later.

'As I was saying, the ground floor also contains the Control Centre, the visitor's room and a staff rest room. While the first floor has the detainee processing centre and a twenty-four hour medical facility.'

She walked up the stairs with Ridpath following her closely.

'Was the medical centre in operation at the time the woman died?'

'I'm afraid it wasn't. We have difficulty attracting trained nursing staff to work unsocial hours, but we have an arrangement with a doctor to be on call 24/7.'

'And was he called on the night of her death?'

They reached another door on the second floor which she unlocked. 'I'm not sure, Mr Ridpath, I can check if you want.'

The door swung open slowly. On the reverse side was another sign with the letters, 'LOCK IT, CHECK IT.'

'Please do. And it's Detective Inspector Ridpath.'

'I thought you were a coroner's officer?'

'I'm also an officer of Greater Manchester Police.'

The door clanged shut as she locked it. Ahead, Ridpath could see a long grey corridor with numbered doors on either side. An uneasy feeling crept from his stomach up through his chest. He instinctively found himself holding his breath as if the simple act of breathing in this place would somehow infect him with despair.

And then he knew why he was having such a strong reaction. The place reminded him of the isolation ward after his chemo – the sense of sheer terror combined with profound loneliness.

He forced himself to listen as the PR Manager carried on talking as they walked down the corridor.

'...Room 7 is the fourth on the right. We have kept it unoccupied since the incident.'

The only background sound to her words was the hum of air conditioning.

'Where is everybody?' he asked.

'Normally from 8 a.m. to 9.15 p.m. the detainees are allowed out of their rooms. On the fourth floor there is a television room, washing facilities, a reading room and a general relaxation area. But as you wanted to inspect the facility, we decided to lock the detainees into their rooms. We couldn't risk your safety by having them wandering around.'

'My safety?'

'Detective Inspector Ridpath. This is an immigration removal centre. There are three reasons why people are here. They have overstayed their visas, they have entered the UK illegally or they have broken the law, served their sentence and are awaiting deportation back to their home country. About half our inmates are in the latter category.' She stopped outside a door. 'This is Room 7.'

She opened the door. The room was small but tidy and showed no signs of a person dying inside. The walls and floor had been cleaned, the bedsheets replaced and a new lamp, still wrapped in plastic, stood on the bedside table. On the left, a clean paper band covered the lowered seat of a toilet. On the band the words 'Disinfected' were printed in bright purple block letters.

'Of course, we had to clean it after your forensics people left. We were given permission by the investigating officer.'

'Detective Sergeant Barnes?'

'Correct.'

'Ms Chen was discovered by one of your guards on his rounds just after 4 a.m.?'

'She committed suicide sometime in the early hours. Our Detainee Custody Officers do their rounds each hour. They have to register on each floor by swiping their card on the reader. The information is recorded on the computer.'

Ridpath didn't say anything at the presumption the death was suicide, asking another question instead. 'But the guard on the earlier round saw nothing?'

'Correct. He signed the logbook at 3.15 saying everything was quiet.'

Ridpath walked into the room and looked around. It stank of disinfectant, but other than the smell, it could have been a room you would find in a student hall of residence. 'So the guard, a Mr Cummings, discovered the body at 4.06 a.m. and he immediately called the police and the ambulance?'

The woman stayed at the entrance to the door. 'No. He immediately called the control centre which you saw on entry. They called the emergency services.'

'Can I talk to the guards who were here that night?'

'I'm afraid none of them are on duty this week. We have given them time off to prepare for the evidence on Thursday at the Coroner's Court. But they are in the Centre receiving training. I'll contact them just as soon as we finish our tour.'

Ridpath wondered what sort of training they were receiving. 'Can you give me the home addresses, tele-phone numbers and personnel files of all your staff?'

'I'm afraid I don't have the information. You will have to ask our HR department.'

'Could you do it? You know them better than I do. And you did say you were here to help in any way possible.'

There was a long sigh from the PR woman. 'I'll see what I can do. Now, if you've finished here, I can show you the common areas.'

Ridpath nodded. Just before they left the room, he stopped. 'One more question: the witness report for Joseph Cummings says he noticed the door was open. How did that happen if all detainees are locked in their rooms at 9.15 each evening?'

'We don't know, Inspector. We've mounted a thorough investigation of our own and we can only put it down to human error. Somebody forgot to lock this door.'

'A coincidence though, don't you think? The one unlocked door is the one to a room where a woman dies?'

'I agree, Inspector, a coincidence. Now if you would like to see the rest of the facility.' She held out her arm to show him the way.

He spent the next half hour being shown around the other floors. The whole place had a soullessness Ridpath found deeply depressing. Plus there was a lingering feeling of human sadness infused in everything: the walls, the chairs, even the curtains.

Finally, after thirty minutes, he was taken back to the control centre. 'Can I see the CCTV for that evening?'

'The tapes were given to the police. We don't keep copies.'

'Not even for your files?'

The woman looked down. 'Not that I am aware.'

A classic politician's non-answer. He would have to dig more deeply.

'If you're now finished, Inspector, I have to get back to my day job. The work is piling up.'

She was rushing him and trying to make him feel guilty for dragging her away from her warm, comfortable office and her important work. For Ridpath, such tactics were like water off a swan's back. 'Just a few more questions, I'm sure your work will still be there when you get back. Where did the knife come from?'

'What knife?'

'The one found in the room.'

The woman shrugged her shoulders. 'I don't know. It wasn't one of ours.'

'So it would have been smuggled into the facility?'

'I don't speculate, Mr Ridpath. That's the job of the police.'

Unfortunately, a job they had done particularly badly, he thought but did not say. 'I would have thought the presence of a knife on one of their facilities was a matter of concern for New Hampshire Detention Services?'

'Not my concern, Mr Ridpath. I deal solely with the public relations matters for the company. I presume other people are investigating how the knife came to be here.'

'And who would they be?'

'The Security Head, Mr Collins, working with the Facility Manager, Mr Carlton.'

'Can I get their numbers and files too?'

'I already gave them to the police.'

Ridpath wrote the names in his notebook. 'If you could add them to the other things you are photocopying for me.'

Ms Bagnall sighed again. 'Anything else, Mr Ridpath?'

He checked his notes. 'Are Mr Collins and Mr Carlton here today?'

She nodded. 'They are in training too.'

'Could I interview them both after the guards?'

'I'll ask but I'm not sure they are available.'

'It would be a great help if they were, otherwise they are going to have to come all the way to the Coroner's Office to chat with me.'

She exhaled. 'Anything else?'

'Just one more question. Which detainees were in the room on either side of Room 7, and could I speak to them?'

'I don't know who they were, but I doubt whether you could speak to them.'

'Why is that?'

'As I have already explained, this is a Short-Term facility. The... incident... happened a month ago. Those detainees would have been deported or sent to another Centre if their deportation from the country had been postponed.'

Ridpath nodded. 'I would like to see a list of detainees, where they were staying in the facility and where they were moved or deported to.'

The woman shook her head. 'Do you know how much work would be involved in your request? It would mean checking the files of 32 different detainees...'

Ridpath nodded. 'The information would be useful in my investigation, Ms Bagnall. You could provide it for me or I could ask the coroner to subpoena your Managing Director to appear at the inquest on Thursday to explain its absence.'

She held up her hands in mock surrender. 'OK, OK, I'll find the information for you even though it's going to take me hours.'

'And send me all the other things I have requested.'

She nodded. 'I will try to email you as much as I can.'

'This evening?'

'As soon as I can.'

'I'm sure you appreciate the urgency of the request, Ms Bagnall, as the inquest starts on Thursday.'

'I will email you as much as I can... this evening.'

'Now, if I could interview the guards who were on duty at the time of the incident?'

Another roll of the eyes. 'Of course, but we prefer to call them Detainee Custody Officers.'

'Of course you do. So can I see them? And afterwards, the Centre Manager and Security Officer.'

'I'll see if they are available.' She pointed to a room on the left. 'If you would like to go into the room over there, I'll bring them to you.'

Ridpath strode towards the door marked Staff Room. He'd had enough of the PR. Now was the time for the real investigation to begin.

Chapter 8

The grey carpet had large coffee stains and the place stank of stale McDonald's. In the corner, a kettle was surrounded by used coffee mugs and opened jars of coffee and Coffee-mate.

If anything, the staff room was even more depressing than the Removal Centre itself. Ridpath sat in one of the armchairs and it squealed loudly under his weight.

The door opened and two men dressed in white shirts, black ties and black trousers walked into the room accompanied by Lucy Bagnall.

'These are the men who were on duty on the night of the demise of Ms Tang.' She pointed to the man on her left. 'This is Joe Cummings, who discovered the body, and this is Tony Osborne, who was in charge of the CCTV that night.'

Ridpath shook both men by the hand. 'My name is Ridpath, Detective Inspector Ridpath, I'm the coroner's officer for East Manchester and I'm conducting an inquiry on behalf of the coroner, Margaret Challinor.'

'Is she the person we'll be seeing on Thursday?' asked Joe Cummings.

'She'll be heading the inquest.'

'What do you want?'

'I'm here to ask you some questions, Mr Osborne.'

'We've already been asked thousands of questions by the police. I'm fed up of answering questions.' He turned to Lucy Bagnall. 'Do I have to answer more questions?'

'I'm afraid so, Tony. We have to assist the coroner, but after Thursday, you'll be done.'

Tony Osborne scowled. 'Right. Get on with it.' He sat in an armchair. 'I'm giving up my break to answer more bloody questions.'

Ridpath sat opposite him, looking at Lucy and Joe Cummings. 'Mr Osborne has decided he wants to be questioned first. If you could leave us, I'd like some privacy.'

'But my boss told me to be present at all the interviews.'

'I need to talk to these men privately now. Or I could do these interviews more formally at the police station.' Ridpath crossed his fingers hoping she wouldn't put up a fight. 'I'll only be fifteen minutes,' he added gently.

'Can we get started?' interjected Tony Osborne.

'Fifteen minutes?' said Lucy Bagnall.

'Twenty tops,' replied Ridpath, buying time.

'OK, I'll be outside if you need me, Tony.'

She left the room with Joe Cummings in tow.

Ridpath took out his notebook and clicked his pen. 'Now, your name is Tony Osborne?'

'She just told you.'

Ridpath ignored the rudeness. 'How long have you worked at the Immigration Removal Centre, Mr Osborne?'

'Two years, three months.'

'And before?'

'I was at HMP Forest Green near Warrington.'

'Why'd you move?'

'Closer to home. I got sick of the travelling. And New Hampshire pays better.'

'You always work in prisons? I can see from the tattoo you were in the Paras.'

'Yeah, did my time.'

'Where?'

'Northern Ireland, Gulf War.'

'Tough places.'

'It weren't no cake walk. You serve?'

Ridpath shook his head. 'Never did. The old man, now he was a Para, jumped over Normandy and the Rhine during World War Two. Never forgot it.'

Tony Osborne sat forward, and for the first time his attitude softened. 'Brave man, jumping out of the arse end of a plane with a bunch of Germans shooting all shades of shite out of you.'

'Aye, he was.' Ridpath stared down at his feet. The closest his old man got to jumping out of a plane was in his dreams. He had been seconded to an Anti-Aircraft Battery during the war. The most fighting he ever did was in the pub on a Saturday night. But Tony Osborne didn't know that.

'In your own words, can you tell me what happened on the night of August 19th and morning of the 20th?'

'I've said all this to the police, twice already.'

'I know, just bear with me. You know what it's like. I have to go through with this otherwise my boss gets the hump. Bloody bureaucrats, hey.'

'Standard operating bloody procedures.'

'Don't I know about it. Anyway, what happened?'

'It was a quiet night until four o'clock. Joe went out to do his round. About five minutes later, he called me on the radio, screaming blue murder.'

'What did he say?'

'Just shouting about blood, lots of it.'

'And what did you do?'

'Honest?'

Ridpath nodded. 'It helps.'

'Never had a suicide before, not on my watch. So I checked the manual and rang my manager.'

'You didn't ring the police or ambulance?'

'That was next. The manual says ring the Centre Manager first.'

'Then what happened?'

'Like I said, after calling him, I rang the emergency services, told them there had been a suicide at the Removal Centre and they said an emergency team and the police would arrive shortly.'

'Did you go to the room?'

'No.'

'Why not?'

'I have to stay in the control centre otherwise nobody can get in.'

'The Emergency Team arrived when?'

'At 4.25. I allowed them to enter and they went to the room, but she was already dead.'

'Who showed them to the room?'

'I did.'

'Where was Mr Cummings?'

'In the control centre.'

'So he returned to the control centre after leaving the room?'

'Yeah, he was pretty shook up. Didn't want to stay anywhere near the place, I guess.'

'So it was left unwatched?'

'Yeah, well she wasn't going anywhere, was she?'

'OK, what about the CCTV? Ms Bagnall tells me it wasn't working outside Room 7 that evening.'

'A lot of the cameras aren't working. They disconnect them.'

Ridpath frowned. 'Who disconnects them?'

'The detainees. Sometimes they don't want us to watch.'

'Why?'

'Because like all cons, they've got their scams going on. Should lock 'em up longer, I think. Like a bloody hotel this place is.'

Ridpath ignored him. 'Why do you believe it was a suicide?'

'What else could it be? A woman cuts her throat. Doesn't want to go home, does she? They don't like being deported, most of them have got nothing to go back to.'

'A couple more things. Joe Cummings says the door was open when he was doing his rounds at 4 a.m. It was how he discovered her.'

'Yeah, I know, that's what he told me too.'

'How could it have been open? I thought all the detainees are locked in their room at 9.15 p.m.'

'They are. I did my rounds at 3 a.m. and I'm pretty sure it was closed then.'

'Pretty sure?'

'I don't know. If I tell the truth, by that time in the morning I'm pretty bushed and it was supposed to be my day off.'

'But you were working?'

'Yeah, we're always short-staffed. But in the early hours of the morning, I'm not paying much attention, just making sure I swipe my card and trying to get the round over as quickly as I could. I was starving.'

'Last question before you go. Did you speak to the Chinese woman?'

'Wendy Chen?'

Ridpath nodded.

'Nah, why would I speak to any of them except to tell them what to do?'

Ridpath closed his file. 'Thanks, you can go now.'

Tony Osborne got up to leave. 'You'll be there on Thursday at the inquest?'

'Probably.'

'See you then.'

As Osborne left the room, Ridpath reached for his notebook. If Osborne hadn't talked to the dead woman, how did he know her real name?

Chapter 9

The interview with Joe Cummings was just as short. He confirmed all the timings given by Tony Osborne, only adding a little more detail about why he left the woman alone.

'Well, there was blood everywhere, wasn't there? And she was lying in her bed with a gash in her throat and I saw her eyes and I just couldn't stay there any longer. I suppose I should have stayed with her, but she were dead, weren't she?'

Ridpath had to clarify one point from the police report. 'You told the police the door to Room 7 was open?'

'Right. I noticed the difference in the colour...'

'The difference in the colour?'

'A thick, black line. The door should be tight to the jamb. It wasn't.'

'Pretty good at that time of night.'

'I'm a bit of a night owl.'

'So you went in...?'

'Yeah, wish I hadn't now. Should have let some other idiot discover it.'

'Who was responsible for locking all the doors on the second floor?'

'After we do the count at 9 p.m., they all go back to their rooms...'

'The detainees?'

'...And we lock them in. I did the lock up for the second floor and Tony did the third floor that night.'

'You're sure?'

'Definite. And I'm also sure I locked all the doors on my floor.' He stared into mid-air for a long while. 'But I can't have done, can I?'

'One last question. Did you ever speak to the woman?'

'Well, I came on at six and I remember seeing her sitting all alone in the Recreation Room, just staring at the wall.'

'So you didn't talk to her?'

'I did. I asked her if she was OK. But she didn't answer me, didn't even turn around to look at me. Sometimes, they get like that, especially when they are about to be deported. Best to leave them alone.'

Just then Lucy Bagnall burst into the room.

Chapter 10

'I'm sorry to bother you, Inspector, but if you want to see Mr Carlton and Mr Collins it has to be now. They have to leave in ten minutes.'

Ridpath peered across at Joe Cummings. The man's hands were trembling and a sheen of sweat glistened on his forehead. Was he telling the truth? He would have to follow up later. 'Thank you, Ms Bagnall, I've finished with Mr Cummings.'

The custody officer stood, shook Ridpath's hand and was out of the room in a few seconds. Lucy Bagnall returned a minute later with David Carlton and Stuart Collins.

Ridpath shook their hands and asked them to sit. It was Collins who spoke first, the bright lights of the staff room reflecting off his bald head. 'So you're a DI? I was the same, but in West Mercia.'

'When did you leave the job?'

The bald-headed man nodded. 'Must be three years ago now. Don't miss the shifts or the bloody weekends on call. Which division are you in?'

'I'm attached to the Coroner's Office at the moment.'

Collins nodded his head. 'You seem a bit young to be doing the job, plus it's not usual for somebody of your rank.'

Ridpath wasn't going to go into long explanations with this man. He checked his watch. 'If you've only got ten minutes, we'd better get started.' He turned to the man. 'Your name is David Carlton?'

'Correct.'

'Take me through the events of August 19th and 20th.'

'Not a lot to say.' Carlton loosened his tie. 'I was called at home by Tony Osborne at 4.08 in the morning. He said there had been a suicide in the centre.'

'He called it a suicide?'

'Yes.'

'Go on.'

'That's all really. I arrived around 4.40 but following standard operating procedure, Osborne kept the medical team and the police in the control room area.'

'What if somebody were dying?'

'In the case of suicide, it is the procedure detailed in the manual. I took the emergency services to the room but the woman was already dead. The detective arrived at 6.20 or thereabouts I think.'

'Did you go in the room?'

'No. I let the emergency services handle everything.'

'Mr Carlton, your custody officer, Joe Cummings, told me the door to Room 7 was open. How is that possible?'

'I don't know. Cummings was supposed to have locked it the previous evening. He has received demerit points for his dereliction of duty.'

'Could anybody have entered the room when it was unlocked?'

'Impossible.'

'Why?'

'All the other doors were locked at both ends of the corridor and for each individual room.'

'Thank you. And now Mr Collins…'

The armchair creaked loudly as the sat back and relaxed.

'But just one more question, Mr Carlton. Why was the CCTV outside Room 7 not working?'

'I don't know, but there were six cameras out of order that night. It's the bloody detainees, they keep pulling the wires out. Costs us a fortune to get them fixed. You should see my maintenance bills…'

'Could I see the tapes from then?'

'I'm sure we have them somewhere, don't we, Stuart?'

'We sent them over to the police,' replied the security manager.

'But you kept copies?'

'Of course, never send anything to the police without keeping a copy. Most nicks are like black holes: stuff vanishes inside and never comes out.'

'Could you send me the tapes?'

'Sure, I'll dupe them off for you. But be warned, there are a lot.'

'Thank you. Were you in the Centre that day?'

'No, I was in London at a meeting, didn't get back until two days later.'

Ridpath made a note in his book to check this later. 'And the knife, how do you think it got into the Centre?'

He shrugged his shoulders. 'I don't know, but the woman must have smuggled it in with her.'

'Was she searched on entry?'

'Of course, it's part of our procedures when any detainee is processed.'

'But still she managed to bring it into the Centre.'

A long pause. 'We've tightened up our processing procedures since the… incident. Now, all detainees are searched twice before they are allowed in the Centre.'

'Bit like closing the door after the horse has bolted.'

'It is, but it's all we can do.'

Ridpath closed his notebook and put his pen back in his top pocket. 'Well thank you, gentlemen. I won't keep you any longer.'

He held out his hand, which was grasped firmly by Collins. He felt a strange pressure in his palm as the man said, 'I'm a good friend of the Assistant Chief Constable, Dave Downton. You should join us for a round of golf one day.'

The pressure on Ridpath's palm increased. Was this man a mason? Then the handshake was released and Collins said, 'I'm sure I could square it with the club.'

'Sorry, I'm not a golfer,' replied Ridpath, putting his hand back into his pocket.

Lucy Bagnall escorted him back downstairs to the Control Centre, leaving the two men in the staff room. 'I haven't had time to find the things you wanted. I'll email them across to you when I've compiled them.'

'When will that be?'

'By tomorrow morning at the latest. You must realise Inspector Ridpath I have other work to do.'

'Anything more important than the death of a young woman in the custody of your Centre?'

The woman stayed silent.

'No, I thought not. Thank you for your help and for escorting me around the facility. I'll look forward to seeing the information ASAP.'

Ridpath was met with a cold face as he was given back his mobile phone, his car keys, his wallet and loose change, and shown out of the facility.

'Thank you, Miss Bagnall.'

The door closed.

As it did, Ridpath's body relaxed as if he had been holding his breath all the time he was in there.

He inhaled a vast lungful of Manchester air.

He had never been happier to cough it back up.

Chapter 11

As his tour of the Centre finished at 5.30, Ridpath decided to go home instead of driving all the way back to the Coroner's Office.

On arrival, he went straight up to see Eve in her bedroom. 'How did it go?'

'Pretty good.'

'Is pretty good, good or just OK?'

She thought for a moment, her black hair falling across her eyes as she twisted her head. 'It means pretty good, Dad. Go ask Mum, she knows more about this stuff than me anyway.' With that, she put her headphones back on and continued watching her iPad.

His wife was in the dining room, her books spread all over the table as she wrote her lesson plan. He asked her the same question. 'How did it go?'

'Pretty good.'

'Is this a wind-up? Did you two get together and decide, "Dad's had a difficult day, let's make him even more stressed"?'

Polly rose from the table and put her arms round his neck. 'You've had a bad day?'

'Visited an immigration removal centre. Not a good place, made my skin crawl.'

'I've heard bad things about those places in the Chinese community. People have done nothing wrong and get locked up.'

'It's worse. So how did she do?'

'I thought you didn't care?'

'Well, I don't but if she's going to do these tests, I want her to do well.'

'Look, you can never tell, but knowing your daughter, if she said she did OK, it meant she aced the exam. She's not one for exaggeration.'

'Unless she's talking about the singing abilities of BTS.'

'True. I brought a takeaway from Marks and Sparks, one of their meal deals, came with a free bottle of crappy wine. You hungry? Eve's already eaten.'

'Ok, what is it?'

'Chicken fried rice with a side order of broccoli and corn. Looks better than the stuff we used to serve in my dad's restaurant.'

They had met twelve years ago in the restaurant when Polly was a waitress and Ridpath needed a lining of carbohydrates before a night out with his mates. They had been together ever since; for richer, for poorer, in sickness and in health. Without Polly, Ridpath would never have made it through the endless rounds of hospital stays, chemo and the rainbow of different pills he had to take. She was his rock, his pillar, his prop forward in the battle against the cancer. It had put so many strains on his marriage, even leading to a separation for six months, but in the end, it had brought them closer, made them stronger.

'I'll put it in the microwave to heat up.'

'Great. I'm off down the Horse and Jockey later, quiz night.'

She took her arms from around his neck and walked through to the kitchen, shouting over her shoulder. 'You going to lose again?'

He followed her. 'Nah, Dave's back so at least we'll have music covered. Those bloody students have to screw up one night.'

She pricked the top of the packet with a fork and popped it in the microwave. 'Do they? When was the last time you beat them? Six months ago, wasn't it? And only because you had the ringer from University Challenge.'

'Don't worry, we have a strategy tonight.'

'What? You're going to give the correct answers?'

'Something like that. You want me to open the wine?'

'Yeah, I need a glass. Oh, and there's one more thing.'

Ridpath looked up from twisting the screw top off the bottle.

'Your daughter is going on strike this Friday.'

'Strike?'

'The school strike stuff for the planet. Her and her mates want to join the demo in Manchester.'

'Isn't she a bit young for that stuff?'

'She's ten going on twenty-seven, Ridpath. She makes me feel young sometimes. But I wouldn't stop her. It could be more than your life's worth.'

He poured out two glasses as the microwave hummed noisily. 'Wouldn't dream of it. I'm kind of chuffed she's thinking of something other than herself.'

'Good, I'll tell her you approve.'

He handed one glass to Polly and took a sip of his own wine, wincing as he tasted its sourness. 'But let her know, if I have to come and bail her out of the nick, she's going to get her arse tanned.'

Chapter 12

Yang May Feng was scared.

She hadn't left the flat for five days now, not daring to go out in case she met him again. Even in the last month, she could count on the fingers of her hand the number of times she had been outside.

But at least she was safe here. Nobody knew about this place.

It belonged to one of her customers, the one who was back in Hong Kong and only came to Manchester every couple of months. She had taken his spare keys and made copies one evening when he was snoring loudly after drinking too much at the club.

And now she was here alone.

The last of the packet noodles lay empty on the table. The fridge was bare, the shelves empty, not even a leaf of tea remained.

Could she take the risk and go out to get some food?

What about money? If she went to the ATM, how much would be left? She was sure there was less than nothing.

She had to do something and soon. Her next payment was due on Wednesday and if she didn't go to work, how was she going to pay them?

She checked the front door was bolted and all the windows were closed, going through all the rooms once again after she had finished.

But still she felt uneasy.

She crept into bed and pulled the covers up to her neck, listening to the sounds of the night as they cut through the silence.

A dog barking. The clack, clack, clack of mah-jong tiles being mixed – swimming, the Chinese called it. Two doors away a couple was arguing, the woman yelling at her stupid pig of a husband.

A sharp sound off to the left.

Was somebody trying to get into the flat? She picked up the knife and hid it beneath the covers, close to her chest.

She listened.

No other sounds.

Silence, but no peace.

Did he know where she was?

TUESDAY

SEPTEMBER 17

Chapter 13

Ridpath was early for the weekly Major Investigation Team meeting, managing to grab something resembling coffee and a cheese toastie from the canteen before it began.

He had been up bright and early, making breakfast for Eve and coffee for Polly. Eve was her normal chatty self.

'What are you going to do today?'

Silence.

'Do you have PE?'

The crunch of cereal.

'I've made a sandwich for your lunchbox.'

'Hmmph.'

'Is that good or bad?'

'Hmmmph, hmmmmph.'

He was used to her inability to talk for the thirty minutes after she awoke. Often he asked her questions just to see if she would engage with him.

She never did.

Polly, on the other hand, was a bundle of energy. Flustered energy but energy nonetheless.

'Where's my lesson notes?'

'Can you pick up the dry-cleaning?'

'Have you seen my necklace? You know the one I always wear in September.'

'What happened to the toothpaste?'

A series of random questions fired off as she rushed around the house without any expectation of an answer.

Ridpath finally packed them both off in the car to go to school, leaning in just before they left.

'We won last night.'

'The quiz?'

'Yeah, I answered four questions correctly, including one on Chinese history.'

'What happened to the students?'

'We slayed them.'

'You mean they didn't turn up?'

'Something like that.'

'Ok, we'll celebrate with something from the chippy this evening. See you later.'

And with a wave they were both off to school, leaving Ridpath free to drive to his meeting.

As he entered with his cheese toastie and the hot liquid resembling coffee, he noticed the meeting room was already packed but he only knew a few of the people. The department had changed considerably since it was run by John Gorman and Charlie Whitworth.

In his head, Ridpath made a sign of the cross for Charlie, killed by Terry Dolan in a fireball two months ago. He still thought of him every day. He supposed he always would, particularly when he spent so much time in their old offices.

'All right, let's be having you.' Detective Superintendent Claire Trent stood at the front of the room and immediately everyone quietened or scurried back to their seats. 'Before we start, there are a couple of announcements. You may notice DCI Lorraine Caruso is not with us today. I'm delighted to announce she has been promoted to Head of Force Liaison, starting immediately. I'm sure you'll all wish Lorraine a great time in her new job. I will be announcing the new operational head of the department in due course. Until then, I will manage it myself. Secondly, before we go through the active caseload, I've asked DCI Dawson from the ridiculously named TITAN squad aka the North West Regional Organised Crime Unit to talk to us about the rise of Albanian gangs in Manchester. This is a growing threat as they have expanded out of London and the South East in the last few years.' She turned to the tall, austere man on her left. 'If you'd like to start, Paul.'

'Thanks, Claire. Titan is a bloody stupid name for what we do, chosen by the mob in London, but it's a deadly serious job. The National Crime Agency has estimated £90 billion of black money is laundered through the UK every year, 4% of the country's GDP. London has become the global capital of money-laundering and the beating heart of European organised crime. English is now the international underworld's lingua franca and crime is an essential part of the British economy, providing hundreds of thousands of jobs, not just for professional criminals – the NCA reckons there are 4,629 organised crime groups in operation – but for prison officers, lawyers and court officials, and security businesses employing more than half a million people. Not to mention ourselves, of course.'

The detectives dutifully laughed.

He stopped for a moment and gazed out over the assembled heads.

'Now knife crime is deadly serious, but the real villains don't go around with blades. Organised crime is run like any other business, and its leading figures look like every other broker or tycoon. It's become "anonymised" crime. The underworld has become the overworld.'

Harry Makepeace sitting next to Ridpath leant over and whispered, 'Far too deep for me, I just stick the bad 'uns in the nick.'

'Britain was once dealing with drug imports from half a dozen countries; now it is more than thirty. A young person who would in the past have sought an apprentice-ship in a trade or industry may now find drug dealing offers better career prospects. And, apart from drugs and guns, gangs now facilitate the trafficking of women from eastern Europe and Asia for prostitution and children from Vietnam as low-level drug workers. Pretty much all of the National Crime Agency's most significant operations now involve people, commodities or transferring money across international borders. Sometimes all three at the same time. The container lorry harbouring forty illegal immigrants may also hide drugs and arms.'

A detective put her hand up. 'But as a force, sir, we tend to deal with crimes in departments: vice or drugs or people trafficking. Won't these new gangs make that a waste of resources?'

'Silly girl, you've just killed your career,' Makepeace whispered, 'don't make the case for a National Police Force, not in GMP.'

'Great question – to combat the gangs, we have to change our structure and operations. For example, the Albanians. There are currently around 700 Albanians in British jails. The UK criminal has a get-rich-quick mentality while the Albanians' strategy was get-rich-slow. Originally based in the East End of London, they are gradually expanding to Manchester, Birmingham, Liverpool and Glasgow.'

'But won't they come up against the existing gangs in those places?'

'But that's where they have been clever in the last few years. They have formed alliances with other gangs – the homegrown mobs, the Chinese, the Vietnamese and others – particularly in the cocaine and people-trafficking crimes. It helped that their reputation preceded them. The Albanian criminals may be ruthless and potentially murderous when controlling their organised crime, but when it came to the UK, they tried to be more amenable – "We're here, we need to get on," that sort of approach. To sum up, the Albanians are coming here and when they do, these gangs will require a different set of skills to deal with the threat. Skills we have been frankly slow at developing in Britain. Any questions?'

Everybody kept their hands down. Ridpath could see the woman DS was desperate to ask another but didn't. She had more sense.

'Well, if there's no more, thank you for your time. I know you're busy at the moment, but these updates are important. Crime is changing every day, so be careful people.'

There was a short round of applause before Claire Trent returned to her feet.

'Right, thank you, Paul. I want you all to keep a look out for these thugs. Tap your grasses and put a bit of pressure on. I want to nip these bastards in the bud before they get a foothold in Manchester. Right?'

There were murmured grunts and nods from the assembled detectives.

'It's nice to see such enthusiasm for your jobs. I want to hear it.' She held her open palm against her ear.

'Right, boss.'

'Will do.'

'On it.'

'Report back at next week's meeting. And woe betide anybody who doesn't have something for me, even if it's just a sniff of some rancid Albanian underpants, I want to know about it. Understand?

'Yes, boss,' chorused the detectives.

'Right, let's get to business. Tommy, how are you with the Urmston stabbing?'

'The papers are with the CPS and just waiting for their response, guv'nor. Looks like he'll go down for a long stretch.'

'Good work, I'll get onto the force publicist. We need to let the public know we're with them in the fight. More important, we need to let any young thug know he won't get away with carrying a knife in my city.' She turned to a detective at the end of the table. 'Emily, how's the work on the County Lines investigation?'

The young detective coughed once before she spoke in a soft voice. Ridpath recognised one of the new fast-trackers immediately: university graduates whose promotion and elevation through the ranks was assured as long as they kept their noses clean, attended the right courses and licked enough boots.

'We're liaising with DCI Dawson's team at Serious and Organised Crime as well as the National Crime Agency and the National Crime Intelligence Service to identify individuals involved in the drugs trade and will be organising raids in the near future, ma'am.'

Why did these people speak like they were reading from a manual, thought Ridpath. Perhaps it was the way of modern policing. Charlie would have just said, 'We're on to the bastards and we'll be nicking them soon.'

The answer seemed to annoy Claire Trent. 'It's boss or guv'nor, Emily. And keep me informed of any developments. I don't want them southerners from the NCA on our patch, nicking our criminals. That's our job. So no surprises, OK?'

'Yes, ma'am... I mean boss.'

'And keep Paul here copied on all correspondence too. He hates the NCA almost as much as I do.'

'More,' said Paul Dawson.

'Yes, boss.'

'And now some good news. I'll be away next week giving evidence at the trial of Terry Dolan, the Fireman as he's come to be known. CPS are happy with all the evidence we've gathered and it looks like he'll be put away on multiple counts of murder. A big thanks for all your hard work putting the case together and a round of applause for the coroner's officer on my left, DI Ridpath, for putting us on to the bastard in the first place.'

Ridpath could feel his face reddening as all the eyes watched him and he heard a polite round of applause.

'Talking of Ridpath, anything from the coroner this week?'

'Nothing much. We're looking into the death of a young woman at the Wilmslow IRC. Any help with the investigation would be appreciated.'

It was DS Emily Parkinson who spoke up. 'I thought the case had already been investigated by Rowley CID and they thought she had committed suicide.'

How did she know so much about the case?

'The coroner wants to check the decision and that's why I've been asked to investigate. She wants to be able to give a more definitive verdict for the family.'

'It's my ex-nick and I remember the case coming in…' DS Parkinson was about to say more before Claire Trent cut her off. 'If Ridpath requires any assistance in this case, you are to give it to him. Understand?'

Ridpath couldn't believe his ears. How had he suddenly become flavour of the month with the guv'nor? His surprise was only compounded by the next thing she said.

'Please come to my office after the meeting, Ridpath. Right you lot, meeting over. Take care out there.'

She picked up her papers and motioned for Ridpath to follow her. He glanced back at Emily Parkinson. He would have to chat with her later. There was something about what she said. It was almost as if she were being defensive. But it wasn't her name on the final report.

Claire Trent was waiting at the door, snapping her fingers.

Chapter 14

'You want coffee, Ridpath?'

Claire Trent was holding one of those glass and metal jugs with a large amount of black sludge in the bottom. To Ridpath, the coffee at HQ always tasted like it had been dredged from the bottom of the Mersey.

He shook his head.

She poured herself a cup of mud and then sat behind her tidy desk with its pristine white blotter. She took a file from a drawer, put on her glasses and began to read from it. 'Detective Inspector Thomas Ridpath, joined Greater Manchester Police in 2007, passed out from Edgehill. Ok marks, nothing to shout about. First posting at Greenheys and helped capture Thomas Dalbey, aka The Beast of Manchester. Promoted rapidly despite not being a fast-tracker...' She paused for a moment and peered out at him over the top of her glasses. 'Looks like you were one of John Gorman and Charlie's boys, Ridpath.' The she returned to reading the folder out loud, picking out snippets. 'Passed detective exams and joined CID in Stockport before being seconded to MIT in 2014. Solid performance and good reports, smart according to this but developing a reputation as being a bit of a one-man-band. Promoted to Detective Inspector in 2016 and then it all fell apart.'

She closed the file, took off her glasses and sat back. 'Cancer, wasn't it?'

She knew it was.

'Myeloma. Cancer of the bones. But I'm in remission now, have been since 2018.'

'When you were cleared to return to duty and seconded to work with Margaret Challinor as a coroner's officer.'

Ridpath wondered where she was going with all this. None of it was exactly secret.

'Usually it's the kiss of death for any career. A place to see out your days until retirement, filling out forms and dealing with grieving families. But it wasn't for you, why?'

He shrugged his shoulders. 'I had a point to prove. I wanted to show them I could still do the job. I was a bloody good detective who just happened to get ill.'

'So prove it you did. Great work on finding the real killer in the Beast of Manchester murders, stopping the gang wars from erupting again and recently spotting the links in the Fireman killings. You have been a busy little detective, haven't you? Enjoyed the freedom, have we? Mrs Challinor gives you a lot of latitude I hear.'

Ridpath didn't say anything. *Where was she going with this?*

'But your career's blocked. Your promotion to Detective Inspector is still not confirmed, is it? Still probationary after over two years?'

'I've been wanting to talk to you...'

Detective Superintendent Claire Trent held up her hand to stop him speaking. 'I won't mess you about any longer. We'd like you back, Ridpath.'

Was he hearing correctly?

'What?'

'Don't be so surprised. We'd like you to return to MIT and your promotion to Detective Inspector will be confirmed.' She adjusted the files in front of her so they were properly aligned. 'Frankly, between you, me and the four walls, Lorraine Caruso wasn't right for MIT. Don't get me wrong, she's a fine copper, just wrong for our sort of work. She lacked the right…' Claire Trent struggled to find the word.

'Imagination,' suggested Ridpath.

'…application,' the detective superintendent finally said. 'To her credit, she realised as much and we've found a more suitable post for her undoubted talents in GMP.'

'Force Liaison, where she can't do any damage?'

Claire Trent stared at Ridpath. 'She didn't like you Ridpath, and I can understand why. You are undisciplined, disrespectful and downright disruptive, but you are a fine copper with a dogged determination to get to the truth. I like that in a detective and I'm willing to put up with the rest of the shit. Let me lay my cards on the table. You've seen the group of detectives we have now. Lorraine was right to get rid of many of the boys hired by John Gorman and Charlie Whitworth. They were old, slow and couldn't keep up with modern policing. But my own view is she went too far with her changes…'

Changes sanctioned and approved by you, thought Ridpath without voicing the words.

'…We have a group who is young, keen and energetic but lacking in experience of practical police work; the grind of an investigation, the complexities of gathering evidence, the leaps of imagination required to nick the thieves, murderers and con men, otherwise known as the inhabitants of Manchester.'

'So... let me get this right. You want me to come back to work for MIT?'

'Got it in one. You'll be a Detective Inspector running your own team.'

A year ago, Ridpath would have snatched her arm off for the opportunity to return to MIT. 'Who would I report to?'

'Me initially, until I appoint a DCI to run the department operationally. Between you and me, I don't think anybody in GMP is good enough. I'll be looking outside the force. Which is another reason I want somebody who knows Manchester backing him, or her, up.'

'What about the coroner, does she know?'

'Not yet, I thought I would ask you first. So what's your answer?'

Ridpath thought fast, his eyes moving from left to right. 'I'm in the middle of an investigation...'

'So are we. You saw the work in progress. The county lines case worries me and I'd like somebody more senior involved. Emily Parkinson is a good detective but she doesn't have the experience to manage an investigation involving multiple forces and operational units. So what's your answer?'

Why was she pushing him so hard? Why was she in such a rush? Ridpath knew Claire Trent well. No decision was ever so straightforward with her. There had to be a political angle he knew nothing about.

'Well?'

'I'll need to talk to my wife...'

'The wonderful Polly, how is she these days?'

'Fine.' Ridpath forgot she and Claire Trent had met when they finished the Connolly case.

'Do you want me to call and have a chat with her?'

She was in a hurry. 'That's ok, I'll chat with her.'

The smile vanished from Claire Trent's voice. 'Don't take too long, Ridpath. I need your answer by next Monday at the latest.'

'You'll have it, boss, and thanks for thinking of me. I'm flattered.'

'Don't be, Ridpath. You're a good copper. I'll expect your answer by next Monday. That will be all.'

She switched on her computer and stared at the screen. The interview was over and Ridpath left the room quietly.

What the hell was he going to do?

Chapter 15

After the meeting with Claire Trent, Ridpath felt an over-whelming desire for a cigarette. He had stopped smoking over a year ago now, but occasionally the urge to smoke again filled his body and mind.

This was one of those times.

How would he tell Polly? She liked the fact he didn't work overtime or shifts now and was always home at weekends to spend time with her and Eve.

And what would he say to the coroner? Margaret Challinor had supported him through thick and thin. When everybody else doubted him, she was always there, encouraging him and never questioning his judgement.

A year ago, he would have given anything to get back into MIT, to prove the cancer was just an illness and nothing more. Now, he didn't know what to do.

He forced himself to concentrate. He had a case to work on and it must come first, particularly when the inquest would open two days from now.

He spotted Emily Parkinson sitting at a desk in the far corner and walked over to her. 'Hi, I'm DI Ridpath.'

She looked up from her computer. 'I gathered. So you're her blue-eyed boy are you?'

'What's that supposed to mean?'

'Well, ever since I joined MIT, she's been singing your praises. Ridpath this, Ridpath that. Ridpath, the detective with the halo round his head. I heard the Pope has you down for sainthood next week.'

Ridpath recognised another lapsed Catholic when he saw one. He also recognised the pack of cigarettes sitting beneath a lighter next to her computer.

'Look, I need to have a chat. How about we go out for a fag? I need to bum one off you anyway.'

She picked up her lighter and cigarettes. 'Come on, I'm dying for a quick fix myself. Those meetings can be hell.'

He followed her out of the detective's room and into the lift. They went out of the back entrance and round the corner where two other coppers were gathered round a concrete ashtray filled to the brim with dimps and discarded matches.

She gave him a cigarette and lit it, shielding the flame of the lighter from the wind with a practiced curve of the hand. It was a beautiful late summer's day; clouds scudded across the blue sky, cutting across the contrails of the aircraft headed for Manchester Airport.

After a long throat-clenching tug at the cigarette and the expelling of a cloud of smoke above her head, Emily Parkinson said, 'What can I do you for?'

Ridpath decided he was wrong about her. She *was* one of the fast-track university tossers GMP insisted on hiring these days, but there was a hardness there too. This woman was on the way up and nobody was going to get in her way.

'You seemed to know a lot about the investigation into the death at the Wilmslow IRC?'

She gazed at him over the top of her cigarette. 'Do I?'

'Back in the meeting, you asked me questions about it. Were you part of the investigating team?'

She took a minute to think and shook her head. 'I was on another case, but it was the same CID office and people talk, you know how it is.'

'What did they say?'

She stared at him. 'Why should I tell you?'

'Because we're on the same side.'

'We're not on the same side. You work for the coroner, Ridpath, a woman who has just reported one of my ex-colleagues to the Professional Standards Branch.'

Ridpath didn't know. All he could do was mouth, 'What? PSB?'

'Detective Sergeant Barnes is now under investigation. He's only got three months to his pension and you bastards are out to get him.'

'We're not out to get anybody.'

She threw the cigarette on the floor and crushed it out with her heel. 'You know as well as I do if it was a complaint from Joe Public, they would bury it until he retired but coming from a legal officer like the coroner, they have to act. A good man could lose his pension after 30 years in the force because of one mistake.'

'What mistake did he make?'

'Find out for yourself, I'm not your nark.' And she stormed off, vanishing back inside the glass and concrete cube known as GMP headquarters.

He was left standing there, holding the cigarette in his right hand. He took another drag, but suddenly it tasted bitter, like an old shroud instead of tobacco.

The two detectives on the other side of the ashtray were smirking at him. 'Lover's tiff, hey?'

'And you two can bugger off as well.'

Chapter 16

'Of course I reported him to the Professional Standards Branch. You saw the police report he produced. It was lazy at best and incompetent at worst.'

'But what was the point? The PSB were investigated themselves by the Met in 2016 for wrongdoing. It's not *Line of Duty*, they are just a waste of time.'

'It doesn't matter, incompetence should be reported.'

Ridpath stood in front of Mrs Challinor. 'But by doing so, it means we will be lucky to get any co-operation from him or his colleagues to help my inquiry.'

She stared up at him. 'You forget who you are, Ridpath. You are a coroner's officer, investigating the death of a young woman while under the protection of the crown. If you don't receive "co-operation" from the police, remind them of the penalties for obstructing an officer of this court in the prosecution of their duties. If they still refuse to assist you, I will happily call the Chief Constable to complain about the intransigence of his force. I haven't got the reputation of being a bloody difficult woman for nothing.'

Ridpath knew she was right but by referring Barnes to Professional Standards, she had just made his job ten times harder.

Her voice softened and she said, 'Sit down. How was the visit to Wilmslow IRC?'

He pulled out a chair and sat in front of her. The light was streaming in through the sash window behind her head. Stockford almost looked pretty on a day like this if one ignored the trash on the streets, the old abandoned mills, the wind racing through the empty roads and the ugly grey of the concrete monstrosities surrounding the Coroner's Court.

'They didn't reveal a lot.' He thought for a moment. 'It wasn't as if they were hiding anything, it was just if I didn't ask the right question, I wouldn't get an answer. They were more interested in their company's reputation than in the death of one of their detainees. One other thing disturbed me...'

'What?'

'I saw nobody else during my visit other than the Centre's officers.'

'Nobody else?'

'Not one. They were all locked up during the time I was there.'

'Perhaps they were scared you would talk to the prisoners and discover something you shouldn't have known about.'

'It's detainees, Coroner. The PR woman was keen to correct me on my use of language.'

'It's all becoming positively Orwellian, isn't it? Prisoners are detainees. Prisons are removal centres. War is Peace. Freedom Is Slavery. Ignorance is Strength. The world worries me, Ridpath. Language has become so debased...'

'Nothing we can do, Mrs Challinor.'

'Isn't there? I've been doing some investigating myself. You know Stephen Shaw, the former prison ombudsman Stephen Shaw, told MPs that deaths in Removal Centres were being kept a "state secret" by the Home Office. As a coroner, I tried to find anything published by the department and ran up against a brick wall. It's almost as if they keep quiet about them, nobody will ever ask. No statistics on deaths, none on self-harming, nothing on suicides in detention. They seem to be operating a policy of denial, delay and obfuscation. You'd have thought they would have learned from the Windrush scandal, but the opposite seems to be the case.'

'What about the press? Aren't any journalists asking questions?'

'Our newspapers are more interested in which celebrity got divorced this week. And anyway, it doesn't suit their editorial line. Remember all immigrants are bad and those that are possibly illegal are even worse.'

The coroner tapped the desk with her index finger emphasising every word. 'But we can find the truth about this death, and that's what I intend to do, despite everything. What are your next steps?'

An image flashed into Ridpath's mind for a moment. The coroner dressed as Rule Britannia holding back the hordes of uncultured savages, protecting the truth and the rule of law.

'I asked what are your next steps, Ridpath.'

'There should be a package of photocopies from the PR woman. I asked her for the processing document for Wendy Chen...'

'Processing document? Sounds like we're dealing with a can of peas rather than a human being.'

'That's what they call it, Mrs Challinor. Plus I wanted the names and addresses of the officers, the security chief, a Mr Collins, and the facility manager, Mr Carlton. Finally, I asked the names and destinations of all the detainees in the centre that night. Somebody must have seen or heard something.'

'The police didn't interview them?'

'Ron Barnes didn't meet any witnesses other than the staff at the Centre.'

The coroner shook her head. 'I believe we already have the names and addresses of the officers of the Wilmslow IRC. We have subpoenaed them to testify during the inquest.'

'I wanted her to provide them anyway. You never know, we may find out something new.'

'Good, Ridpath, I don't have to remind you we only have two days before the inquest begins.'

'I may not have an answer by then. Can you postpone it?'

'Not any more. The relatives are coming from China. They want to collect the body. I can only release it if I have concluded my inquest.'

'When do they arrive?'

'Tomorrow.'

'We're not going to be ready, Coroner.'

She checked her watch and took a pink file from her inbox. 'So you better get moving, Ridpath.'

Once again, he had been dismissed. He was starting to get used to it.

Chapter 17

'Sophia, has anything come from the woman at the IRC yet?'

'Five minutes ago, while you were with the coroner, delivered by courier.'

A large package lay on Ridpath's desk. He picked it up and pulled apart the white plastic courier bag. Inside was a bulky A4 envelope. He unwound the string binding it, removed all the packing and pulled out just six sheets of paper.

The top sheet was a note from Louise Bagnall, cheerily informing him the enclosed was the material he had requested and promising further help if any was needed. 'New Hampshire Detention Services as a company is dedicated to helping the coroner in any way possible to ensure the speedy resolution of this matter.'

She was obviously the person responsible for the copy-writing on the brochure.

Sophia came and stood beside him. 'Is this about the death of the detainee?'

'Six pages. It's not much, is it?' He checked out the next document. It was a photocopy of an admission processing form. At the top on the left was a small, grainy passport-sized photograph of the victim, Wendy Tang, as she was then called. The face had an air of resignation about it, as if she knew she was powerless against the world of bureaucracy.

There were details about her height, weight, colour of eyes and hair. The distinguishing marks box was left blank.

The next box was simply headed **RECEIVED FROM** in bold capital letters. Inside somebody had written.

UK Immigration Enforcement

Dallas Court

Langworthy Street

Salford

'It makes them seem like parcels, not human beings. UK Immigration Enforcement were the same bastards that snatched my cousin one morning at 7 a.m. She was seeking asylum, having escaped Pakistan to avoid an arranged marriage.'

'What happened to her?'

'They sent her back. She's married now. The man is 53 years old and has two other wives.'

'I'm sorry, Sophia, but we must remain dispassionate about this case. Whatever we feel, our job is to investigate and try to understand what happened. We mustn't let personal feelings intrude.'

'Be dispassionate? When people are being snatched off the streets, imprisoned without trial and deported, without leave to appeal a bureaucratic decision? Did you miss the Windrush case, Ridpath? That was just the tip of the iceberg.'

'Sophia, if you can't be dispassionate, I will have to take you off the case. Getting angry and arguing with Carol Oates helps nobody.'

'She's such a cold fish.' She held up her hands in mock surrender. 'But I'll do as you say. Dispassionate is my new middle name.'

Ridpath turned back to the document. There was a scribbled signature for the receiving officer; it was Tony Osborne, the same officer who had been working the night of her death. The time of receiving the detainee was recorded as 9.15 a.m. on August 19th.

The final box was headed **ACTION**. Beneath this section somebody, presumably Tony Osborne, had written in block, capital letters.

AWAITING DEPORTATION

Another sheet attached to the processing document was full of boxes with nothing written in them. All seemed to be headed with acronyms and numbers.

'They're billing codes, to be completed later.'

Ridpath stared at Sophia.

'What? I worked in an insurance office for one summer. It's a standard corporate charging sheet. There will be fixed rates charged for the number of days she is detained, meals, medical services, special dietary requirements, uniforms and all the rest of the stuff these companies can charge the government. It's their way of milking the system.'

'But it's all empty.'

'Maybe they didn't get round to filling it in or, more likely, they've attached a blank one instead of letting you see what they've been charging.'

Ridpath turned to the final two sheets. The first was a list of the officers employed by Wilmslow IRC at the time of the death of Wendy Tang aka Wendy Chen Hong Xi, with their names, addresses and telephone numbers. Two of the men listed were Joe Cummings and Tony Osborne. Each name had a passport-sized headshot next to it, obviously a copy of their ID cards.

The last page was a list of the detainees confined in the IRC that evening, their room numbers and what had happened to them.

'Our woman was in Room 7 so either side of her were Rooms 5 and 9, opposite was 6 and 8.' Ridpath searched through the list. Here's Room 5.

Mehmet Ali SYRIAN deported 20/08/2019

'He was deported the day of her death. What about Room 9?' Ridpath searched through the list. There was no Room 9 listed.

'Perhaps it wasn't used that night?' suggested Sophia.

'But they told me the facility was full. What about Rooms 6 and 8?'

Sophia found the numbers on the page next to each other.

Nicolai Ciobanu ROMANIAN deported 20/08/2019

Roman Popescu ROMANIAN deported 20/08/2019

'So all the people in the surrounding cells were deported the day of the incident. Were they getting rid of possible witnesses or was this normal procedure? After all this is a short stay facility.'

Sophia shrugged her shoulders.

'Right, I want you to get onto Louise Bagnall. Check whether there was anybody in Room 9.'

'Ok, will do.'

'And the security officer, Stuart Collins, was supposed to send me the CCTV tapes from that evening, can you get on to him?'

'I'll chase them up.'

Ridpath grabbed his jacket.

'What are you doing?'

'What I should have done yesterday. Going to see Detective Sergeant Ronald Barnes. Perhaps he can tell me what the hell is going on in this case.'

Chapter 18

Tony Osborne glared at his half-drunk pint and realised he didn't want any more. At the bar, a student was ordering a shandy, much to the disgust of the barman. Next to him, an old man sat staring into mid-air, his nicotine-stained fingers tapping on the box of matches next to his pint.

The hands were rough and hard with manual work, while the man's face was etched with the wrinkles of old age, his flat cap nestling over a hedge of bushy eyebrows.

Tony Osborne didn't want to end up like that; sitting in a dreary pub, guarding a glass of frothy brown suds, waiting for death to strike.

He couldn't face such a future.

Not any more.

And he didn't have to if he just played his cards right.

The company had given him a week off to prepare for the testimony at the Coroner's Court on Thursday. Yesterday was training at the Centre, today was a morning spent in the solicitor's office in the town centre to prepare for the day.

'Remember to dress well, Mr Osborne, jacket, shirt and tie but not your uniform. You are a human being, not a custody officer.'

'Remember to be on time, preferably come fifteen minutes early. You can sit in the court and listen to the other testimony.'

'Remember to speak up at all times, and make sure the jury can hear you.'

'Remember it's not a court of law. The coroner will ask most of the questions, not a barrister. This court simply wants to know what you did and what you saw, nothing more.'

'Remember you are representing the company. Always state how proud you are to work for New Hampshire Detention Services and always follow the correct procedures.'

It was all bollocks, of course. They had told him what to say and how to say it, even coaching him to answer difficult questions with 'I don't remember' or 'I can't recall'.

He'd had enough. When this was all over and he'd collected his money, he was off. Somewhere warm and sunny with plenty of hot and cold running women. Somewhere like Thailand. Sean had said you could live like a king for ten quid a day out there. He was sick of Manchester; the cold, the wet, the rain and all the bloody people moaning as if their lives depended on it.

He was off as soon as this court date was done and dusted. It had all gone as they'd told him so far. All he had to do was spend another twenty minutes saying the same thing over and over again and he would be finished. Collect his money and go to discover the women of Thailand. Or, more precisely, let the women of Thailand discover him.

It was his love of them which had trapped him in this bind in the first place.

Just two more days and he would be free.

No more prisons for him.

His sentence was over, the jail time done. The only uniform he would wear from then would be Hawaiian shirts, shorts and a pocket full of condoms.

He looked at his pint and pushed it away.

The old man finally moved his head and gazed across at him with rheumy eyes. 'I could have had it all,' he said, slurring his words.

Tony Osborne was going to have it all. And then some more.

Fuck Manchester. Fuck the prison. Fuck everything.

Chapter 19

Rowley station was one of those new brick-built stations with all the mod cons: hot and cold running cells, a canteen, offices for detectives and even working broadband. The problem was nobody knew where the nick was, not even the police. It was hidden out of sight down a back alley at the end of a cul-de-sac.

Ridpath walked into reception. The usual posters were on the walls: fight people trafficking, don't drink and drive, watch out there's a thief about. Next to these posters was another showing Manchester's most wanted criminals with their mug shots lined up as if on an identity parade. It would be difficult to find an uglier bunch of criminals anywhere.

At the end of the wall was a recruitment poster showing four smiling, uniformed plods beneath a headline saying, 'Let the Force be with you.' They were obviously aiming to recruit Star Wars fans this year. He half expected R2D2 to be hidden somewhere in the picture. But given GMP's problems with its new computer system, R2D2 would be a definite improvement.

In front of the posters, on the benches, was a middle-aged woman with a black eye being comforted by her son who couldn't have been older than twelve. She was quietly sobbing while her son whispered something to her. Ridpath observed both of them. She had probably been beaten up by her partner, while her young son was powerless to defend her.

Now that was a truer image of the reality of modern policing than the sanitised poster on the wall.

He walked to the glass-shielded front desk. A burly sergeant who looked like he could lose a few pounds was slouched behind the desk.

'I'm here to see Ronald Barnes.'

'And you are?'

Ridpath took out his warrant card and held it against the glass.

The sergeant immediately sat up straight. 'Right, Inspector, I'll let him know.'

Ridpath hadn't told him where he was from. Rank hath its privileges.

While he was waiting, his phone rang. The woman with the black eye jerked backwards at the noise and had to be calmed by her son.

Ridpath turned away. The call was from Sophia.

'Lucy Bagnall has come back with the name of the man in Room 9. Leaving him off was a mistake apparently. He was a Mr Liang Xiao Wen. He wasn't deported, but transferred to another removal centre, Halverson IRC in Leicestershire. Apparently, some lawyer had appealed his deportation.'

'Great, Sophia, can you push Stuart Collins on the CCTV tapes too?'

'They've just arrived, so I'll get onto them as soon as I can. But Carol Oates is being a pain.'

'Remember, teamwork, Sophia.'

'Teamwork. That's my new middle name along with dispassionate.'

He ended the call. The sergeant was holding the door open and pointing upstairs. 'It's the second on the right.'

When Ridpath walked into DS Ronald Barnes' office, the man was just taking down a picture from the wall and placing it in a brown box.

'You redecorating?'

Barnes held up the picture for Ridpath to see. It was a younger version of himself dressed in a tuxedo shaking hands with Alex Ferguson. '1994, the year we won the treble. Manchester United on top of the world.'

'Do you still go?'

Barnes shook his head. 'Not since Sir Alex left. My son has my season ticket now. For me, all the passion has gone out of the game. It's all about money now. Sanchez on 500,000 quid a week and he still looks like he couldn't run twenty yards without being out of breath. Give me the old days when Hughesy, Scholes, and Becks were scoring wonder goals while Roy Keane was kicking three lumps of shit out of any midfielder who had the gall to get in his way.' He gazed at the photo for a long time and back up at Ridpath. 'You from PSB?'

'No, nothing to do with that shower. I'm from the Coroner's Office. DI Ridpath.'

'So the witch has sent somebody to do her dirty work, has she?'

Ridpath shook his head. 'The coroner asked me to look into the death of Wendy Chen at Wilmslow Immigration Removal Centre.'

'That's what I mean. The witch has asked you to do her dirty work.'

Ridpath sighed. 'Look, Ron, I'm a copper too. I'm not here to bury you, OK? I just want to find out the truth.'

'The truth? Is that what this is about?'

'It's about a young woman who died in a prison with her throat slashed.' Ridpath pointed to the chairs. 'Can we sit?'

Slowly, Ronald Barnes placed the picture of himself and Alec Ferguson in the brown box and walked to sit behind his desk.

Ridpath pulled out a chair and sat in front of him.

'Aren't you supposed to caution me first and shouldn't I have a union rep with me?'

'This is just a chat.'

'That's what they all say. Remember, I was a bloody detective when you were still sucking on your mother's tit. Thirty years in the force and it's come to this. Under investigation because some old coroner with her tits in a mangle complained about me. I only had three months to go and now they're making me work shifts behind some bloody desk, collating bloody force recruitment statistics.' The man thumped his chest. 'I'm a detective, for God's sake.'

'I'm sorry to hear it, Ron. You don't have to go, do you? You could stay and fight. Carry on working here for the next three months.'

'What? And risk losing the whole bloody lot? I've waited thirty years for this pension and now the bastards are playing silly buggers. Not me. I'll go, take what I'm owed and stick two fingers up at the bloody lot of 'em.'

'Can we talk about the investigation into the death of the girl?'

Ron Barnes stayed silent.

'You were the Senior Investigating Officer, right?'

'I was the only investigating officer. Correct.'

'And you went to the Removal Centre, when?'

'It's all in the scene of crime report.'

Ridpath took it out of the folder and checked the details. 'You arrived at 6.25 a.m., right?'

'If that's what it says.'

'Why so long? The death was reported to the police just after 4.00 a.m.'

'As far as I understand it, nobody was available. We'd had a stabbing and the detectives on duty were attending the scene.'

'So a few cars were despatched but no detectives. When did you get involved?'

'I received a message to attend the death at 6.02. I'd only been at work two bloody minutes.'

'Your shift started at six?'

'Correct.'

'There were no detectives available before that time?'

'Check the logs.'

'I will.' Ridpath made a note in his book. 'So you arrived there, what happened?'

'I arrived at 6.25 and was met by the facility manager, a bloke called Dave Carlton.'

'He was already there?'

'Either that or I was seeing things. He told me there was a suicide in Room 7. I went up with him, saw all the blood and immediately called forensics and the pathologist on call.'

'Who was?'

'Look this is all in the report, why don't you just bloody read it?'

'I want to hear it in your own words.'

'Looking for discrepancies, are we? Remember I've been at this game a lot longer than you. Think I'd fall for those old tricks?'

'What time did the pathologist, Dr Ahmed, arrive?'

Barnes smirked. 'So you have read the report? It was at 7.02. He talked first with Carlton and called the death at 7.30 or thereabouts.'

'Talked to Carlton? He's not in your report.'

'What does it matter? He didn't go anywhere near the scene of the crime.'

'Are you sure?'

'Of course I bloody am. I know how to cordon off a crime scene.'

'When did the forensics team come?'

'It took them a while to get through security, so they arrived at 7.45. Joyce Taylor was the scene of crime manager. Know her, do you? She's good at her job, doesn't miss anything.'

'You stayed at the scene?'

'Until the body was moved and I interviewed the guards.'

'And?'

'It's in the report. They all thought it was a suicide. Apparently it's happened before. These people don't want to go back to their own countries and would prefer to kill themselves than let it happen.'

'That's what you thought happened in this case?'

'It looked like it to me, but I kept an open mind, just as you're told to do in the manuals. I presume you've read the manuals, sonny.'

'I'm not your "sonny" Detective Sergeant Barnes, my name is Ridpath and I'm a Detective Inspector.'

Barnes' eyes narrowed. 'Ridpath? I remember the name... weren't you the one who collapsed on the job, cancer or summat? They hived you off to the Coroner's Office when you returned, did they? Somewhere safe and cosy where you couldn't hurt yourself or do any damage?' He smirked again, 'Or are you one of those who has to prove himself? "Despite everything I can still do the job and I'm going to prove it."'

His years on the job had given Barnes insights into human nature which made Ridpath wince.

'Well, don't go proving your manhood with my career and pension, DI Ridpath.'

'You finished?' was all Ridpath said.

Barnes stayed silent.

'So the room was sealed off while forensics went to work, what happened to the detainees?'

'We sealed off the whole floor. The detainees were taken upstairs and kept together in a common area. They were allowed back at 13.30 after the forensics had finished.'

'But not all of them were allowed back, were they?'

'What do you mean?'

'You know exactly what I meant. Why didn't you interview the people on either side of the woman?'

'Because by the time I wanted to interview them, the Centre Manager said they were no longer in the country. They had already been deported. Home Office rules apparently – their departures had been scheduled for that day. And besides...'

'Besides what?'

'It was obvious it was a suicide. She cut her own throat, didn't she? Probably didn't want to go back. Would've been a waste of time and money going abroad to interview them.'

'Not all of them.'

'What do you mean?'

'Room 9 wasn't deported.'

'The Chinese man? But they told me he had already gone.'

'To another Removal Centre, not deported.'

Barnes stayed silent.

Chapter 20

After his interview with DS Barnes, Ridpath drove back to the Coroner's Office, turning over the elements of the case in his mind.

Why was the SIO not called to the scene until 6.02? Was it a question of police resources as Barnes stated? Was there simply nobody available to go to the detention centre to look into a possible suicide? Or was there something else going on?

He had a lot of questions for Ms Bagnall. Perhaps it was time to pay her another visit.

DS Barnes worried him too. He was obviously a competent detective, so why was his investigation so shoddy? Was he more concerned with putting on his slippers than on investigating properly? Or had he simply gone through the motions believing it to be another suicide?

Perhaps this was all a waste of time. The woman, Wendy Chen, had taken her life because she didn't want to be deported back to her own country. Having visited Wilmslow IRC, he could understand how such places could make a person so depressed and downhearted they would end it all.

But it was like the coroner had said. They had to know for certain. They owed it to the family to let them know the truth about their daughter.

Even the pathologist's report had been perfunctory. It was like he had already made the assumption that the woman had committed suicide and was looking for information and proof for that theory instead of performing a proper examination. Where was the toxicology report? Where was the examination of the body?

Ridpath couldn't help but think everybody was just going through the motions. Just doing enough to cover their individual and corporate arses without caring about the woman or her family.

One other question occurred to him as he was parking the car at the Coroner's Office. Where had the knife come from? Lucy Bagnall had said it didn't belong to the Centre so where had Wendy Chen obtained it? Did she smuggle it in?

He was still thinking about this as he ran up the stairs to his office.

Sophia was waiting for him inside.

'Stuart sent over the CCTV from inside the IRC. Not much use I'm afraid.'

'Stuart is it now?'

'A touch of charm and friendliness helps get what you want. You should remember, Ridpath.'

'He was obliged to turn over the tapes, otherwise I would have served her with a writ.'

'But he wasn't obliged to hand over this.' Sophia held out a sheet of paper. 'It's a list of outside calls on the day before our victim died; who made them and what number they called.'

'Why did you ask for this?'

'Because I remembered my cousin saying the only contact with the outside world was through a pay phone. Visits were difficult to arrange at short notice and they confiscate any mobile phones during the admission process. The public phone is the only way to contact friends or a solicitor to appeal against a deportation. The Centre logs all the calls.'

'So he gave it to you...'

'I don't think he knew its importance.'

'And?'

Sophia placed the sheet on the table. 'There were 73 calls listed for August 19th and three from our victim. She arrived at Wilmslow IRC at 9.15, was processed and made a call within an hour of her arrival. See.' She pointed to the seventh name on the list. 'I've checked the number using a reverse directory and it was to a cake shop in Chinatown, Madame Wong's Bakery.'

'Perhaps she fancied some cake...'

Sophia missed the irony in Ridpath's voice and continued on. 'The second call was an overseas number. China apparently, but they don't keep a record of overseas calls, just the country.'

'Ringing home? Or a boyfriend, maybe?'

'But it's the third call six hours later that's more interesting.' She turned the page. 'See, this one. I rang this number and you'll never guess who answered the phone.'

'You're right, I'll never guess.'

'It was the front desk sergeant at Rowley Police Station.'

Ridpath frowned. 'She rang Rowley? The same station which investigated her death twelve hours later?'

Sophia nodded.

'Who did she talk to?'

'I don't know, Ridpath, only that she rang the station and the call lasted seven minutes and thirty-three seconds.'

Chapter 21

Ridpath's mouth opened once but no words came out.

'I think you were about to say "Good work, Sophia."'

He paused for a moment and then said it. 'Good work, Sophia. But why was she ringing Rowley station and who did she speak to?'

'Again, I don't know, Ridpath.'

He thought quickly, his eyes darting left and right, before he said, 'Perhaps a better question would be what did they talk about? The desk sergeant would keep a log of all incoming calls. I'll have to go back and chat with him.'

'You could call?'

'No, they'd just blank me, a personal visit would be much more useful. This has to be done one on one.'

As he was speaking, Ridpath knew this was the second place he would have to return. There was so little time available in this inquiry and he had none of it to waste going back to places he had already been.

'There's one other thing on this list. See here, and here and here?'

Ridpath checked the list and found her finger pointing to the name Liang Xiao Wen.

'He made four calls. One to this number, a solicitor with an office in Chinatown, and three other calls to this mobile number.'

'Who is it?'

'I don't know, the number isn't listed to anybody.'

'A burner phone? Why was he calling a burner phone?'

'And who answered his call?'

This case was getting more and more complicated. 'Have you had time to go through the CCTV tapes?'

With her foot, Sophia pushed a box out from under the table. Ridpath glanced down and could see it was full of black plastic recording cassettes.

'There are 36 CCTV cameras in the IRC, each one has 24 hours of material on it. Stuart told me six of the cameras were inoperative...'

'Which ones?'

'He didn't know, or wouldn't tell me, you take your pick.'

'We already know one of them was in the corridor outside the victim's room. I asked Lucy Bagnall when I visited.'

'That leaves five others, but we'll never know which ones weren't working.'

'How convenient. Have they checked these tapes and that's why they've released them to us?' Ridpath said.

'Possibly.'

'But they might have missed something useful.'

'It still means, if I watched every tape, it would take me 35 days.'

'We don't have the time. And the boxes are not marked with a location just a number.'

Ridpath frowned. 'Is it just me or do you get the feeling the staff at the Removal Centre are playing with us?'

'What do you mean?'

'Well, they went from being cagey with information, to now suddenly giving us far too much of it.'

'You mean burying us under too much stuff?'

'It's a technique. They know there's only two days to the inquest too. Instead of being obstructive, they've decided to be helpful, too helpful.'

'Knowing we'll never be able to go through it all in time.'

'Right again, Sophia.'

She held up more papers, this time with a slightly blue tinge. 'That explains why Stuart gave me these too.'

'What are they?'

'Plans of the centre. From the entrance right up to the fourth floor. He even marked out the position of the woman's room on this one.'

'He *was* being helpful.' Ridpath's eyes narrowed. 'Can you open one of the plans?'

Sophia took the top one and from a single square it opened out to a sheet four feet long by three feet across. She laid it down so it covered her table and the desktop computer. She checked the rubric on top. 'Apparently this is a schematic of the boiler room and related facilities.'

'Good.' Ridpath leant across the table and stared at the technical drawing. He stubbed his finger at the document and said, 'There it is.'

Sophia tried to see where he was pointing but Ridpath was already rummaging through the tapes in the box. He finally pulled one out and held it up. 'The CCTV cameras are all numbered on the schematic. It's the same number on the box.'

'But how does it help us, Ridpath?'

'You mean how does it help *you*, Sophia.'

His assistant stayed silent.

'Because they have given us the tapes, even though they said they didn't keep copies. Through the numbers we can plot a map of the cameras working that night…'

'…and the cameras out of action. We'll know the locations of all the cameras in the Centre, the ones working and those that weren't.'

'One of the first rules of detective work, Sophia: the absence of something is sometimes just as important as the presence of something.'

'The dog that didn't bark in the night.'

'Pardon?'

'Sherlock Holmes. The adventure of the Silver Blaze. The dog didn't bark so he had to know who the thief was.'

'Great, Sophia. I would keep it in mind when you're going through the schematics and finding out the location of the inoperative cameras.'

'And what are you going to be doing, Ridpath?'

'I've got a date with a dead body. We are re-doing the post-mortem on the victim this afternoon.'

Sophia's eyes brightened. 'Can I come?'

Ridpath tapped the schematic. 'As soon as you have found the dog who didn't bark, or in our case, the cameras that didn't film.'

Chapter 22

She had to get out.

She hadn't eaten since last night and she was starving. She'd been through the flat looking for food and found nothing. Not even a tin of out-of-date mackerel.

She put on her coat. If she was quick and ran to the main road, she could check her account at the ATM of the bank on the corner. If she had any money, she could nip into the Tesco Express next door and pick up some bread and some pot noodles, maybe even a few apples.

She longed for some fruit. It had been so long since she had bitten into a crisp apple, feeling the juice drip down her chin. She would get six today. No, maybe ten this time, so she could gorge on fruit.

She slipped on her shoes. Five minutes there. A minute to check the account. Three minutes to buy some food. Five minutes back. She would be out for fourteen minutes maximum. Surely, he wouldn't see her?

She slipped on her shoes and opened the door, peering out onto the landing.

It was quiet. The woman next door had gone to work already.

She stepped outside and stopped.

If he was waiting for her, now is when he would attack.

She listened for footsteps on the stairs.

Nothing. Only the sound of a cat wailing for its mate in the garden.

She had to go now. If she waited any longer, she would lose courage and rush back into the flat, slamming the door behind her.

She took a deep breath and rushed down the stairs to the front door.

Again, she peered out.

The path and garden in front of her was empty. On the road, a car raced past.

She checked again.

A woman with a pushchair, her child asleep inside.

Now. Go now.

She raced out of the three-storey building, running down the short path to the entrance. Go left, it's quicker.

The woman with the push chair was staring at her as she ran past.

Ignore her.

She kept running, feeling the damp road beneath her feet, the first falls of leaves making it slippery underfoot.

She missed Shanghai at this time of year. The long heat of summer had given way to the cool of autumn. The leaves of the Plane trees lining the streets, planted so long ago, beginning to turn grey before the storms of October finally blew them from their branches.

She stared ahead. The main road was just 200 yards away.

Keep running.

Her legs were weakening, but she had to keep going.

Left. Right. Left. Right. Keep going.

She reached the main road. The traffic was busier now. Cars, white vans, buses and bikes trundled along in both directions. The bank was on the other side of the road on the corner.

She judged the speed of the traffic and ran out between the onrushing cars. A white van screeched to a halt and she heard a loud burst of swearing but she was across.

There was a queue outside the ATM! What was she going to do?

She looked at the Tesco Express. There were two ATMs there.

She ran down the street, dodging another mother with a pram. Had everybody just given birth in Manchester and were they all on the street now?

She stuck her card in the ATM. The usual ads appeared followed by the list of services. She jabbed the check balance square three times.

The machine whirred and chortled. She had twenty pounds and fourteen pence! She pressed the button for more options and took out 20 quid, looking over her shoulder left and right as the machine counted out the money.

Nobody watching her.

Nobody taking any notice at all.

She grabbed the money and went into the shop. Quick, grab some bread, some pot noodles and some apples, don't spend more than ten quid. Save the rest in case she decided to go to work tomorrow. Liang needed paying and if she didn't turn up with the money, he would come looking for her.

One bastard on her back was more than enough.

She found an empty till, bagged her stuff and paid with two fivers. 9.78.

She grabbed the change and ran out of the store.

All she had to do now was get home.

Across the street, car horns blaring. Down the road, dodging the prams, panting now, legs tired, the Tesco bag banging against her leg.

Keep going.

The flat up ahead, on the right.

She ran faster, her heart beating harder.

Onto the path, key in the door, and into the lobby. Up the stairs two at a time.

Fumbling for the key for the front door, why wouldn't it go in?

Made it. Turning the lock. Slamming the door behind her.

She was safe again.

The man in the car parked on the street took another drag of his cigarette. He thought this was where she might hide.

Chapter 23

As soon as Ridpath entered the morgue, a familiar sense of dread suffused his bones.

He didn't know where it came from. Perhaps it was the shine of the white tiled walls. Or the peculiar smell of formaldehyde and disinfectant. Or the sound of his shoes on the polished floor. Whatever it was, his body knew what it was going to feel and, like Pavlov's dog, began to react immediately when he entered the place.

Dr Schofield the pathologist was bending over the body speaking aloud into the microphone in his high alto voice. 'Left ventricle normal. Heart is comparatively healthy...' He stopped, hearing Ridpath behind him. 'Good afternoon, Ridpath, I'm so glad you can make it.' He stood up and automatically stuck out his hand.

Ridpath looked down at it, covered in gore and dried blood. He waved back. 'Good afternoon, Dr Schofield and Vera.'

Vera was Schofield's rather dour assistant who helped him during the post-mortem, typing up the notes later.

In the background, he could see another man dressed in the usual pathologist's uniform of green apron, mask, hair net, whites and green wellingtons.

'This is a representative from Dr Ahmed, an observer if you like, Dr Waterstone. DI Ridpath from the Coroner's

Office,' he absentmindedly waved his bloodied scalpel introducing them to each other.

Was that ethical? Inviting another pathologist to attend the second post-mortem?

'And before you ask, Ridpath, I asked Dr Ahmed to send an observer. We can contrast his notes with my findings and agree on a conclusion together. I know you would much prefer it the doctor's office and mine were at each other's throats,' he paused, glancing at the woman lying on the stainless steel post-mortem table, 'but we've known each other a long time and respect each other's work.'

'On the contrary, Dr Schofield, I just want to know the truth. Did this woman commit suicide or not?'

'I can assure you, DI Ridpath, Dr Ahmed has exactly the same desire. He believes she did and has stated so in his report. But he is happy to have his findings confirmed by Dr Schofield,' said Dr Waterstone in a deep, mellifluous voice.

Ridpath didn't reply. Were the doctors closing ranks against the Coroner's Office?

Dr Schofield returned to the woman lying on the table. 'We've just got started. Luckily Dr Ahmed has already sliced into this woman a month ago. He did an excellent job on the ribs even though I say so myself.'

Ridpath peered at the young woman lying on the stainless steel table. Her face was white with just a tinge of green around the nostrils. A brown ooze was seeping from her ears and her torso was discoloured with green, brown and dark blotches. The area around the neck was an open gash.

And then the smell hit Ridpath's nose. He immediately covered it with a hand.

'She's beginning to pong a bit, isn't she? Here's a mask. I'd rub some of this under your nose too.' He passed Ridpath a bottle of Vicks. 'Personally, I don't think it works but some of my students swear by it.'

Ridpath put a dab of Vicks on his top lip where it immediately stung. 'Why is she beginning to decompose? I thought she'd been frozen for the last month.'

Dr Waterstone answered. 'I believe she was left out on a gurney after they completed the post-mortem. No cold lockers were available at the time. And it was the busiest time of the year for us. No excuses, though, it shouldn't have happened.'

'Or they simply forgot about her while the pathologist wrote his report,' said Dr Schofield. 'Normally, if frozen, she would still be in autolysis…'

'Autolysis?' asked Ridpath.

'The first stage of decomposition after death. The cells are cut off from oxygen causing carbon dioxide levels to rise and pH levels to drop. Waste begins to gather and poisons the cells.'

'She's past that stage?'

Dr Schofield gazed at the corpse. 'Well past it. She's well into bloat stage now. Sulfhemoglobin, a green pigment, settles in the blood, causing a greenish discolouration of the cadaver. You see it here and here.' He pointed to the nostrils and to the green blotches on the skin. 'Along with the gasses of decomposition, putrescine and cadaverine work to break down the cell walls. You can see the body is beginning to rupture and the skin starts to slough off around the arms and legs.' He took a spatula from a tray table and pushed it between the lips, opening the mouth. 'We have fungus growing on the inside of the mouth. If we left this woman out for a few days, she would quickly go into the next stage, active decay.'

'Thanks doctor, I've heard enough. Have you found anything so far?'

'Well, I've checked the notes from Dr Ahmed. They are short, almost curt in tone, but so far, accurate. He was unable to come to any firm conclusion about the wound itself; whether or not it was self-inflicted. I can understand this inability given its nature. But I would have preferred to have seen more tests performed. For instance, an X-ray of the chest for the detection of air in the venous system and heart, an examination of the stomach contents and a toxicology test on the blood.'

'Once Dr Ahmed concluded on the balance of probabilities it was suicide, he decided further expensive tests were not necessary,' said Dr Waterstone.

'Ah, there lies the rub. Was it a suicide? Let's examine the wound on the neck…'

Dr Schofield was in full dramatic flow now, aware he had an audience.

'There are three reasons a cut throat occurs. Homicide, suicide or accident. I think we can rule out the latter in this case. Do we agree?'

Both Dr Waterstone and Ridpath said yes.

'I read up on the literature before commencing this post-mortem. Forensic pathologists have a challenging task when ascertaining the manner of death when cut throats are presented with no proper history or witnesses. The OJ Simpson case highlighted this in excruciating detail.'

He leant in closer to Wendy Chen to examine the gaping wound on her throat. 'The suicidal cut throat wound is similar to the homicidal cut throat from behind. The wound usually begins higher on the neck on the side opposite to where it terminates. If the deceased was a right-handed person, the suicide cut throat should typically start from upper third of the left side of the neck and end at a point lower than the origin on the right side.'

He stepped back, examining the gash in the throat from all angles. 'This wound appears to follow those parameters. Suicidal cut throats are usually, but not always, accompanied by hesitation marks.' Again he examined the throat and the back of the neck. 'In this case, no such hesitation injuries can be seen.' He examined the wrists and the arms. 'Nor does there seem to be any evidence of cutting or self-injuries or scars in the usual areas. Further, a fatal suicidal cut throat may be accompanied by a cadaveric spasm with the knife found clenched firmly in the victim's hand. According to the police report, the weapon was found on the floor.'

He stepped back and looked at both Ridpath and Dr Waterstone. 'The jury is so far undecided, gentlemen, on the question of suicide.'

'So does that mean she did kill herself or she didn't?' asked Ridpath.

'It means I haven't made up my mind yet.'

The sudden urge for a cigarette crept over Ridpath. Anything to get away from this body and this smell. But he forced himself to stand there as the doctor continued with the post-mortem.

'Now homicidal cut throats can be created in two different ways, depending on whether they are produced from the back or the front. We can rule out the front given the morphology of the wound.'

'Dr Ahmed ruled out a cut from the front for the same reasons,' said Dr Waterstone.

'We are agreed. A cut from behind is more common anyway. The head is pulled back, and the knife is drawn across the neck, from left to right by a right-handed assailant and from right to left by a left-handed individual.'

The doctor demonstrated using his scalpel and the wild-eyed assistant, Vera, who appeared relieved when he released her after the demonstration. 'The wound deepens at the beginning and tails off at the opposite side of the neck.' He bent over the neck and examined the gash once again.

Ridpath couldn't understand how he could be so close to the body of the woman.

'It is noticeable the deep cut throat found in this case was a single incision without surrounding injuries. There are no hesitations, no starting or stopping associated with suicide attempts. We also see the direction of the cut is left to right, suggesting a right-handed person. Was this woman right-handed, Ridpath?'

The detective thought quickly. 'I don't know,' he finally answered, 'it wasn't in any of the notes.'

'We have the weapon here.' From a stainless steel table, Dr Schofield produced a clear plastic bag. Inside was a small knife with a seven-inch blade found on the floor of the cell.

With his gloved hands, Dr Schofield took out the blade and inserted it into the wound below Wendy Chen's left ear. It seemed to fit almost horizontally. He moved the blade across the throat to where the cut stopped below the right ear. 'I believe we have our weapon, gentlemen. It fits well in the initial strike area beneath the right ear and gradually gets less deep as the blade cuts through the Adam's apple and the carotid.'

He placed the knife back in the bag and picked out a scalpel. 'The only way the victim could have done it herself would have been to hold the knife in her right hand and drive it into the throat, pulling it across so...' He demonstrated the movement.

'Dr Ahmed concluded this is what she did.'

Schofield pursed his lips. 'It is possible if the victim was right-handed, but if she were left-handed, virtually impossible. See.' He demonstrated with his left hand. 'The angles of the wound would have been different. But when I checked her hands just now, I found calluses on the base of her left fingers but none on the right. There's also an inkstain on her left index finger suggesting she wrote with her left hand. Usually, you only see them if a person is left-handed. Look at Vera.'

Once again, Vera reluctantly demonstrated for Dr Schofield. Her index finger had a splodge of green ink on it. 'I'm left-handed, always have been.'

'That's observational rather than proof, doctor,' said Waterstone.

'That's true. I'm afraid you'll have to find out whether she was right or left-handed, Ridpath.'

'Did Dr Ahmed mention this in his report?' asked the detective.

'He didn't, I'm afraid. You have to understand if a pathologist has been told this is a suicide in an Immigration Removal Centre, those are the signs he will be looking for. Margaret's brief to me was different.'

To Ridpath, it sounded as if Dr Schofield was making excuses for his colleague.

Dr Schofield continued to examine the woman's hands. 'No defensive injuries. If she had been attacked from behind, one would have expected to see them as she tried to grab the attacker's hand or the knife.'

'The lack of defensive injuries suggests suicide, doctor.'

'Correct, Dr Waterstone. The left-handedness is not conclusive, Ridpath, but I would check it out if I were you. Now, let's come to cause of death.'

He picked up the heart lying on a stainless steel tray. 'There's no evidence of air embolism such as frothy blood or air emboli in the right ventricle. The mechanisms of death in this case were blood loss and aspiration of blood following the cut throat.'

'From his notes Dr Ahmed reached the same conclusion,' said Dr Waterstone.

'However, there are two things he missed.'

Dr Schofield waited for a second and Ridpath obliged him with the question. 'And they are?'

'The first is bruising just below the right ear, where it meets the jawline. See it's clearly visible.' He pointed to a large green and black bruise.

'How did Dr Ahmed miss it?'

'I don't know. Perhaps he thought she had fallen after cutting her throat and acquired it as a result of the fall. Or perhaps the bruise happened as a consequence of cutting her throat. The hand holding the knife jamming into this area.'

'But surely he would have mentioned that conclusion in his report?'

'One would think so.'

'What caused the bruising?'

'It could have been a fall, but it was more likely this woman was punched.'

'Punched?'

'Hit with the closed fist.'

'I do know what a punch is, doctor. But there are no records of her being in a fight and she didn't have any bruising when she was admitted into the IRC.'

'No, she wouldn't. My guesstimate, and it's difficult to be precise after 28 days in a fridge, is she acquired this bruise any time from two to six hours before her death.'

'You said there was something else, doctor?'

The pathologist bent over and stared at the woman's right breast just above her dark nipple. 'See here, two round marks. I've only ever seen these once before.'

Ridpath had to walk over to stand close to the body. The smell became stronger the nearer he got. He gagged but took a deep breath and bent down to look at the skin. Dr Waterstone joined him. There were two small black punctures close together. 'What is it?'

Without answering, he produced shears and cut a section around the wound. He placed the inch-deep square of flesh in a stainless steel tray and handed it to Vera. 'Can you make slides of this for me?'

She took the tray into a small room off the morgue.

'What's going on, doctor? What were the marks on her chest?'

'I'm not sure, Ridpath. I have a suspicion this woman did not commit suicide, but I need to look at the slides under a microscope and I'll be certain.'

'Can't you let me know more?'

'Sorry, I've only seen it once before and I want do a little more work before coming to a conclusion.'

'I don't want to remind you, doctor, but we only have one more day before the inquest opens.'

'I am perfectly aware of the date, Inspector,' he carefully selected a scalpel, 'now I suggest you do your job and let me do mine.'

He stopped for a moment, the scalpel poised over the stomach of Wendy Chen. 'You might prepare yourself, Ridpath.'

The doctor used the scalpel to cut into the lining of the woman's stomach with one swift stroke. Immediately, a smell gushed out and assaulted Ridpath's nostrils. The smell was visceral, as if dredged up from the depths of some long-forgotten midden. It was a mixture of rotten meat, spoiled milk and decay, like the worst cheese in the world multiplied one thousand fold mixed with top notes of sewage.

Ridpath gagged involuntarily.

'It'll get a bit worse now,' said Dr Schofield as his scalpel poised to cut deeper into the stomach.

Ridpath gagged again and rushed out of the room.

Behind him, Dr Schofield shouted in his high voice. 'I'll send you the report as soon as I can.'

Chapter 24

Outside the morgue on the main road, Ridpath stood and breathed in deeply, trying to rid his nostrils of the smell, but still it lingered. He could taste it in his saliva and smell it on his clothes. Even worse, the odour seemed to cling to him like a shroud, filling his head, clawing at his brains.

'God, I could use a cigarette right now,' he said out loud. He was tempted to stop one of the passers-by and bum a cigarette off them. But he knew if he did, he would be back to smoking twenty a day. The cigarette with Emily Parkinson had to be a one-off.

'No more, no more,' he said out loud again, forcing a female pedestrian to glance at him and subtly increase her pace past him.

He sat on the wall. Where was this case going? He was working hard but the clock was ticking constantly against him. He was rushing things to hit an artificial deadline of the inquest date. Consequently, the investigation was suffering. It was time to slow it all down. Examine everything, question everything. He took out his notebook.

Until he received Dr Schofield's final report, the jury was out whether this was a suicide or something more sinister. Listening to both pathologists, they seemed to be arguing at one moment it was a suicide and at another it could have been something else.

What was it?

'Patience, Ridpath,' he heard Charlie Whitworth's voice telling him. 'Don't rush the bloody evidence, let it speak for itself.'

'Right, Charlie,' he said out loud. The Immigration Removal Centre had to be a good place to start. What had happened between the discovery of the body and the arrival of Ronald Barnes? The first responders from the ambulance service were there. He needed to find out who they were and question them pretty quickly. Why hadn't Barnes interviewed them? There was nothing in the police report.

Second, were there any other suicides in the centre over the last year? Was there a pattern to the deaths? He wrote himself another note.

Third, where did the knife come from? The centre says it wasn't one of theirs, so how did Wendy Chen get hold of it?

Fourth, and this was the biggest question of all, how was the door unlocked? This was supposedly a secure facility, doors don't just open by themselves.

And what about the victim? Why was she detained in the first place? Where was she arrested? Why was she removed so quickly to the IRC? And of course, who had she rung at the police station?

Too many questions, too little time.

For the first time in a long while, Ridpath was overwhelmed by a case. There were just too many unknowns. He smelt the lapel of his jacket; the scent of death lingered over him. He had to get his suit dry-cleaned as soon as he could.

And then there was one of those momentary flashes of insight which occasionally happened to him when he was under stress; he realised what the biggest unknown of all was.

If Wendy Chen hadn't committed suicide, if, in fact she was murdered, how had somebody killed her in the middle of one of the most secure places in Manchester?

Now Ridpath desperately needed a cigarette.

Chapter 25

His assistant was gazing at a computer monitor when he walked back into the Coroner's Office.

'Hi Ridpath, how was Dr Schofield? Sorry I couldn't make it, got stuck with these.' She pointed to the piles of schematics of the IRC on her desk.

'Fine, up to his arms in people's insides as usual.'

'What a fab job. Isn't he great?' And then she corrected herself. 'Isn't he great at his job, I mean?'

Was something going on between them he knew nothing about? He decided it wasn't his business what they did after office hours. He had enough problems to deal with without getting involved in the personal affairs of two adults. 'Did you find anything, Sophia?' he eventually asked.

'While you were away enjoying yourself at the morgue, seeing dead people we always called it at Uni, I've been buried under schematic plans and CCTV cameras.'

'And…?'

'Look at this.' She opened one of the light blue plans on her desk. It showed the total layout of the IRC. 'I plotted the location of the CCTV cameras on this master schematic…'

Ridpath noticed she had put little red Xs where the cameras were located.

'...and added blue Xs for the inoperative ones.'

'Great, Sophia, at least we can see where the cameras were located now and which weren't working.'

She leant over the table, staring at the plan. 'That's the point, there's something about the schematic bothering me.'

'What?'

'If I knew, Ridpath, I would be telling you.'

Ridpath jabbed his finger at the location of Room 7. 'We need to check if that door was opened during the night. The control room will have recorded all movements.'

'Right first time. So I rang Lucy and asked for the information. Apparently, they don't record the opening of the doors to the individual rooms.'

'It would also help to have the guard's movements. What time they tapped their cards against the various readers.'

'Already asked for the information. She said she would dig it up and get back to me.'

'I thought they would have had that information immediately available.'

'It surprised me too. Lucy also tried to quiz me regarding our investigation.'

'I hope you told her nothing.'

'I said less. And anyway, it's the truth, you never let me know what you're thinking.'

It was a common complaint from his wife too. 'If I'm honest, I'm not thinking too much at the moment, just gathering evidence. I see our first step is to work out whether this was a suicide or not.'

'And?'

'I don't know.'

'What did Dr Schofield say?'

'He's being cautious. He's found something but not telling me yet. Perhaps he will be more definite after he receives the toxicology results.'

'Sounds like a pathologist, always playing their cards close to their chest. It reminds me of a joke at Uni. How many pathologists does it take to remove a light bulb?'

Ridpath shrugged his shoulders. 'I give up.'

'None, they're still waiting for the test results.' She smiled at him. 'It's not funny I know, but if you were a nineteen-year-old student who'd just finished her first ever dissection of a human body, it was hilarious.'

'I can imagine. But to take your mind off the dissection of dead people, I suggest you get on with viewing these tapes. Eliminate the ones of no use and check the rest.'

Her eyes glanced at the tapes and back to Ridpath. 'OK,' she mumbled.

'Also call the IRC. The man in Room 9, Liang Xiao Wen, was sent to...'

'Halverson, near Leicester.'

'That's it. Find out all you can about him: what he did, why he was detained, et cetera, et cetera...'

'OK.'

Ridpath walked towards Mrs Challinor's office. 'Oh, and ring Dr Schofield to find out exactly when we can expect his findings and the toxicology results. Impress on him the urgency of the request.'

Sophia's eyes brightened. 'Will do,' she said.

Chapter 26

Ridpath tapped on the coroner's door and walked straight in.

Margaret Challinor was on the phone. 'Yes, I agree, it won't happen again, but you must understand I have requested an investigation into a death in Her Majesty's custody and nothing must stand in the way. The company was being deliberately obstructive and that is why my officer acted as he did.'

She glanced at Ridpath and motioned for him to sit.

The coroner was now holding the phone away from her ear. Ridpath could hear a tinny male voice coming from the loudspeaker. It did not sound happy.

'Fine, I understand. Thank you for your time and your advice.' She put the phone down and ran her fingers through her hair. 'That was the Ministry of Justice. Apparently, New Hampshire Detention Services have made a complaint to them regarding your behaviour, Ridpath.'

'Have they?'

'According to them you were, and I quote "rude, over-bearing and threatening in your manner" and "arrogant and insolent" in your requests. What do you have to say for yourself?'

'It's probably true. But they were being deliberately obstructive.'

'They disagree. In fact, they said, they sent over everything you requested and more. "They are totally committed to the inquest, believing it will absolve them of any responsibility for the death of Wendy Tang aka Wendy Chen Hong Xi."'

So that was their game, thought Ridpath. 'At least they got the woman's name correct. It's the oldest trick in the book: flood an inquiry with lots of useless bumf so they can't find what they are looking for. Wastes time and energy as well as allowing these shits to claim they have been co-operating to the fullest degree.'

The coroner was silent for a moment. 'I agree. This call ups the ante, they are ramping up the pressure on us. What have you found out so far?'

'No much, I'm afraid. Dr Schofield is still sitting on the fence until he gets results back from the tests. He's not certain whether it was suicide or something else...'

'Something else?'

'Could be murder. I think he's found something but he's not telling me what it is... yet.'

'Waiting for test results and toxicology?'

Ridpath raised his eyebrows. 'How did you know?'

'I heard you speaking to Sophia.'

'Anyway, we should get the results tomorrow. New Hampshire have dumped a library of documents on us.'

'I saw. They're blocking the hallway and Carol Oates is complaining.'

'When is she not complaining?'

'Just work with Jenny to move them. They are a fire hazard anyway.'

'Sophia is going through the boxes looking for information but it's like searching for intelligent life in Liverpool.'

'You met the officer from the original investigation?'

'The SIO was Detective Sergeant Ronald Barnes. Just three months away from retirement. After the complaint to Professional Standards, you're not his favourite person.'

'I'll survive.'

Ridpath's forehead creased with a frown. 'I've been thinking about his report. It wasn't a thorough investigation, but I can't be sure whether it was laziness, incompetence or he just assumed Wendy Chen committed suicide and made the facts fit this assumption. Dr Ahmed, the original pathologist, seems to have thought exactly the same.'

'The assumptions determining the outcome?'

'Exactly, from the Removal Centre to the police and the pathologist...'

'It was just another detainee who committed suicide. I've been doing research since our last meeting. Guess how many suicide attempts there were in Removal Centres in 2015?'

'Why 2015?'

'It's the latest figures I can find. The government is never keen on releasing these kind of stats.'

Ridpath shrugged his shoulders.

'393. In the same period, 2957 detainees were on suicide watch, including eleven children.'

'Eleven children? But don't those figures make it even more likely Wendy Chen *did* commit suicide?'

'But we have to be certain, Ridpath. It's our job and we owe it to the family.'

'Well, Dr Schofield isn't certain and there are some aspects of the death worrying me.'

'Like?'

'I don't know. Too many questions, I think, too many unknowns. For example, the victim made a call to Rowley police station twelve hours before she died.'

'Who did she speak to?'

Ridpath shrugged his shoulders again. 'That's what I need to find out. Plus there's the victim herself. We know nothing about her. Why was she detained? What was she doing here? Where did she live? Was she right- or left-handed?'

'Why is the last one important?'

'Something the pathologist said I need to follow up. And finally, there's one possible witness who may have heard what happened and is still in the country. All the rest have been deported already.'

'And he is?'

'Liang Xiao Wen, sent to Halverson IRC. Sophia is trying to find out about him. I hope to God he hasn't been deported too.'

'Sounds like you have a lot to do.'

'And not much time to do it. I need more help, Mrs Challinor. Sophia is brilliant but she's just one person.'

'You've got all the resources I have, Ridpath.'

'Can you postpone the inquest?'

'Not possible. The family have confirmed they want to take Wendy Chen's body back with them to China after the inquest. They are already here in Manchester, Ridpath.'

Ridpath stared at the ground in front of him. There was just too much to do.

'I'm meeting them tomorrow at 1 p.m. I'd like you to be there.'

'I don't know if I have the time, Mrs Challinor.'

'You could ask them about their daughter...'

Rather than spend years going through files, it would be a shortcut. 'One p.m.?'

'I'll let you know later if it changes.' Mrs Challinor stared at him. 'Do you want me to call Claire Trent and ask for her help?'

'Not yet, let's wait for the post-mortem results. We need something more concrete than your suspicions and my questions if we are to involve MIT. You know, if they get involved they may ask you to postpone the inquest under Schedule 1 of the 2009 act.'

'I'll take the risk. If a senior police officer requests a postponement, I am obliged to suspend the inquest for 28 days, but GMP won't want to be put under the spotlight if they screwed up an inquiry, not with the iOPS scandal flooding the papers and a visit from Her Majesties Inspectorate of Police due in November.'

'You are well informed.'

'I make it my business, Ridpath.'

Ridpath paused for a moment. 'I was talking to an old mate last week, he said the iOPS scandal is worse than it is being reported. They've lost thousands of files of data and are now having to input it manually. Overtime rates are soaring...'

'And not because they are investigating crimes. So Ridpath, what are your next steps?'

'Visit Wendy Chen's last known address in Chinatown and the UK Immigration Enforcement offices in Salford afterwards if I have time. I want to know why she was arrested in the first place. And why the hurry to deport her.'

'A lot to do.'

'Coroner, there is another problem. If Dr Schofield finds Wendy Chen didn't commit suicide but was murdered, it opens up a whole can of worms, starting with one question. Why?'

'Why what?'

'Why murder her? She was due to be deported that day. Why go to the trouble of killing her? Even more, why do it in one of the most secure places in Manchester?'

'Remember, it is not our job to discover why, just to work out the how, the when and the who.'

'But unless I know why, I won't be able to understand the rest, Mrs Challinor.'

She stared at him for a long while before saying, 'I understand, but the focus of your investigation should be what happened to Wendy Chen and how we can stop it happening again. Clear, Ridpath?'

He stood up. 'Thanks for reminding me,' he said as he walked to the door, stopping as the coroner called his name.

'And Ridpath, try not to annoy too many people... unless it's really necessary.'

'Of course, Coroner.'

Before he could leave, there was a knock on the door and Sophia walked in. 'Sorry for disturbing you both, but I thought Ridpath would like to see this.'

'What is it Sophia?'

'I've just got off the phone with Halverson IRC. They said Liang Xiao Wen was released back into the community a week ago. You'll never guess where his community is?'

Ridpath shook his head.

'Here, in Manchester. He has to sign in at 6 p.m. every night at Cheadle Heath police station.'

Ridpath stared at the clock on the far wall. 5.20.

'I'd better get a move on.'

Chapter 27

Cheadle Heath was a large police station in South Manchester. Ridpath had been posted here as a newly promoted Detective Constable working CID under Roberts, a Chief Inspector with a reputation for breaking rookie green detectives on a wheel of withering sarcasm and contempt.

Somehow, Ridpath had survived. Chief Inspector Roberts hadn't, though – his own vitriol had eventually consumed him and he died of a heart attack in 2015, a month after he retired.

Ridpath went to the funeral, as did many others, just to make sure the bastard was really dead.

Walking through the front doors of the station immediately sent his heart racing as if Roberts was waiting to give him yet another bollocking. Instead, he was greeted with a friendly hello from the Desk Sergeant.

'Hey, look what the cats dragged in.'

It was Sergeant Mungovan, another one of Ridpath's mentors from the past. Perhaps Cheadle was the station where old cops were sent to see out their days. A kind of police elephant's graveyard.

'Sarge, great to see you again.'

'I thought you'd turned in your badge, Ridpath. The Big C wasn't it?'

Did everybody know his life story? 'GMP doesn't get rid of me so easily. I'm working as a coroner's officer now.'

'Bit of a come-down, isn't it? Weren't you one of Charlie's golden boys?' There was a quick pause, a short cough and a glance at the book. It was obvious Mungovan knew he had put his foot in it. 'Good copper, Charlie. Sorry to hear what happened.' Another cough. 'Anyway, what are you doing in this neck of the woods?'

'You have a signer. Comes in at six o'clock every day.'

'The Chinese guy?'

'That's him. Has he been in yet?'

Mungovan looked at the clock. 5.45. 'Not yet, regular as clockwork that one. Don't have to check up on him. Comes in, signs the book and out again in two minutes. Wish they were all like him.'

'When he comes in, can you keep him here? I'd like to have a word with him.'

'No problem. Anything I should know about?'

Ridpath didn't want to go into a long explanation. 'Not really, one of the coroner's inquests. You know what lawyers are like. Could I snaffle an interview room for twenty minutes?'

'Number three is free. You'll have to give it a clean though. Dave Hardy's been using it...'

Dave Hardy was one of his friends and another of Charlie's boys from MIT. He had been part of the clear out of the department by Claire Trent. 'Is he around?'

'Should be, but you know Dave, best in the business at skiving. If I see him, I'll tell him to look in on you.'

'Ta, Sarge. Room 3 is this way, isn't it?'

'Hasn't changed since you were here, except the table has some new cigarette burns.'

'Nothing ever changes…'

Ridpath was buzzed through to the interior of the station. Interview Room 3 was the first on the right. He walked in and quickly cleaned up the plastic coffee cups, crisp packets, cans of Coke with stubbed out cigarettes floating in brown flat liquid, emptying everything into a large bin in the corridor. Dave Hardy hadn't changed, still as messy as ever.

He'd only just finished when Sergeant Mungovan's voice came over the tannoy. 'DI Ridpath to reception.'

He walked out and saw a small Chinese man sitting on one of the plastic seats. The man was staring at the ground, his black hair falling over his black-rimmed glasses.

'Mr Liang?' Ridpath asked.

The man looked up. He was young, like a student, only there was a hardness, a coldness in his eyes that surprised Ridpath.

'Can you come with me? I'd like to ask you a few questions.'

'What's it about?' The English was clear if accented, with a peculiar Manchester whine to it.

'Just a few questions.'

'I'm parked outside.'

Ridpath pointed to the door leading to the interview room and smiled. 'Won't take long.'

The man shrugged and stood up. Ridpath noted a certain rigidity about the man's body. His arms went behind his back and his shoulders arched backwards, almost as if he was standing to attention. Had this man been in the military or was he just used to dealing with the police?

Sergeant Mungovan buzzed them both through to the interview room.

Once inside, Ridpath was Mr Affable. 'Can I get you anything? Coffee, water, tea? But between you and me, the coffee is undrinkable, the water is from the tap and the tea is the awful powder stuff from the machine.'

The man shook his head. 'Not thirsty. What's this about?'

Ridpath sat opposite him. 'Nothing much. I just want to ask you a few questions. We need some help with our enquiries. Are you comfortable speaking to me without an interpreter? I can get one to come in if you want but we'll have to wait at least two hours at this time of night. Which dialect is best for you? Cantonese or Mandarin?'

'Mandarin, but I can speak English. I don't want to wait. What's it about?'

The third time he had asked, he was keen to know. Ridpath would keep him waiting for a little while longer. He opened his notebook and took out his pen.

Liang's eyes watched him like a hawk.

'You are Mr Liang Xiao Wen?'

'Right. Your pronunciation is good.'

'Thank you, lucky I guess.' Ridpath didn't tell him about having a Chinese wife. 'What's your present address?' The pen hovered over the notebook.

'You know already.'

'We just need confirmation.'

'You're not recording the interview?' Liang pointed to the machine on the desk.

Ridpath shook his head. 'Like I said, just a friendly chat. Your address?'

'Flat 4, 267 Nicholas Street.'

For a second, Ridpath's pen hovered over the note-book. 'Is that in Chinatown?'

'Yeah, close to the Arch.'

'I know it well, great dim sum near there.'

The man just smiled.

'Now, you were recently detained at Wilmslow Immi-gration Removal Centre, is that correct?'

The smile vanished and the man nodded slowly, his eyes narrowing.

'Is that a yes?'

'Yeah.'

'Why were you in there?'

'I was supposed to have overstayed my visa, but they've got the wrong person. They must be after another Liang Xiao Wen, not me.'

Chinese names always gave the police problems. Firstly, there were less than 100 surnames in use, the surname came first and, like the west, the other names were also common. Ridpath translated Liang's name. Xiao Wen literally meant 'little culture'. Which, looking at the man in front of him, was a correct description.

Liang was staring at him. 'Anyway, my brief is sorting it out.'

'But I'm not here about your problems with the Home Office. I'm investigating a death in custody. While you were in Wilmslow IRC, a woman died. A Miss Wendy Chen Hong Xi, but you may have known her as Wendy Tang.' Ridpath paused, looking for a reaction. The face was like stone. 'A countrywoman of yours, I believe.'

'Was she?'

'I believe so. According to our records, you were in the room next to her.'

'The woman who killed herself?'

'The woman who died, that's right. Did you know her? Talk with her at all?'

The man shook his head.

'Really? The only other Chinese national in the Removal Centre and you two didn't talk to each other?'

'I tried but she didn't want to talk. Too upset.'

'Why was she upset?'

'I don't know, we didn't talk.'

'Later on, what happened?'

'What do you mean?'

'That evening, after the doors were locked.'

'I don't know.'

'What do you mean, you don't know? Didn't you hear anything?'

The man shook his head. 'I was asleep when the alarm went off.'

'What time was that?'

'About four o'clock, I think.'

'You didn't hear anything before that time?'

The man shook his head again. 'I was asleep.'

'And afterwards, what happened?'

'There was noise in the corridor, but I couldn't see anything so I went back to bed. I wanted to come out at 8.15 as usual but they kept us locked in.'

'When did you know there was a death in the room next to yours?'

'When they came for me at about ten o'clock. Said they were transferring me because my solicitor had appealed the deportation.'

'And you were taken to another Removal Centre?'

'Yeah, Halverson. Shit place. Got out pretty quickly though. Now I come here every day at six. Waste of time.' Liang stared at Ridpath for a long time before finally saying. 'The girl who died...'

'Wendy Chen?'

'I think she...'

Just as Liang was about to say more, there was a heavy rap on the door and it opened. Sergeant Mungovan stood in the entrance. 'Sorry, Ridpath, his brief is out here, demanding to see his client.'

'Brief, who called a brief?'

Mungovan shrugged his shoulders. A small, bespectacled man carrying a briefcase and a bundle of papers elbowed past the Sergeant into the room. 'You're interviewing my client without my presence, why?'

'And you are?'

'Henry Miller, his solicitor. You know better than to conduct an interview, detective, without the presence of a solicitor. I don't know what the police are coming to these days.'

'Firstly, Mr Miller, your client wasn't being interviewed, he agreed to help me with my enquiries. Secondly, he waived his right to a solicitor. And thirdly, I'm not working for the police but I'm a coroner's officer, investigating a death.'

The solicitor put his hand on his client's elbow and lifted him up. 'Good, as this isn't a police investigation, I am advising my client he should leave this station now.' He turned to Mungovan. 'He has adhered to the terms of his release by signing in punctually at 6 p.m., has he not, Sergeant?'

'He has already signed.'

'Then we will leave now. My client will return tomorrow evening at 6 p.m. as he is required to do. If you try again to interview him without me being present, Mr...?'

'It's Detective Inspector Ridpath.'

'DI Ridpath, I will report your conduct to the Chief Coroner. Do I make myself clear?'

He strode past Ridpath, pushing his client into the corridor like an errant schoolchild. Just before he left the interview room, he turned back. 'Do give my regards to Margaret, won't you? On the other hand, don't bother, I'll call her myself this evening. Goodbye, DI Ridpath.'

Chapter 28

After the solicitor left, Ridpath sat alone in the interview room. He stared at the black glass of the two-way mirror, seeing his reflection in it. He didn't recognise himself. Who was that person?

That man seemed old and tired. The frown line between his eyebrows was deeply fissured and the bags under his eyes could carry a week's load of groceries from Tesco. Did he want to go back to MIT? The pressure was immense and unrelenting. At least now, he had most weekends off to spend time with Eve and Polly. At MIT, he could never be certain of his hours and he would be back on shifts again, or at least on call 24 hours a day.

But isn't that what he did? Isn't that what he lived for? The energy of a team. The tracking down of leads. The painstaking grind of an investigation. The accumulation of evidence leading to the goal of a conviction.

He remembered the highs and lows; there were always more lows than highs. But when those rare convictions and arrests took place, God, weren't they sweet?

He smiled at the memory. 'You can come out now.' He said aloud to his reflection.

A few seconds later the door swept open and Dave Hardy stood in the entrance. 'How did you know I was there?'

Ridpath stood. 'There's always somebody in the listening room, Dave, and knowing how bloody nosey you are, it had to be you.'

'Yeah, makes sense. You always were too clever for your own good, Ridpath. Fancy a quick pint? There's a good spit-and-sawdust pub nearby. Does a lovely pint of Robbos.'

Ridpath checked his watch. 7.05. 'Just a quickie, Polly's cooking a takeaway tonight.'

'Same as my missus. These days it's easier to get on Just Eat than go to the supermarket. Can't complain though. She'd burn boiling water, my missus.'

They walked out to reception, Ridpath leaving his card with Sergeant Mungovan. 'Can you let me know when Liang signs on again, Sarge? I might need to ask him a few more questions and call him for the inquest. I thought he was just opening up when you came in.'

'Sorry about that, Ridpath, but you know the rules. I'll call you when he comes in again tomorrow.'

'Yeah, ain't it always the same. Solicitors turning up like the cavalry when you least want them. Anyway, let's have that pint, Dave.'

They walked out of the station and across to the car park. 'I thought you said it was nearby.'

'Look around you, Ridpath, what do you see?'

Ridpath did as he was told. Around the station was nothing but industrial estates and, off to the right, a disused railway line. Container lorries raced past, belching out exhaust fumes, rushing to make their last delivery for the day.

'You see, the powers that be, in their infinite wisdom, decided to open police stations in areas like this, because land was cheap and they could build their red brick dream palaces. But what happened was they stuck us out in the middle of nowhere, miles away from the local community. So here we are, on an industrial estate.'

'Not a lot here.'

'Community policing, my arse. The only community we've got to police is a couple of forklifts.' Dave Hardy opened the door to his car. 'Hop in.'

Ridpath didn't want to be at the mercy of Dave Hardy when he needed to leave the pub. 'It's all right, I'll use my car and follow you.'

'Suit yourself.'

Five minutes later and they were both sat in the Printer's Arms with a pint of Robinson's best bitter in front of them. Dave Hardy picked his up and stared deep into the clear yellow/brown liquid. 'Still a good pint.' He drank a third of it in one gulp and wiped his mouth with the back of his hand. 'How's the coroner these days?'

'Fine. Busy.'

'Still got you running round like a blue-arsed fly?'

'Something like that.'

'The solicitor was in quick, wasn't he?'

'He was, who called him?'

'I checked outside for you. A man was sitting in a BMW waiting for our signer to come out. I reckon he called the solicitor when chummy didn't reappear.'

'Who was he? Do you know?'

Dave Hardy slipped a piece of paper across the table to Ridpath. 'A Mr Lam Tai Kong. I checked the number plate with DLVR in Swansea. At least, the car is registered to him.'

'Thanks mate.'

'I may be stuck out in some bloody industrial estate but I'm still a good copper, Ridpath, remember?'

'How much did you hear?'

'From the observation room?'

Ridpath nodded.

'Most of it.'

'What do you think?'

'Seems like you're chasing your arse, Ridpath. When's the inquest start?'

'Thursday morning.'

Dave Hardy laughed and said, 'You're stuffed.' He drank another long gulp of beer. 'Fancy another?'

Ridpath shook his head. 'Not for me, mate.'

'You are a good boy these days. I remember when you would suck this stuff down like it was Vimto.'

'Yeah, well, time's change.'

Dave Hardy stood up. 'How's the cancer?'

Shit. Ridpath suddenly remembered he was supposed to go in and check his blood work. 'Same as ever. Gone but not forgotten.'

'I'll drink to that.' And off he stumbled to the bar.

Ridpath was left alone to work out what to do. First thing tomorrow he'd ring the hospital and arrange an appointment. After that, it was time to follow up on the victim. Perhaps a visit to Madame Wong's Bakery was on the cards.

Dave Hardy returned. 'I was just thinking when was the last time I saw you. Wasn't it Charlie's funeral? I heard you got his killer. Well done, mate, Charlie would have been proud. Here's to Charlie.'

The policeman raised his pint and swallowed half of it. Ridpath took a mouthful of his own. Charlie's face popped into his head, a hand stroking the moustache, and his ex-boss saying, 'We seek evidence, it's all that counts. The truth always lies. Only evidence is clear. Pure, unadulterated evidence.'

'I miss the times at MIT. It was a bloody good team Charlie and John Gorman put together. Do you ever see the gaffer?'

Ridpath shook his head.

'Off on his bloody allotment, growing weeds. What a bloody waste. Meanwhile, the rest of us are hoovering up overtime, manually entering information on the new computer system.'

'How is iOPS?'

Hardy stared at him. 'Put these words in the correct order. Organise. In. A. Brewery. Piss-up. A. Couldn't.' He took another swallow of beer. 'It's a nightmare, Ridpath. Intelligence is all over the place. The plod are going to addresses not knowing who is there or what they'll find. Meanwhile, back at the stations, they're spending half their time doing data entry.'

'The more things change, the more they stay the same.'

Dave Hardy stared at him.

'Jean Baptiste Alphonse Karr. A Frenchman.'

Dave Hardy finished his pint. 'Charlie always said you were too clever to be a copper. You having another?'

Ridpath shook his head, finishing the last dregs in his glass. 'Nah, need to get off home.'

Hardy shrugged his shoulders. 'Suit yourself. Good seeing you, Ridpath.'

'And you.' Ridpath stood up. 'Can you do me a favour, Dave?'

'Ask and it will be granted, my Lord Ridpath.'

'Can you check those two men on the computer for me?'

'The two Chinese?'

'See if they've got any form, any priors.'

'Looking for anything special?'

Ridpath shook his head. 'Nah, it's just the solicitor was too quick and too good. He wasn't your common or garden bottom feeder from the Yellow Pages. This guy was expensive, know what I mean?'

Chapter 29

Yang May Feng wriggled into her tight red cheongsam, daubed her mouth an even brighter red and stepped into her high heels. The Uber was coming in three minutes to take her to the club. She had to go out tonight to work and make money. With luck, there would be some businessmen in town who wanted her company and would leave her a large tip.

She only slept with the customers if she liked them or if she was particularly short of cash.

Like tonight.

Going back to their hotel rooms, their sticky hands pawing her like a piece of fish in the market, disgusted her. But there was no food and no money to buy food. Yesterday at the ATM was OK and anyway, she needed money to give to Liang. She couldn't have them looking for her as well.

'Money, always money,' she said out loud to her reflection in the mirror.

She brushed her hair back and tied it in a ponytail. She was aiming for the Maggie Cheung look in Wong Kao Wai's picture. A sort of sophisticated elegance with a touch of innocence. It had worked on men in the past and it would work tonight.

She knew leaving the flat again was a risk. What if he was there? What if he asked her about Hong Xi? What if he was the one who wanted to buy her out?

The thought sent a shiver down her spine. She would never leave with him, not after what he had done to Hong Xi.

And now her friend was dead.

It would be better to stay here tonight. At least here she was safe; nobody knew where she was. What if he followed her home?

She threw off her coat and sat down. She wouldn't go out tonight, she couldn't risk it.

She checked inside her purse. Just ten pounds and a few coins. Enough for some rice and noodles to keep her going for another couple of days. She would stay at home. At least she would be safe.

A car horn sounded from the road outside her flat.

She forgot she ordered an Uber and would have to pay the man anyway for coming.

She stood again and put on her coat. She would be OK. He never visited the club on a Tuesday, so he definitely wouldn't be there. She'd find a businessman quickly, ask the *mama-san* for a favour, tell her she needed the money and she would be picked first.

The car horn blared again.

'All right, all right, I'm coming.'

She picked up her purse, turned off the light and tottered down the stairs to the waiting Uber.

Once inside the Toyota, she uttered the words 'Elephant Club' and the driver nodded. He had taken girls there before.

She didn't notice the man in the dark car who was still parked across the road from her apartment.

Chapter 30

By the time Ridpath arrived home, Polly and Eve had already eaten. 'Sorry, had a quick one with Dave Hardy.'

'No worries, Eve was hungry so we ate. I'm afraid your fish and chips are a bit cold. I can heat them up if you like.'

'Thanks, I'll just take a shower. And can you get my suit dry-cleaned?'

'At a post-mortem again?'

Ridpath nodded.

'Who this time?'

'A young Chinese woman.'

'Really? Who was she?'

Ridpath couldn't answer. The only information he had on Wendy Chen was from her processing document at Wilmslow Immigrant Removal Centre. Barnes' police report was singularly lacking in any information about the victim. He didn't even have a home address for her. 'That's what I need to find out.' he finally answered. 'All I know is she had something to do with Madame Wong's Bakery.'

'The one in Chinatown? Great char siu sou, daan ta, bo luo bao and jian dui.'

Ridpath made a face.

She struck her Chinese waitress pose. 'For the uneducated *gweilo*, barbecued pork pies, custards tarts, pineapple buns and fried sesame balls. Even talking about them makes my mouth water.'

Eve walked in the kitchen and gave her dad a kiss on the cheek. 'Hi dad.' She screwed up her face. 'You smell kinda weird.'

Ridpath pointed upstairs. 'Time for my shower.'

'I'll heat up the fish and chips.'

Ridpath had a long and extremely hot shower, but even after he had dried himself off, he could still smell the strange aroma of post-mortem on him. He doused himself with Ralph Lauren and went to eat.

His dinner was on the table, so he sat and, without thinking, forked mouthfuls of soggy fish and rubbery chips into his mouth. Upstairs, he could hear Eve and Polly calling to each other, as each of them prepared for bed.

After he finished eating, he washed the dishes, leaving them to dry on the drainer. He walked into the living room and poured himself a large glass of Glenmorangie. The subtle hints of burnt orange, grass, seaweed and peat smoke danced across his tongue as he settled in the chair.

He had just one day left to sort this case out or at least make sense of it. His feeling of being lost hadn't gone away – instead it had intensified.

There were too many strands to the investigation. What had happened in Room 7 between 3 and 4 p.m. on the morning of August 20th? Had Wendy Chen killed herself as the police report said? Or had something else happened? What had Dr Schofield discovered and wasn't telling him?

Ridpath took another sip of whisky. Upstairs everything had gone quiet. Eve and Polly must have gone to bed. In the old days, Eve would always give him a hug and kiss before she went upstairs. He always used to laugh at how high she pulled her Frozen pyjama bottoms. They were almost up to her armpits. 'But it's comfortable, Daddy.'

Apparently, she was too old to kiss him goodnight now. Soon, she would be embarrassed to be seen with him and after that, the dreaded 'You don't have to come with me. I'm old enough to look after myself now.'

He raised his glass in a mock toast. 'Here's to the day being far away.' But he knew it was close and there was nothing he could do to stop it.

And then it occurred to him: the dead woman in Wilmslow IRC had been a young girl once. Had her father sat in his room, wishing the day of her independence wouldn't come too?

Probably.

The image of her body lying on the mortuary table forced its way into his mind, followed by a sharp reminder of the terrible stench as Schofield cut into her stomach.

This woman wasn't a victim. She was somebody's daughter.

Mrs Challinor was right. They needed to find out what happened to Wendy Chen, whatever it took.

She was a young woman who deserved a better end to her life than lying on some cold stainless steel table in an even colder mortuary.

She deserved to have somebody care for her.

Like Eve.

He took another swallow of the Glenmorangie, feeling its bite in the back of his throat. A final thought forced itself to the front of his mind and wouldn't leave.

Did Wendy Chen commit suicide or did somebody murder her?

WEDNESDAY
SEPTEMBER 18

Chapter 31

The next morning he decided to get into the Coroner's Office early, making a breakfast for Eve of scrambled eggs and an extra large pot of coffee for Polly before leaving while they both slept.

He arrived at eight to find Sophia already at her desk staring at the screen of the laptop she had brought from home. 'You haven't been here all night, have you?'

'No way, came in at six. I can't look at this stuff at home. Mum goes all snippy on me. "You'll ruin your eyes. No boy will look at you. You should be making yourself look pretty instead."' She sighed loudly. 'I had to get away.'

'Find anything?'

'Nothing, except…'

'Except what?'

'Well, mum might be right, it could be my eyes, but look at this.'

Ridpath bent over her desk and stared at the screen as she rewound the disc and pressed play. 'Is there a shadow there or am I seeing things?'

'Play it again.'

She rewound it once more. Ridpath stared at the screen. The image was of a camera outside the DCOs restroom on the ground floor where Ridpath had interviewed Osborne and Cummings.

'I guess the bosses put the camera here to check how long their employees were taking for their breaks. But it's the right-hand side you should look at. See the light there?'

'Yes.'

Sophia stared at the time counter at the top of the screen.

03.27.18

03.27.19

03.27.20

'Watch... now.'

The light flickered for an instant and shone constantly again.

'What was that?' said Ridpath. 'A faulty light...?'

'Or somebody's shadow crossing quickly in front of it?'

'Where's the location?'

Sophia tapped the schematic of the Centre. 'On the stairs leading to the first floor.'

'Don't tell me...'

'The camera on the stairs is out of order.'

'Could it be one of the guards?'

'According to their statements, at this time Osborne was in the control room.'

'Can we confirm it?'

'I can check the control room camera.'

'Do it. What about Cummings?'

'He said he went to the toilet.'

'No cameras there?'

'Even New Hampshire Detention Services wouldn't go that far.'

'Is there a camera close to the entrance of the staff toilets?'

'I'm just looking for it now.'

'Good work, Sophia.'

'How was the interview with the man from Halverson?'

'Interesting but not terribly informative. Is the coroner in?'

'I heard somebody banging around.'

'And before I forget, did you follow up with Dr Schofield?'

'The post-mortem results will be in at three this afternoon, he promised me.'

'Let's hope he keeps it.'

A quiet smile crossed her face. 'Oh, I'm sure he will.'

Ridpath decided not to ask her why. Some things were best not investigated.

Chapter 32

'Good morning, Ridpath. You're in early.'

'So it seems is everybody else, Coroner.'

'Including Carol Oates. We are busy this morning.'

'I just thought I'd fill you in on last night's meeting with the man who was in the room next door to Wendy Chen.'

'His name was Liang Xiao Wen. His solicitor, Henry Miller, rang me last night to complain about you.'

'He said he would.'

'Don't worry, the solicitor is a plonker. He knows my ex-husband better than me. They are two peas in a pod. Both as trustworthy as politicians.'

'That bad, huh?'

'Worse. Anyway, what did Liang say?'

'He saw nothing apparently, slept through it all. All he remembers is hearing the alarms go off.'

'Shall we call him as a witness? Did he see her in the Removal Centre?'

'He did see her, but didn't talk to her. According to him, she was crying and wanted to be alone, seemed depressed.'

'Depressed enough to kill herself?'

'He didn't know.'

'We'd better call him as a witness. At least he can talk to her state of mind on the day.'

'I'll send a subpoena over to Cheadle Heath and ask Sergeant Mungovan to give it to him when he signs on at six this evening.'

'Could we do it earlier?'

'Well, I guess I could do it. He lives in Chinatown and I'm going Madame Wong's Bakery this morning.'

'Why?'

'It's the last address given by Wendy Chen when she was processed into the Wilmslow IRC.'

'I hate that word. Processed.'

'What I shall I say?'

'Admitted. Entered. Booked into. Whatever you like, but not processed. I'm meeting the parents this afternoon. What shall I say to them? Your daughter died in one of our prisons the day after being processed?' Mrs Challinor ran her hands through her long grey curls. 'Sorry, Ridpath, the more I read about what happens in these IRCs, the more angry I become. Human beings treated like bits of meat.'

'I know, Mrs Challinor, but becoming emotional doesn't help our victim. As you said, our job is to find out what happened to her and make sure it doesn't happen to anybody else.'

'Quoting my words back to me?'

'They are right, particularly when you are meeting the family today.'

'And afterwards, preparing for the inquest. Have the test results come in from Dr Schofield?'

'Not yet, but Sophia is chasing him. This afternoon apparently.'

'Good. We've got nothing so far except the reports written by Barnes and the first coroner, Dr Ahmed.'

'I know.'

'So I'm relying on you, Ridpath. Unless you find something, I can offer the jury only two possible findings: suicide or an open verdict. But I know in my water there is more to this case, I just know it.'

'I don't disagree, Mrs Challinor, but it takes time.'

'Time is the one commodity we don't have.' She went back to reading her file. 'Don't let me keep you, Ridpath.'

As he walked out of her room, Ridpath looked back at Mrs Challinor, her grey hair dangling in front of her face as she wrote in green ink on the report.

Would he let her down this time?

Chapter 33

After waiting for Jenny Oldfield to type the subpoena for Liang Xiao Wen, Ridpath headed for the small area of Manchester just south of the City Centre, bounded by Mosley Street to the west, Portland Street to the east, Princess Street to the south, and Charlotte Street to the north, known as Chinatown.

He backed his car into a space in the car park right in the middle of the area. Surrounding him were the sights, sounds, smells and beeping car horns of a busy Chinese city. He came here occasionally, when Eve or Polly needed their fix of Cantonese food, particularly dim sum. Or when Polly's mother needed to stock up on the salted eggs, tree fungus, goji berries and assorted dried bits of animal she needed for her soups.

He walked out of the car park and saw the bright red sign in electric neon for Madame Wong's Bakery next to the bright red Chinese arch. He walked in and instantly the distinctive smell of a Chinese bakery hit him. It was different from those in the West – the strong aroma of yeast was missing. Instead, there was a sweetness with a hint of aniseed suffusing the place.

An old woman turned her head and stared at him, as if saying, 'What's the *gweilo* doing here?'

Polly had explained long ago that *gweilo*, the slang word for westerners in Cantonese, literally meant 'ghost man'. The Chinese, on seeing the pale, white skins of the first westerners in their country had been so shocked, they thought they were being confronted by ghosts. The description had stuck and, seeing the wrinkled face of the woman staring at him, he could see she still believed it.

He ignored her and walked up to the counter, flashing his warrant card to the young server. 'Can I see your boss?'

The old woman spoke in a thick Cantonese accent. '*Chai yan, hai-m hai?*'

Ridpath recognised the words for policeman. Polly had taught him some Cantonese so he could understand when she was arguing with her mother.

The server replied. '*Hai ge wo.*'

Instantly, the woman put down the tray on which she had been placing her pastries and walked out of the shop without looking back at him.

Ridpath smiled. The old distrust of the police and the authorities in general was still alive and kicking. 'Can I see your boss?' he asked the server again.

'He not here.'

'When will he come back?'

'Dunno.'

'Guess.'

The woman's shoulders shrugged. 'By and by.'

Ridpath took Wendy Chen's picture from his wallet. 'Have you seen this woman before?'

The server nodded. Finally he was getting somewhere. 'Did she work here?'

'No.'

'Where did you see her?'

'Policeman, he showed me picture.'

'When?'

'Maybe month back. August sometime.'

Had Barnes been here? But there was no address for Wendy Chen on the police report. 'Which policeman?'

'I dunno. A policeman. They all look the same.'

Ridpath was getting nowhere. 'What's your boss' name?'

The woman's eyes flashed from side to side as she weighed up the pros and cons of telling Ridpath. Eventually, she decided a name didn't matter.

'It's Chen Tai Kong.'

The same name as the man in the car last night. A coincidence? Probably not. He placed his card on the counter. 'Get your boss to call me? Tell him I'm not a policeman, I'm from the Coroner's Office.' A little half-truth but Ridpath could live with it. 'Get him to call me.'

The woman took the card and stared at it without answering.

Ridpath walked out of the door, the small bell ringing above his head.

In the reflection of the glass, he saw the woman throw his card into a bin next to the till. He didn't think he was going to get a call after all.

Chapter 34

Ridpath stepped outside and was greeted by Hong Kong in all its garish glory. Bright red and yellow street signs, the noise of traffic, pedestrians looking into windows and always the aroma of Chinese food everywhere.

Time to find Liang Xiao Wen. Last night at Cheadle nick, the man seemed to be on the point of saying something when the lawyer arrived. Perhaps if Ridpath cornered him alone, the man would talk.

He checked Liang's address. 267 Nicholas Street. He turned left past the Wing Fat Supermarket, where Polly's mum shopped, through the arch and right onto Nicholas Street.

In front of him, the burnt-out shell of a building was the only memorial to two dead street sleepers who had been caught in the fire in 2016. Nobody had ever been imprisoned for causing their deaths.

He stopped for a moment, thinking of another fire not far from here. The death of another street sleeper, Sam Sykes. At least Ridpath had caught the killer, but it had been touch and go. He had been lucky. One piece of evidence had helped turn the case, changing a wild goose chase into a successful prosecution.

Luck was all it was. That and the relentless grind of finding evidence.

'The truth always lies. Only evidence is clear.' Charlie's words came back to him again. Was the man haunting him?

He hurried along Nicholas Street looking for the address. A betting shop on the left, the name repeated in Chinese characters, a casino, another betting shop with a restaurant on the second floor. It must be here somewhere, but there were no numbers on the doors, as if nobody wanted to be found.

Ridpath retraced his steps, heading down a back alley with metal fire escapes climbing to the floors above. It reminded him of New York – even the buildings had the turn of the century solidity of that city.

He stopped in front of a six-storey building. Was this it?

He searched for a number above the door.

Nothing.

He walked round one side to see if there was an entrance. On the right was another bookie with a big sign saying BET HERE in English and the message repeated in Chinese.

He had never understood the lure of gambling. For him, there was a reason bookies and casino owners were some of the richest people in the world: the odds were always in their favour.

Polly tried to explain the importance of gambling to the Chinese once. 'It's the belief in fate; one day, the heavens will be aligned, the sun will shine, the skies open and your numbers will come up. The Gods have bestowed their good fortune on you.'

'And if you lose?'

'The Gods weren't listening. Or they were asleep. Or you had simply chosen the wrong numbers. There was always another day when it could happen. It's always a "could".'

'Your dad was a gambler, wasn't he?'

'Lost everything and then lost it again. He was always hoping for the big win when it would all come back. He died hoping.'

Ridpath walked past the bookies and saw a small entrance on the right, with the number 267 above the door in faded red letters.

Inside, concrete stairs led up past an import/export company on the ground floor. Ridpath climbed them. He was looking for Flat 5, according to the address. He passed Flat 2 on the left and climbed higher. Flat 3 had a picture of a young woman dressed in a red nightie outside, probably a knocking shop.

Ridpath climbed more stairs, past a kid's tricycle and a stand for shoes outside another door. Flat 4.

Just one more flight of stairs. He was already out of breath. Either he needed a lot more exercise or there was something wrong. The visit to the hospital should sort it out.

In the back of his mind lurked a fear dressed in black carrying a scythe. He hoped the cancer hadn't come back. He prayed it was just tiredness from overwork and lack of exercise. Nothing more, please let it be nothing more.

He climbed the last flight. Flat 5 was right in front of him. A door painted in one of those Farrow and Ball greys, so different and stylish compared with the utilitarian doors of the other flats. A plant in a pot was on the left and a single bentwood chair on the right.

Ridpath pressed the doorbell, hearing the sound echo inside the flat.

No answer.

He pressed it again, longer this time.

Still no answer. Liang was probably out. He should give the subpoena directly into the man's hands, but he didn't have time to waste chasing him all over town.

Instead, Ridpath took out the paper and lifted the flap of the letter box to post it.

As he did, the door swung slowly open, revealing a dark entrance hall, expensively covered in a small carpet and parquet flooring. Ridpath looked up to see somebody staring back at him and he instinctively stepped back, raising his arms to ward off any blows.

But none came.

He looked up again and saw his own image reflected in a wall-length mirror opposite the door.

Feng Shui. Ridpath should have known. Never have an opening directly behind the door otherwise money will flow out of your life.

He shouted, 'Hello, anybody in?' hearing his voice break halfway through the sentence. He shouted, 'Anybody in?' Stronger now, more like a policeman.

Still no answer.

He crossed the threshold, wiping his feet on the mat. On the right, a small cupboard with open shelves for shoes. Ridpath could see expensive brands of trainers, all lined up in a neat row.

'Anybody here?' he shouted again.

A corridor led into the flat on the right. Ridpath stepped forward, hearing his shoes on the parquet flooring. A door open on the left. He peered in. A bed already made with an expensive suit, shirt and tie lying on top, waiting to be put on by somebody going out. The bedroom itself was neat and tidy; expensive lamps on small tables either side of the bed, built in wardrobes, a print of Marilyn from Andy Warhol, her bright orange skirts billowing around her body. Was that real? thought Ridpath. Worth a pretty penny if it was.

'DI Ridpath, coroner's officer. Anybody here?' he shouted again, walking slowly towards the living room.

And then he saw Liang Xiao Wen.

He was lying on a red carpet in the middle of the floor, his arms spread wide like Jesus on the cross and a smile plastered across his face.

Ridpath gradually realised it wasn't a smile. It was a large gash where his mouth had once been.

And the carpet wasn't red.

It was blood.

Liang's blood.

Chapter 35

'Hello, Ridpath, didn't want to see you again.'

Detective Sergeant Ted Jones climbed the stairs to where Ridpath was standing outside the door with a medic. It was just twelve minutes since Ridpath had called the emergency services.

'You were quick, Ted.'

'As soon as I heard you were involved, I thought I'd better get here sharpish and City 3 is my patch.' He stared past Ridpath into the darkened flat. 'Matey in there, is he?'

'Yeah, on the floor of the sitting room. I've sealed off the crime scene waiting for your mob to come.'

As he finished speaking, there was the sound of heavy boots running up the stairs. A sergeant and two constables appeared on the landing.

'Nice to see you, John. Can you get your lads to close off these stairs?'

'Will do, Ted. There's a crowd gathering outside.'

'Already? The word's got out quick. Better push the cordon out to the top of the lane. Nobody in or out unless they're part of the investigation.'

The uniformed sergeant turned to give instructions to his team.

'And John, see if you can find my oppo. He was only supposed to be parking the bloody car.'

'Right, Ted.'

The Detective Sergeant fished a pair of blue plastic gloves from his pocket and slid them over his hands. 'Come on, Ridpath, let's see what you've found for me.'

He stepped across the threshold and Ridpath followed. 'Why were you in this neck of the woods?'

'Checking something for the coroner and serving a subpoena on this man to appear at an inquest tomorrow.'

They walked into the living room. Jones took a long look at the body lying on the floor. 'Looks like he won't be able to make it. What time did you discover him?'

Ridpath checked his watch. 'Exactly 11.05.'

Another detective walked in to join them, panting heavily. He was wearing blue gloves too. 'Sorry I'm late, Sarge.'

'No worries, this is Ridpath, he discovered the body.'

The young detective checked Ridpath out. 'Should he be in here with us?'

'Sorry, Ridpath, I can't get the staff these days. I don't know what they are teaching them at Edgely Park any more.' He turned back to his young detective. 'I'll repeat myself. This is Detective Inspector Ridpath, currently attached to the Coroner's Office. He discovered the body.'

The detective reddened. 'Sorry, sir.'

'Don't worry…?'

'Hunter, sir, Detective Constable Rob Hunter.'

'Just call me Ridpath, everybody else does. The only people you call sir are the Chief Constable and the Mayor and only if they can hear you.'

'When's the pathologist getting here?'

'Should be in the next ten minutes, Ted. It's Dr Schofield.'

'The one that sounds like a young kid?'

'Think so.'

Ridpath interrupted him. 'He's good, Ted, give him a chance.'

Ted Jones smirked. He nodded his head towards the dead man lying on the floor. 'What's matey's name?'

'Liang Xiao Wen. I interviewed him last night about a death in Wilmslow Immigration Removal Centre. Sergeant Mungovan over at Cheadle Heath has all his details.'

Ted Jones frowned.

Ridpath explained. 'He was signing in daily at 6 p.m. Arrested for overstaying his visa.'

'Well, I guess it'll be one less they'll have to deport. Rob, can you take Ridpath's statement? Better get it over and done with.'

Hunter took his arm and led him outside to the lobby. He took his notebook out and spent the next thirty minutes going over Ridpath's statement. The young detective was at least thorough.

Dr Schofield arrived when they were halfway through.

'I heard this was one of yours, Ridpath. Not busy enough in the Coroner's Office, you go out looking for bodies?'

Ridpath stayed silent.

'And I've finished the post-mortem on your woman, Ms Chen. I've checked out the test results and I'm just waiting for toxicology to come in. I'll send them over to Sophia this afternoon.'

'Can you give me a heads-up?'

The pathologist leant in and whispered. 'Not now. I'll be finished here in about an hour,' he checked his watch, 'come to the morgue at three. I want to show you something.'

'All very cloak and dagger.'

'Not really, but when you see, you'll know why it's important. Anyway, I think I have another customer waiting, so if you'll excuse me.'

What did the pathologist want to tell him?

Chapter 36

Yang May Feng slammed the door behind her as she entered the apartment, leaning back on it, out of breath.

She had run from the Uber along the path and up the stairs, hoping against hope he wasn't outside waiting for her.

Last night she had gone to the club and reported to the *mama-san*.

'You haven't been here for nearly a week and you expect me to put you to work?'

She put on her best sad face. 'I'm sorry to have let you down, but I had flu. It's the English weather, it's supposed to be warm now but I'm wearing a coat.'

The *mama-san* sniffed. 'You're lucky. Mamie has called in sick tonight and I'm short of girls.'

'Thank you, mama. Can I be picked first? I can work hard tonight to make up the time I lost.'

'We'll think about it. Go and redo your make-up.'

Of course, she was called soon after: a group of buyers from Beijing with their English clients. She made sure she was placed next to the Beijing boss and a few deft touches under the table soon had him interested.

The evening was going well. She'd sang a few karaoke songs and the boss had already suggested they go back to his hotel. She, of course, had demurred. When you land a big fish, it's always better to reel him in slowly.

They'd drunk a lot of whisky and her head was beginning to feel the effects of the alcohol. She made her excuses and went to the bathroom to drink some water and have a break.

It was on her way back that she saw him.

He was sitting at the bar, with his back to her, drinking alone. Had he spotted her in the private room? Or maybe heard her voice?

She didn't know, but she couldn't stay there any longer. She rushed into the room and made a pretence of falling into the boss' arms.

'I'm so tired, let's go back,' was all the inducement she needed. She took him out the back way to avoid being seen, lying that it was easier to get a cab.

They went back to his hotel, where after a glass of whisky, he fell asleep.

That morning he apologised as if it had been something wrong, and gave her a large tip in compensation. She liked these sorts of men: easy to control and embarrassed in the morning. They always paid the best.

Kicking off her high-heeled shoes, she unzipped the tight cheongsam and wriggled out of it. She needed a shower. She stank of cigarettes, whisky and cheap cologne.

She walked to the bathroom and stopped.

What was that?

A noise, like something she remembered from her childhood. A scraping sound in the kitchen.

And it came to her. The sound was like a knife being sharpened on a whetstone.

Her father used to do it every Saturday, taking out the knives and choppers in the morning, wetting the stone with water and sharpening them slowly and rhythmically.

The sound was like music to her young ears.

But what was it doing in there? She grabbed an umbrella from near the door and crept towards the kitchen.

Holding her breath, she pushed it open, hearing her heart beat loudly in her chest as if it was ready to burst. Part of her expected to see her father's face sitting at the table with his array of knives, looking up from the whetstone and smiling.

Instead, there was nobody there.

The edge of one of the metal blinds was being blown by the draught to scrape down the plaster of the wall.

She breathed out, dropping the umbrella. She couldn't go on like this, not any more. She had to get away.

And then she realised the draught came from an open window.

Had she left it unlocked when she went out last night?

Chapter 37

After DS Hunter had finished taking his statement, Ridpath waited around for fifteen minutes to see if he was needed.

Around him, the forensic technicians in their white suits were unpacking their gear. The crime scene manager, Tracy Millward, recognised him. 'Ridpath, what are you doing here? I thought you were still with the Coroner's Office. Your lot normally come after we've finished, not before we've started.'

'I discovered the body, Tracey.'

'Oh, did you touch anything inside?'

Ridpath thought for a moment. 'I don't think so,' then he remembered, 'I touched the door though.'

'Better fingerprint you anyway, just to eliminate your dabs.' She called one of her technicians over. 'And, if you went inside, we'll need those.' She pointed to his shoes.

'Do you have to?'

'You know the rules, Ridpath. There may be footprints on the floor. We have to eliminate your shoes. I've got a pair of flip-flops in the van if you want.'

So here Ridpath was, driving back to the Coroner's Court wearing a pair of bright pink flip-flops. He parked and ran up to the office, passing Jenny Oldfield in a vivid purple dress at reception. 'Love the colours, Ridpath. Grey and pink, my sort of style. Have we converted you?'

'No, my shoes are at a crime scene,' he shouted over his shoulder.

Sophia was waiting for him. 'You're late, Ridpath. Mrs Challinor is already with the family. What's with the…?' She pointed to the pink flip-flops.

'Don't ask. Get on to Dr Schofield, confirm I'll go to the morgue at 3 p.m. Ask him to compare his preliminary findings from the crime scene with Wendy Chen.'

'Preliminary findings? Crime scene? What crime scene, Ridpath?'

But he was already gone, down the corridor to the meeting room. He knocked on the door and entered. Inside an old Chinese couple were sat next to a younger Chinese woman with glasses. Mrs Challinor was sitting opposite.

As soon as he entered, the coroner stared at him for a moment before saying, 'This is my coroner's officer, Detective Inspector Ridpath. He's been investigating the death of your daughter.'

'Sorry I'm late, held up.'

The young woman translated the coroner's words for the parents of Wendy Chen as Ridpath sat next to the coroner, carefully hiding the pink shoes under the table.

Ridpath noticed the interpreter was using Mandarin not Cantonese. These people were from mainland China, not from Hong Kong.

Mrs Challinor leant closer to Ridpath and whispered to him. 'I've filled in the family on the procedures and explained the nature of the inquest. They've decided not to be legally represented, even though I would prefer it if they were. I think it's a question of money. Is there anything you want to ask them?'

'I need to know more about their daughter and what she was doing here.'

'Be gentle with them, Ridpath. I think they are both in a state of shock, the mother in particular.'

Ridpath studied the old woman. Her head was down as she listened to the interpreter. In her hand, a sodden paper tissue was gripped tightly.

The interpreter finished speaking and Mrs Challinor continued. 'My investigating officer would like to ask you some questions about your daughter, if he may?'

The interpreter spoke and the old man nodded once, no sign of emotion on his face.

Ridpath brought out his notebook and smiled at the old couple, receiving a blank look from the old man. 'Just a few details for our records. Your daughter was 23 years old, is that correct?'

The old man glanced at his wife as the interpreter translated the question. He answered slowly and deliberately in Mandarin.

The interpreter spoke for him. 'That's right.'

'And where was she born?'

Again the interpreter answered after he spoke. 'In Shanghai, she was born in Shanghai.'

'The name she used in the Immigration Centre was Wendy Tang. Is this her correct name?'

The old man shook his head. The interpreter shook hers also. 'No, it's not right. As we told the other policeman, her name is, was,' the interpreter corrected herself, 'Chen Hong Xi, but she likes to call herself Wendy Chen, like a westerner. I'm sorry, this man is using the present tense when talking about his daughter, not the past. How do you want me to translate?'

Mrs Challinor spoke. 'Tell us his exact words, please.'

The interpreter nodded.

Ridpath continued. 'How did she get a different surname?'

'I don't know.'

The old woman next to him sniffed and brought the sodden handkerchief up to her face.

'When did she come to England?'

'She left us in Shanghai about three months ago. I don't know when she arrived in England.'

'You don't know when she arrived here?'

The man shook his head. The interpreter spoke. 'No, I don't think she came straight here.'

'Where did she go first?'

'I don't know.'

Ridpath made a note in his book. This wasn't going well. He tried a different tack. 'Did she contact you when she was in England?'

The man nodded. 'She rings us every Sunday. It's great to hear her voice. She's our only child, you see. China, one child policy.'

'So when was the first time she rang you?'

The man glanced at his wife again. 'June, I think, the middle of June.'

Ridpath pulled out his phone and checked the calendar. 'So it would be June 14 or June 21?'

The interpreter translated and there was long conversation between the two of them. Finally, she answered, 'He doesn't know the exact date. They are old, they don't keep track of time so precisely.'

'OK, and when was the last time she rang you?'

As the interpreter translated, the woman began to sob quietly.

'She last called us on August 19. She said she had been arrested again, and was inside a prison…'

'She called you from the prison?'

The man continued to speak as the interpreter translated. 'That's what she said. She might be coming home but Xiao Feng was fine. She was going to try to stay. She knew what to do.'

'Xiao Feng? Who was Xiao Feng?'

'Her friend, the one who she left Shanghai with.'

As the man spoke, his wife reached into a bag on the floor. She pulled out an album, flipping it forward to a photograph of two girls, arm in arm, standing in front of a river with a futuristic building in the background. The woman touched the girl on the right. 'Xiao Feng.'

'And this is your daughter?'

The interpreter answered yes.

'Can I keep this photograph?'

The woman took it out of the album and gave it to Ridpath. 'Do you have any other pictures of your daughter?'

The woman turned to the first page and showed a close-up of a young woman smiling at the camera, her face happy and radiant.

'My daughter…' the interpreter said as the woman looked down and sobbed again. Her husband put his arm around her but didn't pull her closer. There was still a formality, a stiffness between the two of them.

There was a pause before she slumped forward on the table, the interpreter and her husband both trying to hold her up, as she said the same words over and over again. 'My poor daughter. My poor daughter. My poor daughter.'

Mrs Challinor glanced across at Ridpath as the interpreter tried to calm the woman. Gradually, the crying subsided.

All Ridpath could see was a hunched back over a table, occasionally trembling as if shaken with a profound grief.

He checked his notes. One word was underlined. He had to ask the question now.

In front of him, the woman drank some water from a cup held by her husband. Her eyes were red and sore, the salt of the tears white against her skin.

'I'd just like to ask a question,' Ridpath spoke softly. 'You stated your daughter had been arrested again. What did you mean?'

The old man's face didn't betray any emotion. 'I don't know.'

With a speed and a violence belying her small stature, the woman slammed her small fist down on the table and shouted at her husband in Mandarin.

Both Mrs Challinor and Ridpath looked to the interpreter.

'She's telling him to tell the truth. Their daughter is dead and it's too late for lies now. Too late. They've come all this way to this ugly country to take their daughter's body back home... no more lies. Their daughter is dead, they'll never see her again, never speak to her again, never hold her in their arms.'

The man said nothing throughout the tirade from his wife. He just sat there, his eyes blinking, holding back tears.

Finally, the woman turned to Mrs Challinor and Ridpath and spoke in Mandarin.

'It's time to tell the truth,' the interpreter translated.

Chapter 38

Ridpath could see the pain in her eyes. She spoke in a softer, more lilting voice than her husband as the interpreter translated.

'Even though we saw our daughter, white and cold at the house of the dead this morning, my husband still thinks Hong Xi is alive somewhere and she is going to come back soon to give him a hug and a smile.'

A long pause.

'I know she's dead.'

Mrs Challinor handed over a fresh packet of tissues which the woman took with a whispered, 'Xie, xie' before continuing.

'My daughter is 26 not 23 and she changed her name because she had already been deported from England before, and thought the computers might recognise her if she used her real name.'

'She was deported before?' asked Mrs Challinor softly.

The interpreter repeated the question in Mandarin and immediately translated as Mrs Chen replied.

'She first came to England as a student. She was a bright girl and had so many dreams. China is such a big place, but in her eyes, it was too small. My daughter had big dreams; she wanted to see the world, experience the world and everything all at once.'

'So she came to England. When was this?'

'In 2015. She applied to study in a language school in Manchester. Her friend Xiao Feng was already there. It cost a lot of money, we're not rich and we had to pay for the visa, the permits in China, the air fare and the school fees. We thought, this is our daughter, we should help her achieve her dreams, even though it meant we were going to lose her to a country far away. But isn't that what parents do? Give their children a better life than the one they had?'

As the interpreter spoke, the woman was staring at Ridpath. He felt she was looking into his soul, seeing all his dreams and hopes and desires for Eve, talking directly to him.

The interpreter continued after a short pause. 'So we took her to the airport and saw her off, smiling all the time while inside our hearts were crying.'

'She came to England to study, what happened next?'

'All went well for the first year. She said her English was getting better and she was studying hard. She wanted to go on to university here when her English was good enough. In the evenings, she was working in a Chinese restaurant to make money...'

'Do you know which one?' asked Ridpath.

The woman shook her head. 'She never said. It seemed to pay well as she never asked us for anything.'

'Where was she living?'

'We didn't know. She was sharing an apartment with Xiao Feng and some other students to save money, she said. We never saw the other students, but when she rang on Sundays, her friend sometimes said hello.'

'You never rang her?'

The woman shook her head. 'She said it was too expensive, cheaper for her to ring us.'

'A question about your daughter. Was she right- or left-handed?'

The woman appeared surprised. 'Why do you ask? She was left-handed. My husband tried to force her to change when she was young, but she continued to write with her left hand whatever he did.'

Ridpath felt Mrs Challinor touch his arm lightly and say, 'Let her tell her story.'

'So after a year, she was supposed to come back, but she didn't. She told us she wanted to stay in England, study more English, become better, make money working so she could pay for university herself. She stayed for over one year, she seemed happy and she still rang us every Sunday evening. I noticed she was getting thinner, but I thought it was just English food and she wasn't eating correctly, but she said she was happy and had met someone…'

'Did she say who?' asked Ridpath.

'No, just he was a good man, older than her but a good man…'

'And what happened?' Mrs Challinor interrupted.

'We had a phone call one Tuesday, late in the evening. It woke me up. She said she was in prison. The English didn't like people staying in their country without permission and she was coming home.'

'When was this?'

'December 2017. I remember because it had just got cold in Shanghai and the first snow had fallen. She came home two days later. She was thin as if she hadn't been eating, but we were just so happy to have our daughter back.'

'Was Xiao Feng with her?' asked Mrs Challinor.

'She was. Both of them were so thin. Of course, they had to go to the Public Security Bureau to explain. Hong Xi told them she just overstayed her visa. They didn't care, she had done nothing wrong in China.'

'So she came home?'

'But she was restless, as if she couldn't settle any more. She avoided her friends and didn't go out much. The only person she spent any time with was Xiao Feng. And there were the calls to England...'

'She was ringing here? Do you know which number?'

'She wouldn't tell us. We saw the phone bills though. It was expensive.'

'And what happened?'

'She told us she was going back to England. We begged her not to go, to stay in China, to stay with us. But her mind was made up and my daughter was always stubborn, once she decided something, nothing could change her mind.'

'If she had already been deported back from England, how was she going to come back here?'

'She said she knew a way, but it would cost money. We got a loan from the bank and gave her the money. Two weeks later, she was a gone... and we never saw her again.'

The woman stopped talking and began to cry, sobbing softly into one of the paper tissues.

Ridpath looked across at Mrs Challinor. 'One last question, Mrs Chen. How long was it from your daughter leaving home until you received the first phone call from England?'

The woman stopped crying for a second as she thought of the answer. 'Three weeks, I think,' the interpreter translated. 'Hong Xi said the journey had been long and painful but she was happy to be back in Manchester with the man she knew. On her last call, she told us she had some wonderful news and she was coming home soon. We were so excited she was coming back. And then on the next call, she said she was in prison again. It was the last time I heard her voice.' Another long pause. 'I just want to take her home, away from this country, take her back to China. We don't ever want to come back to this cold place again. My daughter, my poor, beautiful daughter...' The last vestige of self-restraint vanished and the woman sobbed uncontrollably, her chest heaving and fat tears rolling down her cheeks.

Mrs Challinor stared at Ridpath and shook her head.

There would be no more questions.

Chapter 39

As soon as he could, Ridpath gave his condolences to the family and explained to Mrs Challinor he had to see the pathologist urgently.

He drove from the Coroner's Court into the centre of Manchester, parking in the multistorey car park at Manchester Royal Infirmary before walking to the morgue close by.

Dr Schofield and a new doctor were waiting for him. As soon as he stepped into the room, the familiar tightness stretched across his chest.

'Ah, Ridpath, glad you could make it. I've invited Dr Ahmed to join us as he is the interested party in this review of his first report.'

They were both sitting in front of the microscope looking at the monitor.

'Isn't that unusual?'

'Not really, Detective Inspector Ridpath. I have the right to attend if my report is being challenged. And anyway, it will save you time if I am here to work with Dr Schofield. Dr Waterstone informed me of the preliminary conclusions and of my unfortunate omission.'

'The marks on Wendy Chen's chest.'

'Precisely, detective.'

'Anyway, Ridpath,' Schofield interrupted, 'I am delighted to tell you we are both in agreement and Dr Ahmed has accepted the new findings without reservation.'

Was that good news? Ridpath didn't know. 'And I have some news too, doctor. Her parents told me she was left-handed.'

Schofield glanced across at Dr Ahmed. 'More evidence confirming our finding this wasn't suicide,' he said.

'More evidence it wasn't suicide?'

'You do have a habit of repeating my sentences, Ridpath. I know what I said.'

Dr Schofield pressed a switch and an image appeared on the monitor next to the microscope. It had the appearance of an area of deep-brown, rocky moonscape surrounded by gradations of red earth gradually becoming pink at the edges.

'You're looking at a vertical cross-section of the flesh of the pectoral muscle I took from the dead woman's chest beneath the puncture marks. You remember Vera made the slides for me.'

After five seconds, the image changed and the dark brown area became larger with the pink section diminishing.

'The first section was just beneath the epidermis. We are now going through the fascia, the fibrous fat layer and deeper into pectoral muscle.'

The image changed again and the dark brown area became almost black in colour with the pink area vanishing.

'It looks like it's been roasted.'

'Well, it has.'

'I don't understand.'

'As I've said, I've only seen this once before and it left exactly the same marks on the skin and beneath it.'

Ridpath stared at the image. 'What is it?'

'This woman was tasered shortly before her throat was cut.'

Chapter 40

'What?'

'It was a most interesting discovery, even though I do say so myself.'

Ridpath shook his head. 'What did you just say?'

'Do I have to repeat myself, Ridpath? She was tasered, a stun gun. When I saw the two marks above her breast, it reminded me of a post-mortem I did two years ago. A man had tasered his uncle as a joke, sending 50,000 volts of electricity through the heart. The uncle didn't survive. In our dead woman's case, however, she was relatively healthy. The Taser merely stunned her. It was the cutting of the throat that killed her.'

The doctor sat back and nodded at his colleague.

'What?'

'Before you came, I did some research. I'm not finished yet but I'm certain it was a Taser. The weapon was invented by a man called Jack Cover, a NASA researcher, in America. Interestingly the name is a loose acronym of the title of the book *Tom Swift and His Electric Rifle*, written by Victor Appleton and featuring Cover's childhood hero, Tom Swift.'

The doctor pressed his mouse and a picture of a Taser appeared on the monitor.

'The Taser fires two small barbed darts intended to puncture the skin and attach to the target. The darts are connected to the main unit by thin insulated copper wire and deliver a modulated electric current. In medical terms, it works by disrupting voluntary control of muscles, causing "neuromuscular incapacitation." The effects of a Taser may only be localized pain or strong involuntary long muscle contractions, based on the length of use and connectivity of the darts. The cartridge contains a pair of electrodes and propellant for a single shot and is replaced after each use. With a bit more time, I may even be able to work out which model of Taser was employed.'

'But... how? Stun guns and Tasers are illegal in the UK.'

'But still easy to obtain online from overseas. The man who tasered his uncle bought his in Germany.'

'So let me get this clear. You are ruling out suicide?'

'Detective Inspector Ridpath, it is impossible to cut your own throat if you are unconscious. I would have thought a detective of your intelligence would realise.'

Ridpath stood there open-mouthed. Wendy Chen was tasered? She was murdered? But how? Wilmslow IRC was one of the most secure facilities in Manchester.

'Do you have any other questions, detective?'

Ridpath shook his head.

'There is one other thing, DI Ridpath...'

There was more?

He walked over to one of the stainless steel tables on the right covered in a white cloth. He pulled the material down to reveal the naked body of Liang Xiao Wen. 'I have yet to start the post-mortem on this man's body but even I can recognise the marks when I see them.'

Ridpath checked out where he was pointing. Two small, parallel marks stood livid on the skin in the centre of the chest. 'He was tasered too?'

'Before his throat was cut.'

'It's the same man who committed both murders?'

'Or woman, Inspector. Cutting the throat of an unconscious person requires no great strength, merely a sharp knife.'

The breath left Ridpath's body. He had to talk to the coroner immediately.

Chapter 41

'We have to cancel the inquest, Mrs Challinor.'

'Not possible, Ridpath. You heard those parents – they've come all this way and they want to return with their daughter's body.'

Ridpath and Mrs Challinor were in her room. The parents of Wendy Chen had left a long time ago with the interpreter. They were going to return tomorrow morning at the commencement of the inquest.

Ridpath took a deep breath. 'But this is now a murder investigation, Coroner, and under the 2009 Act, you need to give the police 28 days to conclude their enquiries.'

'You're quoting the law at *me*, Ridpath? And the police have already had 28 days. They reached a conclusion of suicide, remember? And to educate you on the law, I only have to postpone the inquest if requested to do so by a senior police officer.'

'The circumstances have changed. We now have Dr Schofield's post-mortem report. She was tasered and her throat was cut.'

Mrs Challinor stared at him. 'Tasered? A stun gun?'

'According to Dr Schofield, and Dr Ahmed agrees with his findings. The evidence is clear. Also the throat could not have been self-inflicted by a left-handed person.

It all means we have clear grounds for postponing the inquest.'

Mrs Challinor picked up the packet of paper tissues lying on her table left by Mrs Chen. After a long while, she stared directly at Ridpath. 'That's not going to happen. The inquest will go ahead as planned tomorrow morning and will be concluded by Friday evening at the latest.'

'But Mrs Challinor...'

The coroner raised her voice. 'We are not going to keep these people waiting for the body of their daughter any longer, Ridpath. We already have a pathologist's report and we need to release the body.'

'And if Dr Schofield's findings are challenged in any subsequent criminal trial?'

'We will overcome the challenge when we get to it. And Ridpath, a criminal trial could take place up to a year from now. Are you suggesting we keep Wendy Chen's body in the morgue for all that time?'

Ridpath thought for a moment before answering quietly. 'If necessary, Coroner.'

'It's the copper in you thinking, Ridpath. The copper who believes it's more important for a criminal to be convicted than for a family to find closure. Do I have to remind you what our job is in the Coroner's Office? It's to be an advocate for the dead to safeguard the living. We don't chase convictions. We don't kowtow to authorities. We don't worry about what the government thinks. We find out who died, how they died and when they died. That is all. The inquest into Wendy Chen will do exactly that and nothing more. Nobody stands up for these families, Ridpath, except us. We are their last, and only, line of defence.'

'But what about doing what's right, Mrs Challinor? Don't these families also care about arresting the murderer of their daughter? They want to see justice too.'

'But justice isn't blind, it's about people, what's right for them, not what's wrong.' She ran her fingers through her long grey curls. 'Why do you think I became a coroner, Ridpath?'

'I don't know.'

She stared into mid-air, an air of vulnerability encircling her for the first time. 'After completing my law degree and articles, I joined one of the big law firms in London and was spending my life worrying about billable hours and charting the labyrinthine path to becoming a partner.' She took a deep breath and continued speaking slowly and quietly. 'Then, my mother was killed in a car accident. An inquest was ordered and I watched the coroner, a man called Harry Turner, probe and question the driver of the other car to destroy his lies and uncover the truth. The man had overtaken a lorry and couldn't get back to his lane in time. My mother died in the head-on collision…'

'I'm sorry to hear that, Mrs Challinor.'

She finally looked up at him. 'But from that day, I knew what I wanted to do, Ridpath. I wanted to discover the truth for every family out there who can't do it for themselves. Families like the Chens.'

There was a long silence between them, before Ridpath finally said, 'But Coroner, we won't be able to uncover the truth unless we understand not just *how* Wendy Chen died, but also *why* she died.'

'And that's why you will continue your investigation while the inquest is taking place.'

'But it only gives me until the end of the inquest. Can I at least inform Clare Trent, get the resources of MIT involved?'

Mrs Challinor thought for a moment before nodding. 'Do you want me to ring her?'

'Please just tell her I'm coming but not the reason why. I hope she agrees to be involved, otherwise the murder inquiry will remain with the CID at Rowley and Central Manchester.'

'One of whom has already failed in an investigation…'

'That's unfair, Mrs Challinor.'

The coroner frowned. 'Perhaps it was. Brief her as soon as you can.'

'Mrs Challinor, I would like to put on record my profound disagreement with your decision.'

'Duly noted, Ridpath.'

'Moreover, by continuing the inquest, you may be prejudicing the outcome of a criminal investigation.'

Mrs Challinor's hand slammed down on the table. 'I have made my decision, Ridpath. The inquest will continue.'

There was a light tap on the door. Carol Oates popped her head round the door. 'I thought I heard the sound of raised voices. Is everything OK, Mrs Challinor?'

'Perfectly fine, Carol. We were just discussing tomorrow's inquest,' Mrs Challinor said tersely.

'So it will be going ahead. I thought with the new post-mortem findings…'

How had she found out about those so quickly? thought Ridpath.

'The inquest will start tomorrow at 10.00 a.m. as scheduled. Now, Ridpath, I believe you have an investigation needing your attention.'

Ridpath collected his notebook off the table and stepped past Carol Oates to exit the meeting room. As he did, he heard his voice being called by Mrs Challinor.

'If you want to discover who killed Wendy Chen, you have until the end of the inquest, Ridpath. At that time, the jury will give its verdict on the case and I will release the body back to the parents.'

Chapter 42

Ridpath went outside and stood on the street. He was desperate for a cigarette. Giving into his cravings a couple of days ago had been a mistake.

Mrs Challinor was wrong. She had been affected by the testimony of the murdered girl's mother. The inquest should be halted to give the police time to investigate properly, not the bogus going-through-the-motions ticking-the-bloody-boxes investigation completed by Ronald Barnes. The killer had already murdered one more person, Liang Xiao Wen. What if they killed somebody else?

He had to get Claire Trent onside. There was so much work to do, he couldn't even scratch the surface on his own. Wendy Chen's friend, the one she came to Manchester with, had to be found. The Chinese man in the BMW outside Rowley station had to be interviewed. The manager of the Removal Centre and the DCOs had to be screened, and he hadn't even got round to meeting with Immigration Enforcement and finding out more about the reasons for Chen's detention.

He shivered.

He had come outside just wearing a shirt. Shit. The hospital appointment, he had forgotten all about it.

Another thing he had to get done. He would ring them and re-arrange for another time.

Too much to do for one man, and too little time to do it all. Claire Trent and MIT had to get involved.

And it struck him that if he could confirm the murder of Liang was linked to the death of Wendy Chen, they would have to take the case on.

He turned to climb the stairs to go back inside, bumping into Carol Oates standing behind him. 'I saw you standing out here, Ridpath. Are you OK?'

'Fine, Carol, just needed some fresh air.'

She pushed an errant blonde hair that had escaped from her chignon behind her ear. 'You came out without your jacket. Be careful you don't catch cold.'

'I'm just going back in.' He tried to step around her, but she moved into his path. 'I couldn't help but hear the conversation you had with the coroner. It isn't right what she's doing. I agree with you; the inquest should be postponed.'

'Well, it isn't, so I need to get on with the work. We have so little time.' He edged past her up the stairs.

She put her hand on his arm. 'An inquest should never jeopardise a criminal investigation. The coroner has ignored the law. I'm here to help if you want me.'

Ridpath stared at her. 'But to help who, Carol? Yourself or my case?'

Chapter 43

'Sophia, do you know if Dr Schofield has finished his post-mortem on Mr Liang yet?'

'I haven't heard anything, Ridpath.'

'Can you give him another call and ask him to let me know his topline findings as soon as he can? Particularly if he can confirm the killing is linked to Wendy Chen?'

'Will do. And Christie's Hospital called saying you missed an appointment.'

'I'll call them back.'

'Not anything bad is it?'

'No, just routine.'

'A couple of other things.' She handed him a brown file. 'This is Dr Schofield's report on Wendy Chen.'

'Did you read it?'

'Clear cut case of murder. Tasered first and then killed. You can't cut your throat if you are unconscious.'

'You're sure?'

'No. But Dr Schofield is and you can't argue with his conclusions.'

'The fount of all wisdom?'

Sophia's cheeks reddened. 'He's good at his job.'

Ridpath opened the file and scanned through it. 'You're right, this is good.'

'Told you. One other thing. While you were at the morgue, I nipped to the market and bought you these.' She held up a pair of slip-on shoes.

Ridpath stared at his feet – he was still wearing the pink flip-flops. 'You're a godsend. How much do I owe you?'

'6.99. I thought I'd splash out. But I wouldn't go near a fire, they might melt.'

Ridpath took off the flip-flops and slipped into the shoes. 'Perfect fit. How did you know the right size?'

'Years of window shopping and buying for my dad.'

'Right, let's get to work. You get onto the pathologist.'

Sophia hurried back her desk. Ridpath rang Christie's Hospital on his mobile. 'Hi there, it's Thomas Ridpath. I'm afraid I missed an appointment this afternoon.'

There was a loud sniff on the end of the line. 'Which doctor?'

'Dr Morris.'

A few clicks on a computer. 'A blood test. You did miss it.'

'I know, that's why I'm calling.'

A few more clicks. 'Next appointment can be a week today... er, hang on, there's an urgent sticker on your file...'

Urgent, why was it urgent?

'...Right, you're in luck. I've just had a cancellation. Can you do ten a.m. tomorrow morning?'

'Tomorrow?'

'Thursday, September 19th.'

'Well...' Ridpath thought about all the work he had to do on the inquest, the investigation, on everything.

The woman at the call centre interrupted his thoughts. 'There is an urgent sticker on your case file, Mr Ridpath.'

'OK, I'll make it… somehow.'

'Your appointment is confirmed, Mr Ridpath, please don't be late.'

Ridpath rang off. One job done, now he just had to make sure he went there.

Sophia was hovering. 'Mrs Challinor just rang through while you were on the phone. Your appointment with Claire Trent is at six this evening.'

Ridpath checked his watch. 5.30. He'd better get a move on. 'Anything from Dr Schofield?'

'He's still performing the post-mortem on the dead man.'

'Message me when you get some news, Sophia. It's important.'

'Will do.'

Ridpath stood up, putting on his jacket. He had to get Claire Trent to take this case. Without her, there was no way he could do all the work on his own.

'Wish me luck, Sophia.'

'You don't need luck, Ridpath, you're the golden boy.'

'Not after today, Sophia, not after today.'

Chapter 44

'Come in, Ridpath. Seeing you at 6 p.m. on a Wednesday evening after an urgent call from the coroner sends shivers down my spine, and not the sort I enjoy.'

Ridpath took a seat opposite, putting his files on her desk.

Her eyes went to the brown files and back to him. 'Mrs Challinor rang me and said you had something. What is it? I have drinks with the Chief Constable at 8 p.m. One of his "informal" chats, which means he's worried about something and wants my input. The latest computer cock-ups are getting to everybody.'

'It's a murder committed at Wilmslow Immigrant Removal Centre last month.' Ridpath handed over the file with the police investigation carried out by Ronald Barnes with its witness statements and the post-mortem report by the pathologist Dr Ahmed.

Claire Trent opened both files and read through them. 'A competent investigation, if not as thorough as one would hope. The pathologist decided it was suicide and DS Barnes has gone along with that conclusion.'

'Competent? It's a tick the box exercise. No interviews of any witnesses other than the Centre's staff. No follow up with Immigration Enforcement. No investigation into the background of the victim, Wendy Chen aka Wendy

Tang. No checking of CCTV. The Custody Officer who discovered the victim states the door to the victim's room was open and that's why he went inside, but Barnes did not check it out. The same officer says he locked all the rooms at 9.15 the previous evening.'

'No, Ridpath, in his statement, he said he *thought* he locked all the rooms. Human error, he mustn't have locked hers.'

'The one room where a detainee was found dead happens to be unlocked? Bit of a coincidence.'

The DCI shrugged her shoulders. 'They happen. Listen, Ridpath, deaths in Removal Centres happen; people don't want to go back to their countries or they are depressed. We investigate every one but once the post-mortem reports suicide, there's not a lot we as police can do. It's up to the coroner to determine if negligence led to the death.'

'And what if we had a post-mortem stating it wasn't suicide but murder?' He handed over the latest report from Dr Schofield.

Claire Trent read through it. 'He seems to be suggesting she was rendered unconscious by a stun gun or Taser before her throat was cut. This is damning evidence. Is he sure?'

'You know Dr Schofield, he wouldn't make such a statement unless he was. Another pathologist, a Dr Ahmed, the man who carried out the first post-mortem, now admits he was wrong and agrees with him.'

'Still doesn't warrant the involvement of MIT. I presume you've let DS Barnes know of these developments in his case.'

Ridpath's face went blank. In all the chaos of today, it was the one thing he had forgotten to do.

'You haven't informed him, have you? Instead of following basic police procedure, you have come running to me... Jesus, I thought you were smart, Ridpath. I also heard you've been giving Manchester Central more work.'

Ridpath raised an eyebrow.

'Ted Jones' boss rang me. He suggested, politely, you give him notice if you're ever on his patch again. People have a habit of dropping dead when you're in the neighbourhood.'

'He can bugger off. The witness to a death is killed and he's worried because I'm giving him work.'

'Can you prove a link to the death of the man today and the death of your woman in the Removal Centre?'

Ridpath shook his head. 'Not yet.'

'Until you do, we have two unrelated deaths. One investigated by the police with a conclusion of suicide and the other with an investigation launched by Manchester Central and in progress. Why should MIT get involved?'

Ridpath's phone rang. 'I have to take this.'

Claire Trent waved her hands. 'Don't mind me, I'm just your boss.'

Ridpath answered the call. It was Sophia. He listened to what she had to say before switching off his phone.

'I hope you believe in coincidences, boss. The pathologist has just released his preliminary report...'

'And?'

'The same MO was used in the death I discovered today and the woman at the Removal Centre. Both victims were tasered first followed by their throats being cut.'

Chapter 45

'Shit.'

'My thoughts exactly, guv'nor.'

Claire Trent bit the nail of her thumb and stared into mid-air for a long time. 'Right, Ridpath, we're taking this on. Collect all the files and come with me.'

She stepped out from behind her desk and marched out into the detective's room. Heads popped out from behind computers and from Pret A Manger sandwiches. 'Right, you lot, meeting room now. You too, Chrissy.' She pointed to a Police Support Officer wearing a light blue Manchester City scarf and anorak, who was just heading out of the door.

The woman did a U-turn and deposited her bag on her desk. 'Just twenty seconds more and I would have been out of here. I should've known as soon as Ridpath went into her room...'

She picked up a pad and joined the rest of the detectives in the meeting room.

'Right, you lot,' Claire Trent stood at the front next to a whiteboard, 'we have a new case brought to us by DI Ridpath.' She indicated he should speak.

Ten pairs of eyes turned towards the detective. He wasn't sure they were happy at the prospect of more work or pissed off.

'The murder of two Chinese nationals,' Ridpath placed the picture of Wendy Chen from his file onto the whiteboard. 'This woman died in Wilmslow Immigrant Removal Centre a month ago. The second, a Mr Liang Xiao Wen, was discovered by me this morning in the centre of Manchester.' Ridpath had no picture so he simply wrote the name on a blank sheet of paper and posted it next to the young woman's photo. 'I don't have much, but here's what I have on both murders.'

Ridpath detailed his investigation, ending with his discovery of the body of Liang Xiao Wen.

'How can we be sure the murders are connected?' asked DS Alan Butcher.

'Dr Schofield's preliminary report on the second murder will tie the MOs together. I'm waiting for it to be sent across.'

'So we think the same person killed both people?' This was from Emily Parkinson.

Ridpath peered across at Claire Trent. 'Yes. The MO is the same.'

Chrissy Wright put her hand up. 'But one of them happened in a Removal Centre. How does anybody enter, commit a murder and leave a secure facility without being seen?'

Ridpath sighed. 'Great question, Chrissy. And the answer is I don't know.'

'We need to find out and quickly,' interrupted Claire Trent.

'Next steps?' asked Harry Makepeace, one of the few inspectors left over from Charlie Whitworth's time.

Claire Trent looked over at Ridpath. 'Why don't you tell them, Detective Inspector? You've been involved in this case so far and know most about it, why don't you lead?'

Ridpath took a deep breath and stepped forward. 'From talking with the parents of Wendy Chen this afternoon, it is obvious she entered the country illegally after being deported. We need to know how the Immigration Enforcement found her and when they arrested her. Emily, can you do the work?'

The DS made note in her book.

'We also need to know more about the staff at the centre. Chrissy, can you do background checks on everybody, including the Centre Manager? Either the person who committed the first murder was already in the Centre or they gained entry later. Plus the security officer, Stuart Collins, said he was in London on August 19th and 20th attending a meeting. Can we check the alibi?'

'You think the killer could have been one of the staff?' asked Claire Trent.

'I'm not ruling it out.'

'I'm on it, Ridpath,' said Chrissy.

'Alan, can you liaise with Dr Schofield? We need his report as soon as possible.'

DS Butcher nodded his head.

'Harry, can you follow up on Liang Xiao Wen? Who was he? What work did he do? You know the drill. And get onto Ted Jones, they should have completed the house-to-house looking for witnesses by now. With a bit of luck, somebody will have seen something.'

'Aye and pigs might fly knowing Chinatown,' said Makepeace.

'Isn't that what the police helicopter is for?' answered Alan Butcher to laughter.

Ridpath stopped the laughter by raising his hands. 'Three more things, people. First, we have a phone call to Rowley station from Wendy Chen on the day before she died. I was going to get round to it today, but I've had no time. Chrissy, can you find out who she called?'

'I'll call the duty sergeant, he's an old mate. And a City fan.'

'Poor bugger,' muttered a voice from the back.

'Second. There is an added complication to the investigation. The coroner, Mrs Challinor, is starting an inquest into the death of Wendy Chen tomorrow morning...'

'Can't we get her to postpone it?' asked Emily Parkinson.

All eyes turned to Claire Trent.

'I'll call her later tonight. Coroners are supposed to wait for the outcome of a police inquiry before holding inquests.'

'Can she do that? Continue on with the inquest when we're still investigating?'

'I already spoke to her,' said Ridpath. 'She doesn't want to postpone it. She sees it as her duty to the family of the deceased. It means we may lose the body if it's released back to the family after the end of the inquest. We have to work quickly, people.'

Claire Trent checked her watch. 'I have to go to meet the Chief Constable, but I'll be back in an hour or so. He's not going to be a happy camper when I tell him he has two more murders to add to his stats this year. And I'll handle Manchester Central and Rowley, they will be more than happy to hand over the cases to us.'

She walked towards the door.

'I have just one more point, boss.'

'What is it, Ridpath?' replied Claire Trent irritably.

Ridpath wrote a name on a blank sheet of paper and pasted it next to the picture of Wendy Chen. 'I think this person is key.'

'Yang May Feng? Who is she?'

'She came into the country illegally with Wendy Chen but evaded arrest by Immigration Enforcement.' Ridpath fished around in the file for the picture the old woman had given him, placing it on the whiteboard next to the name.

'Why do you think she's important, Ridpath?'

'Because, unless we find her, I think she could be our next victim.'

Chapter 46

Manchester was too dangerous for her now.

Only an hour ago, she had gone to Liang's place to give him the money she owed. The bastard was always asking for more and the interest rate was forever going up. Wendy had argued with him so many times, but he wouldn't listen.

'You two owe us for bringing you here,' he always said. Owed him their lives and their bodies is what he meant.

She didn't want to go out again, but this was the last time for a week. She couldn't risk Liang and his goons looking for her if she didn't pay. One bad man chasing her was enough.

When she got to Liang's place, the area was full of police. The alley leading to his flat had been cordoned off with men in white suits and masks wandering in and out.

She asked somebody in Mandarin what was going on.

'Somebody's dead.'

'Who?'

'I think it was one of Lam's men, stabbed they said. Good riddance to bad rubbish...'

But she was already gone, running away from the scene, looking for a taxi to take her back to the flat before the woman finished her sentence.

Now she was back here, what was she going to do? Was it still safe or did he know where she lived?

Her whole body was trembling with fear.

She ran into the bedroom and buried herself under the covers.

What was she going to do?

Chapter 47

The large clock ticked loudly on the wall, the minute hand making a clicking sound as it advanced. It was already past ten o' clock. He hoped Polly wasn't waiting up for him.

Ridpath sat in the situation room all alone, staring at the pictures of the two people who had been killed.

He was strangely elated. The pleasure of running a team, all working towards a common goal, had left him feeling high. God, he loved the early days in any case when the team were reporting back almost hourly with new information and ideas. Ideas sparking additional lines of inquiry.

After Claire Trent had left for her drinks with the Chief Constable, the team had quickly coalesced around him. There was no questioning his authority, no slacking in their desire to get the job done.

The board had been filled with additional information. The first arrest and deportation of Wendy Chen had been dredged from the files along with a new photograph and an address where she had been found working. It wasn't a restaurant in Chinatown but a massage parlour in Cheetham Hill. One of those places that popped up and closed with all the speed of a cold sore on the lips of an addict.

These places, usually advertised as offering 'Thai Massage,' were nothing more than knocking shops, providing fifteen minutes of what was called 'relaxation' for men. As quickly as they opened, they closed and relocated somewhere else. The police always had problems keeping tabs on all of them. Not that they were first on the priority list for any station; as long as nobody complained, the police were reluctant to take action.

But it did give an insight into the sort of people Wendy Chen was involved with.

This was confirmed when more details came through of Liang Xiao Wen's rap sheet. Arrested for criminal intimidation, living off immoral earnings and twice for affray. In other words, he was a lowlife who made his money intimidating shops and working as a pimp.

Ridpath's eyes drifted across to the only other picture posted on the whiteboards.

Yang May Feng.

Was it linked to their arrival in the UK? Both her and Chen Hong Xi had been trafficked into the country. Was the killer covering up his crimes? Covering up his trafficking operation. But why kill? Why not just shut it down?

He should brief Mrs Challinor before it gets too late. He took his mobile out of his pocket.

There was a rap on the door. Claire Trent and Chrissy Wright came into the room.

'Chrissy's got some news for you, Ridpath.'

'Remember you asked me to find out who Wendy Chen rang at Rowley station? Well, the duty sergeant finally got back to me and he checked the logs...'

'And?'

'The call was put through to CID. To Detective Sergeant Ronald Barnes.'

'What?'

Chapter 48

Ridpath and Claire Trent stood outside a large detached house in Bramall. The street was classic 1930s suburbia: neat lawns, two car garages, solid brick-built homes and as quiet as a stalking cat late on a Thursday evening.

'Not bad on a Detective Sergeant's salary. I wish I could afford a place like this,' Claire Trent said as she pushed open the gate and walked up the rose bush-lined path.

There was a single light on upstairs. Ridpath pressed the illuminated bell, hearing it ring in the hall.

A middle-aged woman answered it almost immediately. 'Can I help you?'

She was slightly unsteady on her feet and Ridpath could detect the tang of whisky on her breath. He showed her his warrant card. 'My name is Detective Inspector Ridpath and this is Chief Superintendent Trent. Could we talk to your husband, Mrs Barnes?'

'Couldn't it wait? He's only just got home from work. He's exhausted.'

'I'm afraid not, Mrs Barnes. We'd like to talk with your husband now if we can?' said Claire Trent forcefully. 'Can we come in?'

'Who is it, dear?'

'It's a Detective Inspector... what did you say your name was?'

'Ridpath.'

'Ridpath,' she shouted up the stairs, 'and a woman here to see you.'

'My name is Claire Trent and I'm the head of the Major Investigations Team. Can we come in?'

Ronald Barnes stood at the doorway. 'Don't worry, dear, I'll handle it.'

'But Ronald, you work so hard, you've only just come back. Won't they give you any time to rest? You only have three months left...'

'Don't worry, dear, it's just work.' He put his arm round his wife's shoulders and helped her walk to a back room. 'You just rest in here, dear, I'll handle this.'

He came back a minute later and opened the front door wider. 'Please come in, Detective Superintendent, and you too, Ridpath.' He stepped aside and said, 'You'll have to forgive my wife. It's not easy being married to a copper. We can chat in the living room. What's this about anyway?'

The both walked into the living room. It was furnished in classic seventies modern-home style: a green IKEA couch, wood and fake-distressed brick surrounding a gas fire, and a carpet covered in a swirling pattern of muddy colours.

'What's this about?' Ronald Barnes repeated as they both sat.

'It's about the death of Wendy Chen,' said Ridpath.

'I've already told you. I did the investigation as best I could given the resources and the time available. The pathologist and all the prison staff said it was suicide. And that's what I'm going to tell the coroner when I'm in court tomorrow.'

'It's not about the investigation, Detective Sergeant Barnes.'

'Well, what is it? The complaint about me from the coroner? But surely it will be handled by Professional Standards not MIT?'

'Correct,' interjected Claire Trent, 'this is about a phone call you received from Wendy Chen on the 19th August, 2019.'

Barnes sighed and his head went down.

'You admit it was you who received the call?'

The detective nodded.

'Why did she ring you?'

The man's head came up. 'Because she thought I could help her.'

'So you knew her before she was arrested by Immigration Enforcement?'

Again he nodded slowly. 'I was the one who told them about her.'

Chapter 49

'You told them? Why?'

'I had to. It's the law.'

'I don't understand.'

'Wendy Chen was one of my CI's…'

'She was a confidential informant?'

'I received a call about a month before her death. She didn't want to come into the station, so we met in a coffee shop. She told me she had information about a criminal gang trafficking people, mostly women, from Asia into the UK. She could give me times, dates, people, routes they used, everything.'

'This is all in a case file?'

'Of course, I wrote it all down, I know how to do my job. I sent the details to Criminal Intelligence and to North West Organised Crime.'

'So what happened?'

'I met her a couple of times, trying to get more information out of her, but she stalled me, saying she wanted payment. I thought it was worth it, so I raised the subject with my boss…'

'And?'

'He said the payment was impossible at the moment. He also advised me as she was an illegal immigrant, I had to inform the Enforcement authorities of her status and her address.'

'What? You shopped her even though she had come to you as a CI?'

Ridpath felt a hand on his arm. 'It's the law, Ridpath. Home Office Rules state all illegal immigrants who come into contact with the police have to be reported immediately to the Immigration authorities.'

'But this woman was reporting human trafficking. Don't we have posters in all our nicks asking people to report this?'

'True, but if they do and they are illegal themselves, they will be deported.'

'But why come forward? I'd bloody stupid to report myself to the police...'

'Look, Ridpath, we don't make the rules, we just enforce them.'

'Even if they are stupid.'

'Even if they are stupid.'

Silence descended on the living room. It was Claire Trent who spoke first. 'So DS Barnes, you reported her address to Immigration Enforcement?'

'Yes, worst thing I ever had to do. They picked her up a week later and that's when I received the call from inside the Removal Centre. She said she would tell everything as long as they would let her stay. There was nothing I could do...'

'Why did you investigate her death? You should have excused yourself, saying you knew her.'

His head went down again. 'I know. I shouldn't have got involved but there were no other detectives available and I thought I could make it easy on her.'

'Easy on her?'

'I thought she'd killed herself because I'd shopped her, you see. I just wanted to make everything smooth for her family. Not have some heavy-handed copper trampling through her life. She was a good person, a sweet person. And I had to shop her.'

'Was that why your inquiry was so superficial? You didn't do any background checks, didn't interview witnesses, didn't dig deeply or investigate properly.'

'What was the point? She'd killed herself and I was to blame.'

'But that's where you're wrong, Ron. She didn't kill herself, she was murdered.'

Chapter 50

Ridpath was at home, sitting in front of the darkened screen of the television, sipping a glass of Glenmorangie.

They had finally left Ronald Barnes' house two hours ago. The man seemed genuinely distraught Wendy Chen had been murdered and he had missed it.

He had asked the question troubling Ridpath too. 'How is a young woman murdered in one of the most secure places in Manchester?'

That was the sixty-four thousand dollar question. It must have been an inside job. One of the guards, the management or the security staff must have helped the killer gain entry.

Or perhaps the killer was already inside and they merely opened the doors for him or her. Or left them open?

They needed the schematics from the Coroner's Office.

He found his mobile and rang Sophia.

'Morning,' she said sleepily.

'Sorry for ringing so late, Sophia, but could you do me a favour and deliver the schematics of the Removal Centre to Police HQ tomorrow morning? And if you have printouts of the CCTV shots of the shadow on the stairs, they would be useful too.'

'What time do you want them?'

'Before 8.30, we have a meeting.'

'Can I join?' The voice was suddenly wide awake. 'I've never seen a police investigation in action.'

'It should be confidential, but I suppose it would be OK. I'll text Chrissy, our Liaison Officer, to let her know you're coming.'

'Thanks, I'll be there before 8.30.'

'And one more thing, can you bring all those personnel profiles and head shots of the staff of the Centre? Ta muchly.'

'You're going to kill me, Ridpath.'

He switched off the call and texted Chrissy Wright. He'd forgotten how much co-ordination there was in running an investigation. It was like keeping twelve balls in the air at the same time, two of which were his.

He sipped the whisky, turning the case over in his mind as the Glenmorangie circled in his mouth. They were still waiting on Dr Schofield's full report but his initial findings into the two deaths indicated the MO was the same.

They were killed by the same man or woman, but why?

And how did the killer get into a supposedly secure place to commit murder? He pulled out his notebook and wrote two questions to himself.

Did Liang and Chen know each other?

How did the killer get into the Removal Centre?

As he wrote those two questions down, a third occurred to him.

Or was the killer already there? *Did Liang kill Wendy Chen?*

His mind raced. Liang was in the room next to her, was his door unlocked as well? Did he simply go next door, kill her and go back to his room?

BUT WHY? He wrote in block letters, underlining it. And if he did kill the young woman, why was he murdered using the same MO? It didn't make sense.

A shadow loomed over him.

'It's late, are you coming to bed?'

'In a minute, Poll, I'm just thinking about something.'

'Ridpath, it's nearly two o'clock. You didn't get home till close to midnight and you left early this morning…'

'I'm working a case, Poll.'

'You're working yourself into an early grave, Ridpath.'

He put the glass down and stood up, putting his arms around his wife. 'I feel great, Poll, and there's only a couple more days left. The inquest finishes on Friday evening at the latest.'

'Look after yourself, Ridpath. You know Eve and I worry. What would we do if you weren't here?'

He tightened his grip around her. 'Don't worry, I'm going nowhere and I promise after this case, I'll take a few days off. How does autumn in the Lakes for mid-term sound, just you, me and a grumpy daughter?'

'It sounds great, Ridpath. But come to bed now, you need some sleep.'

'OK, Poll.' He finished off the last half inch of Glenmorangie in one gulp and, putting his arm around his wife, climbed the stairs to bed.

As he undressed, one more question occurred to him. Why had Liang been killed today? Was it because of his investigation?

It was a question that kept him awake for most of the night.

THURSDAY

SEPTEMBER 19

Chapter 51

The following morning, Ridpath was awake bright and early and, once again, out of the house before either Eve or Polly had stirred from their beds. He left a full pot of coffee on the breakfast table along with a packet of cornflakes and a pint of milk.

Next to both were little drawings detailing instructions on how to prepare the cornflakes: place bowl under open packet, twist wrist, catch cornflakes and stop when bowl full. Pour milk. Get spoon and lift cornflakes and milk to mouth. Chew. Repeat. Repeat. Repeat.

The instructions for the coffee were briefer. Pour into mug. Lift to mouth. Drink. Repeat till eyes open.

He had signed the instructions with a flourish. Knowing how grumpy they both were at that time of day, he doubted whether his sense of humour would be shared by Eve and Polly.

Not at 7.30 in the morning.

He didn't know why he did it. Perhaps because this case was so grim, he had to have some respite. Or maybe it was a desire to remind them he was still there and thinking of them. Whatever the reason, he left the house with a smile on his face. Not something that would normally happen in the middle of a murder case.

The traffic into Manchester was light and he arrived at Police HQ on the dot at eight. A quick coffee and a bacon bap taken away from the canteen and he was ready to plan the day's work.

He was surprised to see most of the team already in, including Alan Butcher, Emily Parkinson and even Harry Makepeace.

He walked into the situation room. Chrissy Wright and Sophia were pasting the schematic and the CCTV images of the Removal Centre on the board. 'Morning, Chrissy and Sophia. I see you two met.'

'Morning, Ridpath,' both chorused as Chrissy stepped back from what she was doing and checked it out. 'We've updated the board with new information that came in overnight and added Sophia's stuff, including the pictures of the Centre's staff. We'll be ready for the 8.30 meeting.'

Ridpath stared at the boards. In the middle, details and images of the two victims were separated by a picture of a Taser and of the knife found at the Removal Centre. On the left were the conclusions of the pathologist in point form. On the right were the now blown-up pictures of the Removal Centre's staff with their names, and a picture of DS Barnes and his initial report.

'Looks great. I'll just make a call.' He put his coffee and bacon bap down on the table and rang the coroner. Mrs Challinor answered after two rings.

'Ridpath, I've finally heard from you. I was expecting an update last night.' The voice wasn't friendly.

'Sorry, Coroner, I was wrapped up in the investigation. Claire Trent has agreed to take on the case.'

'I know, she had the courtesy to ring me last night and fill me in.'

'Sorry once again. I'm at Police HQ now, we're just about to start the briefing.' Detective were drifting into the room, placing folders on the table before leaving once again.

'And I'm in the middle of last-minute preparations to begin the inquest. Since I received Dr Schofield's report into her death, I've decided to call him first. His testimony is key as it reverses all the assumptions about the case. Hopefully it will encourage other people to rethink their testimony.'

'Won't New Hampshire's barrister challenge the new evidence?'

'Of course he will, but I'll handle it.'

Ridpath paused for a moment. 'I also have something else to inform you,' he looked around as more detectives entered the room, 'but I'll do it when I see you later. There are a couple of things you could ask the DCOs. Why was Wendy Chen's door open? And what happened in the missing time between the discovery of the dead woman and the arrival of the police?'

'Those are good questions, Ridpath, but it would be better to know some answers. And so far, I have too little to work with.'

More detectives were drifting in and sitting down.

Ridpath was tempted to say it's exactly why you should have postponed the inquest, but stopped himself. Now was not the right time. 'I'm sorry, Coroner, I'm working as fast as I can. With MIT on board, I'm sure we can make rapid progress. I'll come to the inquest before lunch if I can. One more thing, did Claire Trent ask you to postpone the inquest?'

'No, and I would have refused her anyway, even if it did land me in hot water.'

Ridpath wondered why. It never occurred to him to ask Claire Trent when they interviewed Ronald Barnes last night. He would have to do it this morning.

'And where is Sophia? Carol Oates is asking for her.'

Ridpath glanced guiltily at Sophia, who was just putting the final touches to the boards. 'She's with me.'

There was a long sigh on the phone. 'Make sure she calls Carol Oates. I don't want another complaint from my number two.'

There had been complaints?

'And make progress quickly, Ridpath, we don't have the time.'

The line went dead.

'I do know, Coroner,' he said to his mobile.

'She being difficult?' DS Emily Parkinson stood behind him.

'No more than usual. She wants answers to questions we haven't even asked yet.'

'Sounds like my mother.' She sat next to him. 'Sorry about the other day, I was a bit defensive about Ronald Barnes. Now it looks like his investigation missed a murder.'

'It was almost like he was going through the motions rather than trying to find the truth.'

'Retirement syndrome. Half the nick seems to suffer from it.'

Claire Trent walked into the room and everybody sat a little bit straighter, detectives hurried to their places and a few more squeezed into the room before the door was closed.

'Right, you lot, what have you got for me? The Chief Constable is not chuffed we've added two more murders to his stats. He's got enough on his plate with the computer cock-up and the review by the Inspectorate of Police. He wants this sorted and fast. In addition, the reporters have heard we've been put on the case. I've already had one on the phone this morning sniffing my arse, looking for titbits. Ridpath, you lead with Chrissy.'

Ridpath stood and strode to a place in front of the boards. 'We filled in more information for both victims. Wendy Chen used the alias Wendy Tang and that's the name she was detained under by the Immigration Enforcement. She was a confidential informant for DS Ronald Barnes.'

'What was she telling him?' asked Emily Parkinson.

'She was giving information on people-trafficking gangs. Names, dates, money, apparently she knew everything.'

'So where's the intelligence?'

'She wanted payment and they wouldn't stump up.'

'But if she was a CI, how did she get arrested?'

'Barnes had to tell Immigration Enforcement she was illegal and they arrested her.'

'That's sick!'

'No, it isn't, DS Parkinson, DS Barnes did his job. Until the Home Office changes the rules, you would do exactly the same. Do I make myself clear?'

Claire Trent held the young detective's gaze for a long while. 'Am I clear, DS Parkinson?'

She looked away. 'Yes, guv'nor.'

'Carry on, DI Ridpath.'

He pointed to the schematic. 'This is a plan of the Removal Centre. My assistant, Sophia,' he pointed to her, 'has marked the location of the CCTV cameras. The ones with a blue "X" were out of order on the night of the murder.'

Claire Trent counted the Xs. 'Six cameras out of order?'

'Right, guv'nor.'

'It seems a lot.'

'According to Lucy Bucknall, the PR woman, it's normal,' answered Sophia, before looking down nervously. 'There's one other thing I noticed as we were putting up the boards…'

'What is it, Sophia?' asked Ridpath.

'Well,' Sophia stood up and, taking a black marker from the desk, proceeded to put short black lines from the front entrance of the Immigration Removal Centre to the place where the victim was found, Room 7.

It was Ridpath who reacted first. 'The route seems to pass close to all the blue "Xs".'

'Right,' said Sophia. 'All six CCTV cameras that weren't working lead directly from the front door to the victim's room.'

Chapter 52

'What?'

'None of the CCTV cameras were working on the route, boss.'

'Somebody could have entered the Removal Centre without being seen by the Control Room.'

'Even more important, their movements wouldn't have been recorded.'

Sophia walked over to the board with the picture of the shadow on the stairs. 'Except here, when it was caught by accident.'

'Right first time. Another coincidence in a bunch of bloody coincidences?'

'I also checked the footage of the cameras in the vicinity of the route. They all had nothing except this image and it's not so clear.'

'It could just be a camera fault or dirt on the lens,' said Emily Parkinson.

Ridpath held out the CD. 'It could be, but check out the footage yourself.'

'I'd like to see it,' said Claire Trent.

He passed the footage across to his boss. 'Chrissy, you were doing background checks on the Centre's staff, anything on them?' she asked.

The civilian officer shook her head. 'All seem to be straight, no criminal records and have worked in custodial services for most of their lives. One of them, Tony Osborne, was investigated for being part of a ring smuggling mobile phones into Forest Green. Two other guards were charged but he wasn't. He moved soon afterwards to the Removal Centre, nothing on him since.'

'Can you follow up? Find out who did the investigation and see if you can find the files?'

Chrissy wrote a note to herself.

Ridpath moved along to a picture of the second victim, Liang Xiao Wen.

'Before you move on, Ridpath,' said Claire Trent, 'if you are suggesting there was a path from the entrance of the Centre to the victim's room, with no CCTV cameras working, it means…'

'Somebody on the inside had de-activated the cameras before the killer arrived.'

'Or was already inside the Centre and didn't want to be seen on CCTV,' added Emily Parkinson.

'Correct. Hold that thought, let's come back to it in a minute.' Ridpath pointed to the picture of Liang Xiao Wen. 'He went under the name Bobby Liang and had form for small-time Chinatown stuff: racketeering, pimping, intimidation. Again, I'd like to find out why he was arrested by Immigration Enforcement. I'd also like to know who was paying his legal fees. His solicitor isn't your normal run-of-the-mill ambulance chaser.'

'I'll check with the head of the North West Immigration Enforcement,' said Claire Trent.

'It leads me to my first question.' He picked up a felt pen and wrote on the whiteboard. **Did Chen and Liang know each other?**

'When I questioned him, he said they didn't. Now I'm not so sure. They certainly moved in similar circles. According to Ronald Barnes, Wendy Chen was involved, even if peripherally, in the vice trade. Looks like Liang was too.'

Chrissy jumped in. 'Ted Jones has come back with the results of his house-to-house…'

'Let me guess. People heard nothing. Saw nothing. Said nothing.'

'Right first time, boss. Forensics are rushing through their samples but the preliminary shout from Tracey is nothing. No fibres. No hair. No DNA. She's still got some work to finish yet but it's not looking great.'

'It's almost like the killer wasn't there? Could the pathologist be mistaken and this is just another suicide?' asked Emily Parkinson.

'I've worked with Dr Schofield before and he doesn't make mistakes. And you can't kill yourself after being tasered,' Ridpath answered.

'There's always a first time…'

'No, Ridpath is right. We need to treat this as two linked murders until the evidence tells us differently. We don't seem to have come far yet. Next steps, Ridpath?'

'I was thinking about it last night. He looked across at Emily Parkinson. 'If Wendy Chen was killed in the Removal Centre, if she was *murdered* there, it narrows the investigation. Joe Cummings, one of the officers, reported seeing her door open and so he went in.' He took the pen and wrote on the whiteboard. **Who opened the door?**

'Maybe it wasn't locked in the first place,' said Harry Makepeace.

'Possible, but he thought he locked up as usual at 9.15 the previous evening. And it's too much of a coincidence that a dead woman was found in the one room with an open door.'

'It means somebody must have had keys.'

'Right, DS Parkinson, which rules out another detainee but implicates one of the guards of the Centre or its management. Who had access to the keys?'

Claire Trent laid her hands on the table. 'I think it's time we questioned the Centre's staff.'

'They are all giving evidence at the inquest this morning.'

'Ridpath, I suggest we let them go home. Let them think it's all finished and they can relax. then we bring them in and interview them individually. We can start to put pressure on.'

'I'll organise it, guv'nor. I'm going to the Coroner's Court later.'

'Good, you get along there and make it happen. Somebody was the inside man, or woman, in all this.'

Ridpath was tempted to tell Claire Trent he had a hospital appointment at 10 a.m. but decided to keep his mouth shut. The less she knew about his cancer and the hospital, the better.

'Will do, boss. Let's go back to what we were discussing before. Did someone enter the prison that evening to kill Wendy Chen...?'

'Or was the killer already there in the next room, Liang Xiao Wen? Somebody opened the door for him to commit the murder and locked him in his room again afterwards?' said Emily Parkinson.

'It was an idea I rolled over in my mind last night. But Liang was murdered with the same MO yesterday.'

'Same MO doesn't necessarily mean the same person. Just the same style of death.'

Claire Trent spoke loudly, interrupting their discussion. 'We won't solve this until we get the pathologist's report later today on the second victim. What it does suggest is somebody from the Removal Centre was involved in the murder, either committing it or being an accessory. Either way, we need to question all of them ASAP.'

'Agreed, boss.'

'Next steps on Liang Xiao Wen?'

Ridpath stood in front of the picture on the board. 'Harry, can you contact all his known associates, find out if anybody knows anything?'

'Will do, Ridpath.'

'So to conclude, let's bring in the guards and the manager this afternoon for questioning. Chrissy, can you organise the plods and one team to bring the DCOs, Joe Cummings and Tony Osborne, in from their homes? The Centre Manager, David Carlton, is giving evidence this afternoon. Pick him up as soon as he finishes on the stand.'

'Got it, Ridpath.'

'We want them all here by 4 p.m., Chrissy.' Claire Trent stood up. 'Time to turn the screw on the screws. Let's get this done, people.'

Chapter 53

Mrs Challinor stood in front of the mirror and adjusted the collar of her cream shirt, pulling down her black jacket so it sat level across her shoulders and moved her skirt a little more to the centre.

Appearance was important to her, particularly when she walked out to sit in front of a jury.

She checked the clock. 9.55. Just five minutes to go. She liked to start exactly on time, setting a precedent she would maintain throughout the session. Woe betide any junior barrister, solicitor or witness who was late back into one of her courts.

She leant closer to the mirror and checked her lips. Slightly smudged. She took out her lipstick and re-did the shape of her mouth, making sure the bow was perfect. She was going to be talking a lot today. Her usually unruly grey curls were tied back in a mass behind her head. Most people called this a ponytail, but she preferred to think of it as a mane.

There was a knock on the door and her office manager entered.

'Two minutes, Coroner.'

'Thank you, Jenny.'

The door closed and Mrs Challinor checked her make-up once more. Her hands were clammy. She was nervous for some reason. How many inquests had she held? Thousands in her career but for some reason she was nervous about his one.

Should she have listened to Ridpath and postponed it? Possibly.

But after meeting with the family yesterday, she couldn't disappoint them, particularly the mother. They had to take their daughter back to China on Saturday and she wasn't going to stop them.

She pulled down her jacket once more and chose the correct case files from her desk. 'Let's get this done, Margaret.'

She opened the door on her left and walked straight into court no. 1. Immediately, a hush descended on the packed room.

She placed her files on her table, glanced across at the jury siting on her left and the solicitors in front of her and sat down. 'Today we open the inquest into the death of Wendy Chen, known as Chen Hong Xi, and also known as Wendy Tang.'

She nodded towards the seven jurors. 'There is a jury present at this inquest. I thank you in advance for your service. This inquest should last two days, unless new evidence comes to light.' A quick glance at the papers in front of her. 'Representing the family is a community worker, Ms Heidi Wong.'

A young Chinese woman rose and bowed her head.

'Ms Wong will simultaneously translate the proceedings for the family.' She nodded towards the old woman and her husband sitting next to the interpreter.

'The operator of Wilmslow Removal Centre, New Hampshire Detention Services, is represented by Mr

Ronald Stride, on behalf of the firm of Walker and Walker.' A tall man at the table in front of her bowed his head.

'The government is represented by Mr Archibald Sutton.'

A small, plump man stood up. 'I have a watching brief from the government, Coroner, but don't intend to intervene unless absolutely necessary. I will be joined tomorrow by a representative from the Chief Coroner.'

'Thank you, Mr Sutton. I am always happy to see the government representatives in my court.' She smiled in his direction and turned her head to the gallery. 'A gentle reminder to all those present, including the ladies and gentlemen of the press I see before me.' She gestured towards the group on her right. 'This is not a court of law. I will ask each witness questions as I see fit. The legal representatives of the Immigrant Removal Centre and the representative for the family will then have the opportunity to question the witnesses when I have finished.'

There was a long pause as she opened the case file and found her notes for the first two witnesses. 'This case is unusual, ladies and gentlemen of the jury, as we will be calling two pathologists to the stand. The first, Dr Schofield, has re-examined the body of the victim, Wendy Chen, earlier this week after an instruction from my office. The second, Dr Ahmed, examined Ms Chen in the days after her death. We will hear their testimony before we hear that of the custody officers who found her body, as their findings will have an impact on my questioning of those men...'

The barrister for New Hampshire Detention Services was on his feet. 'Coroner, we only received these new findings from the second pathologist yesterday...'

'You received them shortly after I did, Mr Stride.'

'But Coroner, it has meant we have had no time to digest them properly and prepare a proper defence for our clients. We request with the utmost sincerity you postpone the inquest until we have had time to prepare a defence and advise our clients of their statutory obligations in this matter.'

Mrs Challinor took a deep breath. 'I have to remind you, Mr Stride, this is an inquest into the death of Wendy Chen in Wilmslow Removal Centre on August 20, 2019. Your clients are not on trial so there is no need to prepare a defence for them. As for receiving Dr Schofield's report, all I can say is you received it at the same time as I did, and have had the same amount of time to digest it as I have. I hope it did not give you indigestion.'

There were a few titters from the reporters.

'I will not be postponing this inquest, Mr Stride. The family have flown a long way to attend this court and I have no intention of making the journey a fruitless one.'

'Coroner, I must protest. This ruling affects the rights of my clients...'

'Mr Stride,' the coroner spoke louder, 'I will say again your clients are not on trial. This inquest is to establish how Ms Chen died, when she died and where she died. That is all. Your request is denied. Jenny, can we proceed with calling our first witness, Dr Schofield?'

Reluctantly, the barrister sat down, glancing across at the solicitors representing the company. By making the protest, he had officially lodged a complaint at the way Mrs Challinor was running the inquest. It was now a matter of record. There was nothing she could do anymore except continue and hope Ridpath and MIT could discover new evidence in the next couple of days.

The die was cast.

Chapter 54

Ridpath sat in the hospital waiting room surrounded by other patients in various stages of fear.

He had arrived ten minutes late but, as ever, the doctor was running behind schedule. He had entered, checked out the other patients and, in a couple of seconds, chosen the seat farthest away from anybody else.

He sat down and searched through the pile of magazines next to the seat for one published later than 2016.

There were none, so he picked a Country Life with a cover of a bucolic English village that existed only on jigsaw puzzles. He opened it at the middle and preceded to read it, trying to stop his mind thinking about the case.

Relax, Ridpath, let it go for half an hour. Instead, he stared out over the waiting room, checking out his fellow patients.

He had been coming here long enough to recognise the types. It was the first visit of the cocky guy on his own on his right. For one, he tried to talk to his neighbour, forbidden in places like this by the unwritten rules of cancer wards. Secondly, he wasn't nervous. The doctor hadn't given him the news yet of his cancer stage. The shaking hands, furrowed brow and sweating would come later.

The couple to his left had just received their news about a week ago, Ridpath was certain. They were grim-faced, occasionally whispering to each other but most of the time just staring out into mid-air.

From their faces, Ridpath worked out it was the woman who was the one with cancer, even though it was her partner who was the one who looked more ill. It was always harder on the partner.

He remembered how Polly handled it. A manic-depressive roller coaster of highs and lows; from we're going to beat this together to what the hell are we going to do? Sometimes separated by just minutes.

The final couple on his left were just about to start chemo. He recognised the fear of the unknown on both their faces. Despite the doctor explaining everything, and Christie's were lavish with their information, nobody knew how the body would react to the poisons given to kill the cancer cells. Even worse was the fear it wouldn't work. This man would go through a month of hell and be told the cancer was still there.

A voice calling his name in a foreign accent. 'Thomas Ridpath.'

A nurse, Spanish, he thought, was calling him into to the small clinic where they took blood. He hoped Dracula wasn't working today. She was the nurse who couldn't find his veins and always wanted an extra vial 'for luck' as she called it. But if he had cancer, he was hardly lucky, was he?

The nurse sat him on the end of a day bed and asked him to roll up his sleeves.

Her hands were warm as they tapped the crook of his arm. 'Good, nice big veins. We take some blood now, yes?'

'Take as much as you want, I've got plenty.'

'No, just two vials is enough, yes?'

He loved the way she said yes with a sound like a 'j'. It had a wonderfully positive feel about it.

She found his vein expertly, allowing the vials to fill and pulled out the needle, putting a cotton ball on the mark and bending his arm backwards.

'We finished, yes?'

'I hope so.'

'Yes, we are. You wait now for doctor.'

Ridpath checked his watch. He hoped it wouldn't be too long, he had an inquest to attend and an investigation to run.

When he walked back into the waiting room, the young couple had gone. Had they run off in fright or were they in the doctor's room receiving the good or bad news?

He had his answer five minutes later when they came out. The man had tears in his eyes, but his partner was stoic, her face a mask of nothingness: no emotion, no fear, no reaction.

He remembered that face. He had worn it too when he left the consultation room two years ago. The truth would hit later, Ridpath was sure, and then the panic, fear and terror would wash like a tsunami through her body.

He was sorry for her. And her partner. He knew what they would go through now and he wouldn't wish that experience on anybody.

'Mr Thomas Ridpath.'

The Spanish nurse was calling his name again. He knocked on the door of the consulting room. Dr Morris was sitting behind his desk, his body in profile to the door. Ridpath took a seat beside him. The man was staring at his computer.

'Ah, Mr Ridpath, we've called you back today because your last blood test showed a low white blood cell count. An extremely low count. How have you been feeling recently?'

'Fine, pretty good.'

'Tired? Feeling sleepy? Lacking energy?'

'No, I'm sleeping well and seem to have plenty of energy.'

The doctor frowned and checked back with his computer. 'Been ill recently?'

Ridpath shook his head.

'More stress at work, perhaps. I see you are a police officer.'

Ridpath paused for a moment. 'No, same stress as usual. But I'm now a coroner's officer, so at least I work regular hours,' he lied.

The doctor frowned again. 'It's maybe just a rogue result. It happens occasionally. Or the samples became mislabelled. Anyway, that's why we've retaken your blood. I'll rush through these blood tests and, with a bit of luck, I'll ring you with the results by tomorrow evening. Are you sure everything is OK?'

'Positive, doctor.'

'Good, thanks for coming in and we'll chat again once I see the results.'

That was it, he was done.

Ridpath stepped out of the consulting room and began breathing again.

He was under stress, but he did feel fine. It must be a rogue result as the doctor said.

Mustn't it?

Chapter 55

Dr John Schofield took his seat in the witness box and adjusted the microphone so it was at the same level as his mouth.

Jenny Oldfield administered the oath and, as Margaret Challinor began questioning him, he ran his finger around the inside of his shirt collar, as if giving himself more room to breathe.

'Please state your name and occupation,' asked Mrs Challinor.

'Dr John Schofield. Forensic Pathologist attached to the Eastern Manchester Regional Health Authority.'

'You were asked to re-look at the post-mortem performed by a Dr Ahmed on Ms Chen, were you not?'

'Correct. In fact, Dr Ahmed and myself re-performed the post-mortem together,' he said in his high, school-boyish voice.

'Isn't that unusual?'

'It is, but given the shortness of time in this case, we both believed it would save time if we could reach a conclusion together.'

'And did you reach an agreed conclusion?'

'We did.'

Mr Challinor paused, expecting him to continue but he didn't. Eventually, she was forced to ask, 'Which was?'

'Wendy Chen was murdered in Wilmslow Removal Centre early in the morning of August 20, between three and four a.m.'

A buzz went around the court. The journalists were scribbling in their notebooks. The jurors stared at each other.

On the family's table, the interpreter was quickly translating for the mother and father. When she had finished, both stared at the coroner, their mouths open.

Mrs Challinor waited for the hubbub to die down before continuing with her questions for Dr Schofield. 'How did you form this conclusion, doctor?'

'As you know, the initial findings by Dr Ahmed in his first post-mortem was the victim had committed suicide. My examination at first seemed to indicate this to be the case. The angle, depth and cut along the victim's throat all were consistent with killing oneself. However, three things came to my attention which threw doubt on that conclusion.'

'And they were?'

'Firstly, there was a bruise on the victim's right temple consistent with her being struck.' A picture appeared on the screen of a close-up of Wendy Chen's head. A gasp from her mother, which was quickly stifled. Dr Schofield continued speaking. 'Dr Ahmed presumed this had happened as she hit her head when she fell. But, a careful examination of the body's position, she was lying on the bed, indicated this would have been impossible. The rooms within the Centre are designed to avoid hard edges. There is nothing that could have created the bruise other than another human.'

Another buzz travelled round the courtroom, which was quickly silenced by a glare from Mrs Challinor.

'The second inconsistency occurred when I noticed a mark just above the breast of the victim...'

'A mark?'

Another picture appeared on the screens around the court. It was a close-up of human skin. 'Actually, two marks, side by side. I believe the storage of the body had helped them to become more prominent and explains why Dr Ahmed missed them on his first examination.'

'What made these marks, doctor?'

'I believe it was a Taser, or stun gun. I have checked the research abstracts and files of the University of Tennessee Anthropological Research Facility in America, commonly and erroneously called the Body Farm, and it would appear from their tests the likely candidate as a weapon is Taser, a Raysun X1, made in Taiwan, to be precise.'

The image of a Taser flashed onto the televisions.

'Let me get this correct, doctor. You are saying Wendy Chen was tasered before she was murdered?'

'Correct, Coroner.'

'And does Dr Ahmed agree with your findings?'

The other pathologist rose from his position in the area reserved for witnesses. 'I concur, Coroner, there can be no other explanation. I am sorry I missed these marks in my original post-mortem.'

'Are Tasers or stun guns part of the Centre's equipment?'

'A question you should ask them, not myself.'

'Oh, I will, doctor.' Mrs Challinor wrote a note for herself. 'You said there were three findings...'

'The third inconsistency came from the investigation carried out by your officer, Coroner, DI Ridpath. The cut on the throat ran from the left, just below the ear and went across, cutting the artery and ended at the Adam's apple. Perfectly consistent with a suicide. Invariably, the victim either blacks out through pain or loss of oxygen to the brain before the throat can be completely severed.' He demonstrated on himself. 'However, as it started on the left, the perpetrator had to be right-handed. The family have informed us Wendy Chen was left-handed. Hence, suicide was impossible.'

'Do you concur, Dr Ahmed?'

'The doctor stood at the back of the court. 'I do, Coroner. This information was unavailable to me when I performed my post-mortem.'

The coroner shifted her gaze back to the young pathologist sitting in the witness box. 'So your conclusion, Dr Schofield, is that Wendy Chen was murdered?'

'Correct.'

'But how could such a murder occur in a secure facility like Wilmslow Immigrant Removal Centre where everybody was locked up?'

'With all due respect, Coroner, that is your job to discover, not mine.'

Chapter 56

Sitting at the back of the court, Tony Osborne could hear the pathologist's testimony clearly.

His knee was trembling and his right hand shaking. He put it in his trouser pocket to keep it from view.

Next to him, Joe Cummings leant over and whispered. 'She was murdered. That's why the door was open. I thought I closed it.'

Tony Osborne didn't reply.

This little mess is going to cost the bastard a pretty packet. He told me he was only going to have a chat with her, not finish her off. I thought she committed suicide after he visited her. Bastard.

In front of him, Dr Ahmed was called to give testimony. Osborne listened carefully. The doctor was agreeing with everything the pathologist had just said. It sounded like both of them had reached exactly the same conclusion.

His leg started bouncing of its own accord again.

Calm down, take three deep breaths. Just say the words the company told you to say and get out of here. Tomorrow you are going to be a long way away from the grey skies of Manchester.

Just get through today, that's all he had to do.

Get through today.

Chapter 57

Yang May Feng snatched some clothes off a hanger and threw them into an open suitcase on her bed. She didn't know where she was going, but she just had to get out of Manchester.

She had spent all night worrying, lying in bed awake, working out what to do.

Was he outside waiting for her? If she went to the club again, would he be there? Was he watching now?

She wished Wendy was there. Wendy always knew what to do. She was the bright one, perhaps too bright. Hadn't she decided the only way to get out of their debts was to shop the people who had smuggled them into the country to the police? But look what had happened. Her intelligence had left her dead on the floor of one of their prisons.

When dawn fought its way through the grey Manchester skies, she knew what she was going to do.

She would go to London.

She could hide in the big city; find somewhere to stay in Soho and just vanish into the back alleys and lanes of Chinatown.

Nobody would know she was there. Nobody would follow her. She could just live her life. Work would be easy to find too. There were always waitress jobs going in Soho: cash in hand and no questions asked. She wasn't going to work the clubs any more – far too dangerous. And, if he ever came looking for her, they would be the first place he would look.

Now it was time to go. She'd get the train to London; in just two hours she could be away from here.

Away from him.

She closed the suitcase. Perhaps she could return later to get the rest of her clothes before the businessman made another visit and discovered his flat had been used.

She fastened the latches and rolled the suitcase into the living room. This had been her prison. She had become used to the four walls surrounding her, the kitchen where she cooked her instant noodles and the bathroom, where she threw up with fear.

But it was time to go now. After seeing him the other night she couldn't go back to the club any more.

The weight of the bulging purse in her coat pocket gave her a feeling of security. At least this would give her some money to help her start her new life. Better she should have it than Liang and his grasping boss.

She stopped for a moment, remembering the long journey from Shanghai to here. A flight from China to Budapest, then a long drive in the back of a lorry, thirty-seven hours from Belgrade to somewhere in Belgium, she didn't know where.

Herself and Wendy holding hands throughout the journey, trying to give each other comfort. The rest of the Chinese passengers silent, just staring into mid-air as the lorry lurched from side to side.

Each mile of the journey she continually reminded herself why they were doing this. For her, it was easy.

Leaving China and going to Britain was the only way to escape her marriage to a man who beat her. She was running away from China but Wendy was running to somebody.

Her boyfriend.

Listening to Wendy, she never understood the attraction of the older Englishman. Neither did Wendy, but still she went back, attracted like a moth to a flame.

In Belgium, the terrible men who had made them jump in the back of a container and closed the doors, sealing out the light. Sitting there in the dark, with 40 other people, Wendy beside her whispering to her to stay strong.

Her friend was always the strongest, the one who took care of everyone.

The cold. The hunger. The noise of the lorry as it accelerated. More cold. Voices outside the container. The air stagnant and putrid with the smell of piss from the bucket in the corner. Taking it in turns to use their phones for light until the batteries died and they just sat in the dark.

And then they arrived just outside Manchester. The morning was cold and the men just opened the doors and told them to run. Luckily, Wendy's boyfriend was waiting for them and he took them back to his small flat. They stayed there for a week, just sleeping and eating, happy to be back in the city.

How it had changed. Wendy was dead and she was scared in case he came to kill her too.

She had to run, to get away from here.

'Going somewhere, May Feng?'

She stared at the kitchen. He was standing in the entrance. How did he get in?

'I... I...'

He put his arms out as he walked towards her. 'Don't worry, I won't hurt you.'

She stood in the centre of the room, paralysed by his voice, her suitcase at her feet.

'But you do realise I couldn't risk them knowing about Wendy and I. You do understand, don't you? It would've destroyed everything.'

She opened her mouth to scream but he pulled out a gun from his pocket and fired at her. She expected to hear the explosion of a bullet. To feel the metal explode into her skin and shatter her bones.

Instead two metal wires snaked out from the front of the gun and buried themselves in her chest. A sharp pain shot through her body, followed by a jolt of energy surging into her bones, collapsing her to the floor.

She was still semi-conscious as she watched his feet come closer to her face and a hand grab the back of her neck, while another forced a damp pad against her mouth.

She tried to struggle, to push his hand away, kicking out with her feet, but he was too strong... too strong.

She found herself falling, falling, losing consciousness but still held by powerful arms.

As she fought to stay awake, the last words she remembered hearing were, 'Wendy's gone now, May Feng. What a shame, I do miss her.' A rough hand stroked her face and her hair. 'You need somebody to look after you. Such a pretty little sparrow deserves to be taken care of.'

Chapter 58

The coroner was already interviewing Joe Cummings when Ridpath slid silently through the doors at the back of the court. He caught Jenny Oldfield's eye but the Mrs Challinor was so intent on interviewing her witness she didn't notice him.

'And what did you see, Mr Cummings?'

Mrs Challinor leant forward to hear the witness better. All seven of the jurors at the inquest matched her body language, straining to hear the answer.

'I saw a body lying on the bed.'

'Could you speak up please? It's important the jurors and everybody else at the coroner's inquest can hear your answers. Could you increase the volume on the microphone, Jenny?'

The court bailiff, Jenny Oldfield, adjusted the volume at a machine on the wall. A screech of feedback echoed through the East Manchester Coroner's Court.

'That's as loud as it will go, Mrs Challinor.'

'Very well, you will have to speak up, Mr Cummings.'

The witness leant in close to the microphone. 'I saw a body on the bed.'

'Good, we can all hear you now.'

Even Detective Ridpath standing at the rear of the court near the entrance doors could hear him. Ridpath peered at the clock. 11.35. He hoped Mrs Challinor finished early today. He needed to get back to HQ as soon as possible, otherwise Claire Trent would be demanding to know where he was. His left arm ached slightly from when the nurse had taken blood. Perhaps she wasn't as gentle as he thought.

'A body? Whose body?' asked Mrs Challinor.

Ridpath's attention was drawn back to the tall, thin, tattooed man answering the coroner's questions while sitting upright on a chair in the witness box. Joe Cummings appeared different from the time Ridpath had interviewed him. Now, he was clean-shaven and dressed in his Sunday best, looking like one of those Mormon missionaries.

'The body of one of the inmates… I mean one of the detainees,' he quickly corrected himself. 'There was blood everywhere. On the walls, on the bed, all over her clothes…'

'So what did you do next?'

Mrs Challinor was gently coaxing the story out of him. Ridpath could see the fear in his face as he relived it again, his eyes dancing upwards and to the right. This man would never forget what he had seen.

'I pressed the alarm button on my walkie-talkie.'

'It linked back to the control room?'

Joe Cummings nodded.

'You will have to answer for the record, Mr Cummings.'

'Yes, it linked to Tony in the control room. There were only two of us on that night…'

'Only two for a facility with 32 people awaiting deportation?'

'In reality, there were 34 detainees. Two of the mothers had children with them.'

'Children were locked up too?'

'If they were too young to be separated from their mothers, yes.'

A barrister rose in the middle of the court, wearing his gown and wig. Silly chuff.

'Yes, Mr Stride,' Mrs Challinor raised her eyebrow in annoyance at being interrupted.

'This is as per Home Office guidelines, Coroner. I direct you to the Review into the Welfare in Detention of Vulnerable Persons of 2016 and the subsequent passage of UK Statutory Instruments, 2018, no. 409 on the Rules for Short-Term Holding Facilities. There are no guidelines or rules as to staffing levels in a facility.'

'Thank you, Mr Stride, I am so happy somebody is up to date with the minutiae of government policy.' Mrs Challinor paused for a moment before returning to her original line of inquiry. 'There were only two of you on duty?'

'Right, there should be four, but one person was off sick and another had recently resigned.'

'Two people to manage a facility with 34 detainees. Was that normal?'

Joe Cummings shrugged his shoulders. 'I don't know if it was normal, but it was usual.'

Mr Stride was on his feet again. 'Government policy…'

Mrs Challinor stopped him from speaking with a wave of her hand. 'We will be asking the company's representative when we call him, Mr Stride. You will have your opportunity to explain if two people are enough to ensure the safety and security of 34 detainees. In the meantime, I will continue to question Mr Cummings.' She switched her focus to the witness as the barrister reluctantly sat down.

Ridpath smiled to himself. Mrs Challinor was on fine form today.

'Let us return to the body of Ms Chen. You say there was blood everywhere?'

'Everywhere,' repeated Joe Cummings, 'it seemed to be coming from a slash to her throat.'

'So you called the control room.'

'Yes, and they called the police and ambulance.'

'And what happened?'

'We automatically went into standard operating procedure. All lights were switched on in the facility and all doors were checked. Our paramount concern is the safety and security of our detainees.'

'Did an alarm go off?'

'Yes.'

'And did this wake all the detainees?'

'It did. And the alarm alerted the local police station, who sent three squad cars to the Removal Facility.'

'Why?'

'For additional security in case anybody tried to escape.'

'What time did the ambulance and the police arrive?'

'I would guess ten minutes later.'

'And what did you do?'

'As per operating procedure, after checking the corridor doors were all locked, I returned to the control room on the ground floor.'

'Did you lock the door to the dead woman's room?'

Joe Cummings stared down. 'No.'

'Why not?'

'I didn't think. I wanted to follow the manual and the manual says once the alarm sounds, I am to check the doors and return to the control room if I am not already there.'

'How come the room was unlocked in the first place, Mr Cummings?'

'I don't know.'

'But wasn't it your responsibility to lock all the detainees in their rooms after 9.15 p.m.?'

'Yes, but…'

'But what?'

'I thought I locked the room, but…' his voice trailed off, '…but I guess I didn't. The company has given me demerit points for this error.'

'So you think you just forgot?'

'I don't know. I may have missed this room.'

'Not easy to do, is it?'

'What?'

'Miss a room? I mean there are only sixteen on the floor.'

Joe Cummings shook his head. 'I thought I locked it but…'

'You may have missed it.'

Mr Stride was on his feet again. 'I think the witness has made his point, Coroner. He has been censured by New Hampshire Detention Services for this regrettable error.'

'Thank you for helping me, Mr Stride, but I'm going to ask the witness one more time. Did you or did you not lock the door, Mr Cummings?'

'The truth is I just don't know. I don't remember.' Joe Cummings looked across at his barrister and received a reassuring nod. The training had paid off. 'If you are asked a difficult question, simply answer "I don't remember" and continue with this response until the coroner gives up.'

Mrs Challinor shuffled her papers. 'You said after the alarm was triggered, you immediately returned to the control room.'

'Standard operating procedure.'

'Without locking the room with Wendy Chen's body in it?'

'Correct. I was upset. I'd never seen so much blood before, it was everywhere. I just wanted to get away from the blood.'

'So anybody could have entered the room if you didn't lock it?'

Mr Stride was on his feet again. 'I thought the coroner's duty was to find out who died, how they died and why they died, ma'am. We seem to be stepping into unknown territory with these questions.'

Mrs Challinor stared at him. 'I am perfectly aware of the parameters of my job, Mr Stride, I do not need anybody to tell me what they are. The government and its agents, in this case New Hampshire Detention Services, has a duty of care for all people in its facilities. It is my job to see if this duty of care has been breached.'

'But ma'am...'

'I'll thank you to interrupt me less, Mr Stride, and listen to my questions more. Do I make myself clear?'

The barrister held his hands together in front of his body as if in prayer. 'Yes, ma'am. Please accept my heartfelt apologies.'

Ridpath had never heard a less heartfelt apology.

'Mr Cummings,' the coroner continued, 'so these detainees were locked in their rooms at four o'clock in the morning with an alarm blaring...'

'It's not blaring, ma'am, merely ringing.'

The coroner rolled her eyes. 'So these detainees were locked in their room with the alarm ringing. Was any explanation given to them?'

'Not until after the police arrived.'

'And you made an announcement?'

'Correct ma'am. But they were used to it.'

'What do you mean?'

'The alarm goes off by itself once a week.'

'Once a week?'

'There's something wrong with it.'

'And it's never been fixed?'

'It's been fixed many times, but it still goes off. These days, the police ring us before they come out to check whether it's a false alarm.'

Mrs Challinor shuffled through her papers, finding the correct one and reading out loud, 'This is the police transcript of the call. "Your alarm has gone off again, Wilmslow Immigrant Removal Centre, what is it this time?" That was the police sergeant speaking. "We've got a dead 'un. Topped herself." Who was that?'

'Tony, Tony Osborne, the other guard that night.'

'We will be calling him later, members of the jury.' She turned back to the witness. 'How did Tony know Ms Chen was dead?'

'I must have told him.'

'How did you know she was dead?'

Joe Cummings thought for a moment. 'All the blood, I just assumed...'

'You didn't lock the room after you discovered the body?'

'No.'

'You didn't enter the room?'

'No.'

'Why did you think she killed himself?'

'That's what happens. People don't want to go back so they…'

'Kill themselves?'

Joe Cummings shrugged his shoulders.

'How many people have killed themselves at the facility, Mr Cummings?'

Mr Stride stood. 'The witness is just a detainee custody officer, he can't be expected to know the information.'

'You're correct, Mr Stride, I will be asking the question to the manager of the Removal Centre when we call him. In the meantime, I will rephrase it. In your knowledge, Mr Cummings, how many people have killed themselves at this facility?'

'In the time I've worked there, to my knowledge, three, but this was the first one to use a knife. The other two jumped into the stairwell.'

'Thank you, Mr Cummings. One final question. You heard the pathologist, Dr Schofield, state Ms Chen was murdered. What do you say to that?'

He shrugged his shoulders. 'I thought she committed suicide. How could she have been murdered? This was a secure facility.'

'I keep asking myself the same question. Thank you, Mr Cummings. Any questions from the family, Miss Wong?'

The interpreter spoke to the old man and his wife and they shook their heads.

'Any questions, Mr Stride?'

The barrister was on his feet quickly. 'Just one, ma'am. Mr Cummings, were the standard operating procedures of the Centre followed at all times after your discovery of the body?'

'They were, sir.'

'Thank you, Mr Cummings.' Mr Stride nodded at his briefing solicitors and sat down.

'You may leave the court and go home if you wish, Mr Cummings, but remember you are still under oath and are liable to be called again if this court sees fit. Thank you for your testimony.'

Joe Cummings left the dock and walked over to sit beside his colleagues from the Centre.

'It's time to call Mr Tony Osborne to the stand.'

The tall Custody Officer levered himself off his seat, receiving a pat on the arm from Joe Cummings and a whispered 'good luck.' He walked nervously to the witness box.

Jenny Oldfield handed him the Bible and he swore the oath to tell the truth. Ridpath glanced at his watch. 12.05. This would be the last witness before lunch.

'Could you state your name, age and occupation for the record.'

'Tony Osborne, I'm 46 and I'm a Detainee Custody Officer.'

'Please speak up, Mr Osborne. You have been a Custody Officer for the last thirteen years?'

The man cleared his throat and leant closer to the mike. 'That... that is correct, ma'am, after leaving the army I was employed at Forest Green Prison and just over two years ago, I transferred to Wilmslow.'

'Why did you transfer from Forest Green to the Wilmslow Immigrant Removal Centre?'

Ridpath listened closely to the answer. Would Osborne reveal he had been under investigation?

'I live in Handforth, ma'am, and the Removal Centre is closer to home. Plus the pay, overtime and benefits are better with New Hampshire.'

He didn't mention anything about the investigation. For the first time, Ridpath wondered if he was hiding anything else. They would find out more when they brought them in this afternoon.

'You seem to be nervous, Mr Osborne, why?'

'It's my first time in court, ma'am. It's a bit intimidating.'

'Don't worry, we are just trying to discover the truth of what happened.' A long pause as Mrs Challinor checked her notes. 'Do you enjoy your work?'

Osborne appeared confused. 'Sorry, ma'am?'

'You can call me Coroner or Mrs Challinor. I asked, do you enjoy your work?'

'It's a job, Coroner. But I enjoy the interaction with the detainees.'

'Even when you are deporting them?'

Tony Osborne smiled nervously at the jury. 'It's part of the job, defending the country's borders. Somebody has to do it.'

Mrs Challinor made a note on her blue legal pad. 'Let's talk about the night of the death, shall we? What time did you go on duty?'

'At six, I was working the late shift. It should have been my day off, and I'd only finished at noon on the day, but they were short-staffed so I volunteered for the overtime.'

'Is that usual?'

'Like I said, there's always overtime at the Centre. It's hard to get the staff.'

'So you only had six hours between shifts?'

'I live nearby so I went home, had a shower and slept.'

'You had been on duty the previous day when Ms Chen arrived?'

'That's correct, ma'am... I mean Coroner.'

'So were you tired or exhausted after working such long hours?'

Osborne was looking more relaxed now. He sat back in the witness chair. 'Not at all. I was used to it and anyway, I usually take a nap on my breaks.'

Mrs Challinor made another note. 'So you came on duty at six, and what did you do?'

'The usual.'

'Take us through it, please?'

'I checked the logbook to see if anything had happened earlier...'

'Had anything happened?'

He shook his head. 'It was a pretty quiet day. There was a removal scheduled for the following morning, but he was happy to go so we weren't expecting any problems.'

'Who was that?'

'A Romanian, I think. He had finished serving two years for assault and possession, and we were sending him back. He seemed to think it was a good result.' He smiled at the jury again.

'What else did you do?'

'I had a verbal briefing from the Duty Manager, Mr Carlton, and I walked through the facility, checking all the detainees. Some were doing their washing, others finishing their dinner and a few more watching TV.'

'All was quiet?'

'Yeah, all normal.'

'Afterwards?'

'Myself and Joe Cummings did our roll call at 9 p.m. and locked up for the night.'

'By locked up, you mean locked all the detainees in their cells?'

'We prefer to call them rooms.'

'And the victim, Wendy Chen also known as Wendy Tang, how was she?'

'Seemed fine, I didn't really notice her.'

'Why?'

'She'd only just come in and we hadn't received any information on her yet from Immigration.'

'So you only had a name, you didn't know why she was being detained?'

'Right. Ours not to reason why and all that.'

'I thought it was a statutory rule that a detainee must be told why they are being detained? As Mr Stride so helpfully pointed out, it was decreed in 2018.' The coroner held aloft a copy of the legislation.

'They should be told when they are being processed but the paperwork hadn't arrived from Immigration Enforcement.'

'An unfortunate oversight. Let's move on to later in the night. You commenced your rounds at 3 a.m.?'

'That's correct. We take it in turns to walk round the facility and we need to swipe the card on the readers.'

Mrs Challinor picked up a printout. 'I see you were slightly late when you got to the victim's floor. The printout on the readers says you arrived at 3.08.'

'I went for a pee. We're allowed a ten-minute leeway to touch our card to the reader. Standard operating procedure.'

'All was quiet?'

'Very.'

'The victim's door was locked?'

'I don't know. I don't check each door. Standard operating procedure is to check the doors at the end of the corridors only. I usually just look at the doors as I'm walking along the corridor. I would have noticed if it was open.'

'But you can't be sure.'

'No.'

'And you didn't look inside her room.'

'No. Standard…'

Mrs Challinor held up her hand to stop him speaking. 'We understand, Mr Osborne. How do you think the door was left unlocked?'

Tony Osborne shrugged his shoulders. 'Beats me. Joe must have forgotten to lock it. He did the second floor and I did the third floor that evening.'

'So you did your check but didn't notice an open door.'

'No, I didn't notice it was open.'

'What time did Mr Osborne go on his rounds?'

'Bang on 4 a.m. Joe was always on time.'

'What were you doing?'

'Watching the cameras in the control room. A few were on the blink, but all the rest were working.'

'How many cameras were not working?'

Tony Osborne counted on his fingers. 'Six, I think, but it may have been more. The incident happened over a month ago.'

'Was the camera in the corridor outside the victim's door working?'

'No, it's one of the ones on the blink. We reported it but nobody was going to come out to fix them late at night. It was probably just a fuse.'

'Let's move to the discovery of the body now, shall we? You received a report on the walkie-talkie from Mr Cummings at 4.06 a.m. What did you do?'

'I followed procedure.'

'Which is?'

'Activate the alarm button, check all the cameras, check all doors are locked and secured and ring the police and the ambulance service.'

'You told the emergency services the victim had topped herself, why?' The coroner seemed to remember something, and turned to the jury. 'Topped in this case is slang for suicide. Please answer the question, Mr Osborne.'

'When Joe told me there was blood everywhere, I just presumed, didn't I?'

'Because it had happened before?'

He nodded. 'Some of them cut themselves. They don't want to go back, see. They're looking for a Section 35.'

'Section 35?'

'A medical report on their mental and physical state. It's a way of getting out of it.'

'Out of what?'

'Out of deportation. Some of them try it on.'

'Miss Chen wasn't trying it on, though, was she?'

He shook his head. 'She was a goner.'

'You sat in the court when the pathologist, Dr Schofield, gave his evidence Ms Chen didn't commit suicide, but was murdered. What do you think, Mr Osborne?'

Mr Stride was on his feet. 'Mrs Challinor, this officer is not a medical practitioner or a pathologist, he cannot be expected to "think" anything. His presumption of suicide was based on information relayed by the discoverer of the victim, Mr Cummings.'

'Thank you, Mr Stride, you are, of course, correct.'

Ridpath could see Mrs Challinor had made a mistake with the question. It immediately put her on the defensive.

'What happened next?'

'The police and ambulance arrived. I let them in and showed them to her room.'

'You left the control room?'

'I had to. With only two of us on, Joe was in no fit state to help. I got a demerit notice too.'

'A demerit notice?'

'During an emergency, as the officer in charge I wasn't supposed to leave the control room, but I couldn't see any way of dealing with the police and ambulance unless I did. When the police came, they took over the scene and I could go back to the control room.'

'Thank you, Mr Osborne. Any questions, Mr Stride?'

The barrister rose to his feet. 'Just a few, ma'am.' He turned to the witness. 'Mr Osborne, did you at any time go into the victim's room?'

'No. When the police and ambulance arrived, I opened the door at the end of the corridor for them but didn't go any further.'

'So you never saw the body of the victim at any time?'

'No, sir.'

'One more question, Mr Osborne. You said you received demerit points from the company. Why?'

'Like I said, I was the officer in charge and I shouldn't have left the control room.'

'Because it was against standard operating procedure.'

'Yes, the company is strict about following SOP. I guess it's for the good of the detainees, so everybody gets treated in exactly the same way.'

'Thank you, Mr Osborne.'

Mrs Challinor looked at the clock on the far wall. 'I think we will break there to allow the jurors to eat.' She turned to them. 'This inquest into the death of Ms Chen will continue after the break. Please do not discuss this case with anyone. We will return at two o'clock to continue questioning Mr Carlton, the Centre Manager, and other witnesses. Thank you for your time and diligence this morning, jurors.'

Mrs Challinor rose, bowed and exited through the rear door.

There was an audible sigh of relief from the court and everyone spoke at once.

Ridpath watched as the barrister and his attending solicitor immediately rang somebody on their mobile phone.

Somehow he knew this phone call wasn't good news for the coroner.

Chapter 59

'How much did you hear, Ridpath?'

'Quite a lot. I came in midway through Cummings's testimony. It was word for word what he told me before. Almost as if he had memorised it.'

'He's been coached.'

'New Hampshire?'

'Who else?' Mrs Challinor took off her jacket. It was one of those unusually warm September days; the sun was streaming in through the large picture windows in her office and the air conditioning was struggling to cope. 'The morning didn't go well. They have kept to their stories and even when I introduced the new post-mortem evidence regarding her murder, they just stalled me.'

'How did they explain the open door?'

'Joe Cummings said he didn't know. He thought he'd locked it, but he must have been mistaken.'

'You still have the Removal Centre's manager, the CCTV maintenance company, the emergency medics, the security officer and DS Barnes to interview.'

'The manager is a lifer, somebody who's spent time in the prison service and knows every bland pontification ever published. The security officer wasn't there. And as for the policeman, his investigation was shoddy as if he didn't care and was just ticking the boxes.'

'We spoke to him last night, Mrs Challinor.'

She looked up from her notes. 'And?'

'He knew Wendy Chen. She was one of his confidential informants who'd called him about a gang of people smugglers. She also called him from the Centre the day before her death.'

'What? Why did he investigate her and why am I only just hearing about this?'

'It gets worse. He was the one who reported her to Immigration Enforcement. Home Office rules...'

'What?'

'If an illegal immigrant comes into contact with the police they must be reported immediately.'

'Even when that person is helping with another crime, helping to stop trafficking?'

'Yes.'

Mrs Challinor threw her file on the table. 'Tell me that's not screwed up, Ridpath.'

He stayed silent.

'But why run the investigation? He should have excused himself immediately.'

'He said it was to help protect her. He was afraid if it came out she was an informant, the gang would harm her family in China.'

'Jesus, it gets worse. So, if I ask him about this, it may lead to problems for the family?'

'I don't know, Mrs Challinor.'

Ridpath walked over to look out of the sash window. Carol Oates was in deep conversation with the government solicitor, Archibald Sutton. He turned back to the coroner. 'The use of a Taser might be worth pursuing.'

'I've checked, it's not part of the standard equipment in the Centre. I'll ask but again I'm not hopeful.'

She put her head between her hands and sighed. 'It's the blandness of the denials, the explanations and the semi-truths that annoys me. And the smirking face of the PR lady as she sits watching…'

Mrs Challinor slammed her hand on the desk.

'A woman was tasered and had her throat cut. Answer me this: how is anybody murdered when she's locked up in a supposedly secure facility? A facility that has cameras everywhere yet they see nothing. Why was the door to Room 7 unlocked when all detainees are behind locked doors from 9.15 to 7.00 a.m.? Why has nobody been charged with murder?'

'I don't know, Mrs Challinor, but it's what I intend to discover. This was an inside job. Somebody let the killer into the Immigrant Removal Centre and disabled the CCTV cameras.'

'It feels like nobody cares, Ridpath. It's just another girl from China who was due to be deported.' She stared at him again. 'It's like she was a non-person, Ridpath, like she didn't exist.'

'They don't know it yet, but I'm going to officially interview them again at Police HQ this afternoon as part of the MIT investigation. We're sending cars to their homes as we speak. Perhaps, if they are lying, I can break their stories. Somebody on the inside helped murder Wendy Chen. We'll come for David Carlton, the Centre Manager, after his testimony, arrest him outside the court. Just to shake him up a little.'

'I wouldn't count on breaking them, Ridpath.'

He glanced at the clock. 'It's time to go back in, Coroner.'

She pulled on her jacket. 'Sorry, Ridpath, for the argument yesterday, not like me at all.'

'Not like either of us.'

'You still don't believe I'm right to continue with the inquest, do you?'

'No, Coroner, I think you should wait till we've completed our investigation.'

'You're not the only one.'

Ridpath raised an eyebrow.

'I had a phone call from the Chief Coroner's Office this morning. Apparently they have received reports I have been acting "inconsistently" as they euphemistically put it. They're sending an observer from London tomorrow.'

'I haven't made a complaint to them, Mrs Challinor, nor has Claire Trent to my knowledge.'

'I have an inkling who it was, Ridpath. But the great thing about being a coroner is we are difficult to remove unless they can prove I am no longer in charge of my faculties.'

'And how would they do that?'

'There are ways. But coroners can always fight back.'

'Mrs Challinor, if I could say one thing.'

She waited for him to speak.

'You can't solve all the world's problems.'

'I'm not trying to, Ridpath. Just this one.'

Chapter 60

After his meeting with Mrs Challinor, Ridpath returned to his office to see Sophia.

'Hiya, I enjoyed the work this morning. So that's how a real investigation runs. Exciting.'

'Most times it's boring grunt work. Chasing down leads. Following up on dead-ends. Checking through paperwork. Preparing submissions for the CPS. And always, always, collecting evidence.'

'It was good, felt like a team working together.'

'Do you have anything for me?'

'Dr Schofield gave me a brief heads-up on his report on the murder of Liang Xiao Wen.'

'And?'

'The MO is exactly the same as that of Wendy Chen. The actual report will be here soon. He's couriering over a copy to MIT too.'

'Right, I'm heading back there now. Call me later and tell me how it went this afternoon in court.'

Before she could answer, he was out of the door and heading towards the car park. On the way, he bumped into Carol Oates again. Why did he have a feeling she was watching him and these accidental meetings were not accidents at all?

'Hello Ridpath, I wanted to have a chat with you.'

'I'm in a hurry, Carol, can we do it later?'

She shrugged her shoulders. 'Of course we can, but I thought you'd like to know we have a visitor from the Chief Coroner coming to Manchester tomorrow.'

How did she know? Was she the one who had reported Mrs Challinor? Ridpath decided to play dumb. 'Really, why are they gracing us with their presence? I thought they never left London.'

'Something about Mrs Challinor's handling of the immigration case, I think? But you can never be sure with the Chief Coroner's people. I'd keep my head down if I were you.'

'What do you mean?'

She smiled coyly. 'You know what it means when they bother to make a visit...'

'No...'

'Well, it's never good, let's put it this way. The Chief Coroner would prefer never to get involved with the cases of an area coroner. The mere fact they are coming...'

She let the insinuation trail away like her sentence.

'So they prefer coroners didn't investigate deaths properly, didn't rock the boat and just toed the government or corporate line?'

'No, of course not, but if a coroner is embarrassing the department, they have to step in, don't they?'

'Is Mrs Challinor embarrassing the department?'

She shook her head vigorously. 'I'm not saying that at all, but sometimes mud sticks and the last thing they want is for mud to stick on their new three-piece suits.'

And you would be the one slinging the mud, wouldn't you? It's what Ridpath thought, but he said, 'Look, I'm late for a meeting.'

She stood aside. 'Don't let me get in your way. But one more thing. I needed Sophia but she wasn't in this morning.'

'She was with me.'

'Oh, I suppose that's OK, but she should have let Jenny know where she was. I can't be expected to do my work and track down her whereabouts too. It's a rule Jenny has to know where everybody is all the time.'

It was a rule Ridpath broke every day of his working life at the Coroner's Court. 'I'm late...' He edged past her.

As he did, she spoke softly, 'Remember, I would keep my head down if I were you in the next couple of days. We don't want them to make too many changes around here, do we?'

Chapter 61

'Now, Mr Carlton, you are the manager of the Wilmslow Removal Centre, are you not?'

The man was wearing a bland grey suit and an even blander grey smile. He had already been sworn in and Mrs Challinor was questioning him.

'That is correct. I have been in charge of the Centre for the last two years and have worked for New Hampshire Detention Services for fourteen years.'

'So you are in charge of the day-to-day running of the operations?'

'I am.' He smiled at the jury. 'New Hampshire have a rigorous set of standard procedures that must be adhered to at all times.'

'Even when these procedures come into conflict with the needs of the detainees?'

'The operating procedures are designed to meet the needs of everybody in the Centre, Coroner, from the detainees to the staff, the visitors to the doctors and nurses. They have been designed in accordance with govern-ment policy and, in many cases, surpass that policy in the generosity with which they treat everybody associated with the Centre.'

Mrs Challinor sighed. Questioning this man was like reading the human version of a corporate brochure. It was time to ruffle his feathers. 'And yet, according to your own staff, three people have died in the Centre in the last four years.'

The bland smile again. 'While it is regrettable anybody has passed away while under the care of New Hampshire, it must be remembered, at the same time, over 3764 individuals including 128 children have passed through the door of our facility. All have been treated fairly and supportively, according to the relevant government policy of the day.'

'Tell me what happened on the night of August 19th.'

'Actually, it was the morning of August 20th. I received a phone call just after 4 a.m. that there had been a suicide in the Centre...'

'But we now know it was murder, don't we, Mr Carlton?'

'We didn't at the time, Coroner, the Custody Officer reported it to me as a suicide.'

'What did you do?'

'I came immediately to the Centre from my home, arriving at 4.45 a.m. The police and an emergency medical team were already there. I consulted with the two officers on duty and we switched off the alarm.'

'It was still ringing since it had been pressed at 4 a.m.?'

'Yes, it is standard operating procedure. Once activated, only myself or the police can switch it off. The police didn't, so I did.'

'And the detainees were still locked in their rooms?'

'Standard operating procedure...'

The coroner held up her hand and the man stopped speaking. 'We get the message, Mr Carlton. 'What happened after you switched off the alarm?'

'I questioned the paramedics. They told me the woman was dead and nothing could be done.'

'Did they tell you she had committed suicide?'

'No, I simply presumed she had because of the information from my custody officers.'

'What happened?'

'I went to the corridor and checked the room.'

'Did you go in?'

'No, I closed the door. I thought the woman should be left undisturbed, so I waited in the control room until the police detectives arrived just after six. I then briefed the lead investigator, a Detective Sergeant Barnes.'

Mrs Challinor stopped for a moment, checking her notes. 'Mr Carlton, you just said you didn't go into the room. Did you look in?'

There was a pause and a glance towards the solicitors sitting at the table close to him. 'I quickly checked it out. The dead woman was lying on the bed. There was blood everywhere and a knife on the floor close to the bed.'

'So this persuaded you it was a suicide.'

Another pause. 'It was one of the factors, yes…'

'But we heard this morning Dr Schofield has confirmed it was murder. How do you think murder was committed in your Centre?'

Mr Stride was on his feet. 'This witness is not a detective, Mrs Challinor. He is here to report what he saw, not what he thinks.'

'Mr Stride, I will remind you once again this is not a court of law. I can ask Mr Stride anything I want, even if it is an opinion he may or may not hold.' She turned back to the witness as the barrister sat down reluctantly. 'Please answer the question, Mr Carlton.'

'I have no idea how a murder may have been committed at the Centre. It is New Hampshire's policy that all detainees, regardless of creed, colour, race or offence committed, are treated with dignity and respect within the parameters of government policy.'

'Mr Carlton, do you think your standard operating procedures in any way contributed to the death of Ms Chen?'

'At New Hampshire, we are constantly reviewing our procedures based on new information or new government policy. This is a continuous process...'

'Do these new procedures involve having CCTV that works?' the coroner interrupted him.

Again a glance across to his solicitors. 'Of course, it was regrettable some of the CCTV cameras were not working that evening, but in a facility as large as Wilmslow Removal Centre, we are bound to have some machinery that isn't operative. It is our standard operating procedure that these cameras should be repaired as soon as possible.'

A long pause as the coroner wrote his answer on her pad. 'Mr Carlton. How was it possible a murder was committed in a secure establishment such as Wilmslow Removal Centre?'

'I have no idea, Coroner, but it must be remembered deaths happen in all detention centres across the UK. In fact, in 2017, six deaths occurred, and only one in a New Hampshire facility I am happy to report. Incarcerating any individual, depriving them of their liberty, is always going to lead to difficulties. But as long as it is government policy to detain illegal entrants to the UK, New Hampshire will strive to maintain the best service possible, for both the detainees and our government employers. I am confident our standard operating procedures do this.'

'One final question, Mr Carlton. Does the Removal Centre carry Tasers or stun guns as part of its standard operating equipment?'

'We do not, ma'am.'

'How was it one was used on Ms Chen?'

'I have no idea. It is not part of our equipment.'

This man had been too well coached in his answers. Mrs Challinor was never going to get anything resembling a human response from him.

Two uniformed police officers entered the court at the back. What are they doing here? Were they the ones who were going to take Carlton off for questioning?

She decided to let them get on with their job. Perhaps Ridpath or Claire Trent could achieve more than her.

'Thank you, Mr Carlton. Any questions from the family?'

The interpreter shook her head.

'And from Mr Stride?'

The barrister stood. 'None from us, Coroner.'

'Thank you, we will now take a ten-minute break before we call the Emergency Medical Team that attended the death of Ms Chen.'

As Mrs Challinor rose to exit the court, she saw Mr Carlton wink towards the New Hampshire table.

At the back of the court, the police officers were waiting.

Chapter 62

Ridpath felt a little dirty after his conversation with Carol Oates. If she hadn't reported Mrs Challinor to the Chief Coroner, she would know who did. What a waste of time and energy when there was so much work to be done.

He drove too quickly to HQ, realising she had managed to get under his skin. If Mrs Challinor was sacked, would he survive?

He thought not. Despite Carol Oates' concerns for his well-being, he knew she disliked him intensely. The only person she hated more was Sophia. Their mutual antipathy was out in the open and it wasn't going to be put back in its box. He would have to talk with his assistant again.

He parked outside Police HQ, realising once again he couldn't remember driving there. This would have to stop. He must concentrate on the road and not on what was bothering him.

He ran up the steps, hurried through security flashing his badge and caught the lift to the third floor where the Major Investigation Team was based.

Claire Trent was waiting to pounce as soon as he stepped into the office. 'Where have you been, Ridpath? You're supposed to be running an investigation not running all over town. Brief me in my office, now.'

'Yes, guv'nor.' As he walked through the office, Chrissy Wright gave him a discrete thumbs up while Emily Parkinson stopped him, saying, 'Can you sign this, Ridpath?'

He took the file and was about to sign when he noticed, written in block letters across the top was:

LAM TAI KONG. SHALL WE BRING IN FOR QUESTIONING?

He looked at the Detective Sergeant. 'That's good, DS Parkinson, please proceed.'

Claire Trent was waiting for him at the door to her office. 'Get a move on, Ridpath.'

He walked in, closing the door behind him. Before he had sat, she was in his face. 'What the hell's going on? You held a briefing this morning and disappeared for the rest of the day. Working part-time are we now?'

Ridpath had forgotten Claire Trent was renowned through GMP as a demanding boss. 'Not at all, guv'nor, but I thought I'd check in with Mrs Challinor at the inquest. The arrests are happening as we agreed and all the staff who were on duty or at the Removal Centre that night will be here at 4 p.m.'

He was winging it a little, hoping Chrissy's thumbs up meant what he thought it did.

'They'll all be ready to be interviewed at 4.30 but I suggest we let them take a quick look at each other and then leave them to stew in separate rooms. Time to put some pressure on.'

Claire Trent seemed to be mollified by his answer, so Ridpath carried on.

'We are also looking to bring in an associate of the dead man, Lam Tai Kong, and I've just authorised his detention for questioning. It will be interesting to find out if any of the guards know him. Sophia tells me the pathologist's report is being couriered over, I'm sure Chrissy has a copy. Can I check with her now?'

Claire Trent pressed a button on the intercom. 'Chrissy, can you come in?'

Thirty seconds later, the Manchester City support worker walked through the door. 'Have we detained the Removal Centre's guards yet, Chrissy?'

Behind his back, Ridpath crossed his fingers.

'Two of them are on their way here, boss. We picked up Joe Cummings at home and David Carlton after he finished testifying at the Coroner's Court. He was not a happy bunny.'

'They never are. What about the last one?'

'The plod are at his house now, with Alan Butcher. There's no answer at the door but the light's on so they think somebody is at home. And before you ask, I just called the pathologist and the report on Liang Xiao Wen is on its way. We should have it in ten minutes.'

'Good work, Chrissy.' Ridpath winked at her.

'I've had a heads-up from Sophia; the MO is the same in both murders. But let's wait until we read the actual report.'

'How does your assistant get information before we do?'

'Beats me, boss.'

'Can you send DS Parkinson in, Chrissy?'

Two minutes later there was another tap on the door. 'Hi guv'nor, you asked for me?'

'Ridpath tells me we've located Lam Tai Kong.'

'Yes, boss, wasn't difficult, the local plod said he's well known in the area. A bit of a lowlife; flashy, but cheap apparently. Anyway, he spends most afternoons at the Toronto Pool Hall and the betting shop next door. A creature of habit is our Mr Lam.'

'Send a car to bring him here. It's about time we knew more about him and his oppo, Liang Xiao Wen.'

'Already done, boss. Ridpath sent the request in a while ago. The local plod are on their way. Only too happy to oblige.'

Claire Trent narrowed her eyes and said one word. 'Good.'

'Is that all, guv'nor? 'Cos I'm just following up a lead on the activities of Liang Xiao Wen from a mate in City 3. Apparently, our dead man ran some girls out of a Chinatown nightclub.'

'Yeah, go on.'

She left the office. Claire Trent waited for the door to close. 'You're either bloody lucky, Ridpath, or everybody is covering for you. I don't know which.'

'Neither, guv'nor, the team is working well together.'

'Aye, and pigs might fly. Stay tight on this one, Ridpath, I've got the Chief Constable asking for an hourly update, so if I get hassle so will you...'

A sharp rap at the door.

Before Claire Trent could say enter, it opened to show Chrissy Wright. 'We've just had a phone call from Alan Butcher. They were sure somebody was inside Tony Osborne's house, so they busted the door down...'

'And?' asked the detective superintendent.

'They found him on the floor with his throat cut.'

Chapter 63

Ridpath and Claire Trent arrived at the crime scene near the centre of Handforth. They had blue lit all the way from Police HQ down Kingsway and along the A34.

It was a time Ridpath loved. The screeching modulation of the siren above his head. The roar of acceleration down the outside lane in normally packed roads. The quiet, calm concentration of the driver at the wheel.

It was heaven, pure heaven.

By his side, Claire Trent was on her phone to Alan Butcher at the scene. 'We'll be there in five minutes. Establish a perimeter, I want nobody going in or out of there.' She clicked off the phone as if snapping somebody's neck. 'Ridpath, has Chrissy contacted the pathologist and a forensics team? I want them there yesterday if not sooner.'

'I'm sure she has, guv'nor.'

The car lurched to the right as the driver took it round a bollard in the middle of the road into the opposite lane and back onto the right side of the road again.

'Sure ain't good enough. Check.'

It was one of those times when adrenalin was flowing. Ridpath called Chrissy to confirm they were on their way.

'Seven minutes, Ridpath.'

The car screeched to a halt, sliding sideways.

Claire Trent jumped out, running past a startled copper in her high heels, followed by Ridpath flashing his warrant card. On the left the neighbours were standing around, arms folded, trying to find out what was going on. Next to them, the ambulance car, in bright emergency yellows and blues, was parked, a medic dressed in green leaning on the door.

Alan Butcher was standing at the gate to the garden.

Claire Trent slowed to a brisk walk. 'What happened?'

'As I told you, guv'nor, we came to take Tony Osborne in for questioning at 3.30. We banged on the door but got no reply. We heard music coming from inside the house. Young Dave here,' he pointed to the uniformed copper standing next to him, 'went round the back to check and saw the victim lying in the room on the floor. So we kicked down the front door.'

Ridpath gazed at the front of the house. The door was half-hanging off its hinges. 'Any sign of forced entry when you arrived?'

'None, Ridpath. Place was quiet as a grave.'

'Are you sure it's Tony Osborne inside?'

The DS shook his head. 'I only took a quick look before getting on the blower to you lot.'

'Right, you stay here, nobody is to go in, is that clear? Come on, Ridpath, you're with me.'

She pulled on a bright blue pair of plastic gloves and opened the gate, walking slowly and carefully up the garden path. Ridpath borrowed a pair of gloves from Alan and followed her.

The door was open leading to a small hall with a garish Lempicka print hanging on the wall. The Chief

Superintendent stepped across the entrance and checked in a small room on the left.

Empty.

She walked on, followed by Ridpath. Music was still playing from a room in the rear.

On the left, stairs led up to the upper floor. In front of them, a door led towards a rear room. Ridpath checked out the white wallpaper. 'No signs of blood in the hall, guv'nor,' he whispered.

Claire Trent checked the walls and nodded. She pushed open the rear door.

It led into a large room with a built-in kitchen on the left, a bar table with three chairs next to it, and the bloodied body of a man lying in the centre, with his throat slashed from ear to ear.

Chapter 64

'Is it him?'

The body lay on the floor, a bloody gash where the neck should have been. The front of his Hawaiian shirt was drenched with red, clotted blood.

Above his head a long arterial streak of blood traced across the white wall.

'Is it him, Ridpath?' the detective superintendent repeated.

Ridpath nodded. 'It's Tony Osborne. I saw him giving evidence this morning.'

Claire Trent turned back to stare at the body. 'Well, he won't be giving evidence any more. Check out upstairs, Ridpath, but don't move anything. Where's the bloody pathologist and the forensics team?' she said walking back to the front door.

As Ridpath climbed the stairs to the landing, he heard her on the phone, shouting for the forensics team to get here yesterday.

The house was clean and tidy, almost spotless, but lacking in any character. A new grey, hardwearing carpet clung to the stairs. The walls were freshly painted and the whole place had the distinct smell of newness.

Had Tony Osborne ever lived here?

On the left was a small bathroom. The shelf below the window had no toiletries, shaving cream, toothbrushes or toothpaste on it. He opened a cabinet door.

Empty.

Strange.

He walked out and pushed open a small bedroom on the left. Nothing but a new single mattress and bedside table, both from IKEA, and a built-in wardrobe.

He strode over to it, opening the door with his gloved hands.

Empty again, save for a few cheap metal hangers on the rail.

He retraced his steps into the hall and stared at a closed door. Tentatively, he pushed it open. A strange smell came from inside.

Ridpath leant forward and put his head round the edge of the door, seeing a larger room, the master bedroom.

Next to the door, the source of the smell. A black plastic bin bag full of old, unwashed clothes. Ridpath peered inside and saw the blue trousers and white shirts of Osborne's uniform lying on top. The clothes smelt like they had never been cleaned.

On the bed was a suitcase with a used brown envelope resting on top. Ridpath walked over to the bed, checking the rest of the room.

Unlike the rest of the house, this room had been used. There were toiletries on the dressing table sitting next to a small leather bag. A fresh set of clothes were hanging over the back of a chair. Ridpath saw a new floral Hawaiian shirt and shorts. On the seat of the chair, a black carry-on bag lay open. He looked into it: a UK passport and a wallet were lying inside.

Ridpath picked up the passport, seeing a new picture of Tony Osborne on the inside page, a broad smile plastered on his face. It had been issued from Liverpool only two weeks ago. He took out the wallet. Inside was over two thousand pounds, more American dollars, travellers cheques and a small blue currency with funny squiggles as well as western numbers on it.

He checked in the bag again. Beneath the wallet and passport was an airline ticket. Tony Osborne was due to fly business class to Bangkok Airport tomorrow morning on British Airways.

He put them back in the carry-on bag exactly as he had found them.

He glanced around the room one more time. His eyes kept coming back to the used brown envelope lying on top of the suitcase.

He reached over to pick it up.

Heavy.

He opened the flap and peered inside. The envelope was full of a mass of new, shiny keys with handwritten labels attached.

Outside door. WRC.

Stairs. WRC.

Corridor 2. WRC.

WRC? Could that be Wilmslow Removal Centre?

Chapter 65

Mrs Challinor sat in her room, staring at the files on the telephone. The afternoon hadn't gone well at all. The CCTV supplier and maintenance company had confirmed New Hampshire's story that the six cameras had been reported at 6.30 p.m. on August 19th as being out of order. Apparently, it was as Tony Osborne had stated; one of the first things he had done.

Even worse, the CCTV company said the cameras were always breaking down because they were continually interfered with by the detainees. Apparently, simply putting a piece of metal across the points at the back tripped an internal fuse. Nothing they could do about it.

The Emergency Medical Team had also confirmed the testimony of both Joe Cummings and Tony Osborne. They had been let into the facility by Osborne who unlocked doors to let them into the Centre. He had stayed at the end of the corridor while they entered the room and checked on Wendy Chen. When they arrived at exactly 4.25, the young girl had no pulse and they thought she was dead. With the amount of blood in the room, the obvious marks on the throat and the presence of a knife on the floor, they assumed it had been a suicide too and informed Tony Osborne of this belief and David Carlton when he arrived.

Of the two, the more senior, Lawrence Royston was the most definite.

'Did you have any reason to suspect foul play?'

'No.'

'You have heard Dr Schofield's testimony that Ms Chen was in fact murdered. What do you say to this?'

'We were surprised, given the scene when we entered. I've seen a few suicides in this job, not many cut their throat, and most that try, fail. I just thought this one had succeeded.'

'You saw no suicide note?'

'No.'

'The door was open when you entered?'

'It was. I closed it after I had finished examining the body.'

'Why?'

'It wasn't the sort of scene that anybody should enter. It seemed to be the right thing to do for the young girl.'

At these words, Mrs Chen sobbed so loudly, she was escorted from the court by the interpreter with her shoulder around the old woman's. The husband remained, his face as stoic as ever.

'One last question, Mr Royston. What happened when the pathologist, Dr Ahmed, arrived?'

'We briefed him on our observations, told him the girl was dead and gave him our impressions of the scene.'

'And those impressions were it was a suicide?'

'Correct.'

Mrs Challinor had called an end to the proceedings for the day after cautioning the jury about discussing the case at home.

The only witnesses to call tomorrow were the police officers who attended the scene, Detective Sergeant Barnes who had led the investigation and the security officer of the Centre, Mr Collins.

Unless Ridpath and Claire Trent produced new evidence, there were only a couple of possible determinations available to her: an open verdict where the cause of death was unknown or a verdict of murder. Since 2009, she had more flexibility to voice a narrative verdict, particularly where the death happened in prison custody, and she was certain she was going to do so in this case. New Hampshire's attitude throughout the inquest was disturbing.

If the jury came back with the determination Wendy Chen was murdered, the police could still apply to retain her body as evidence in an investigation. The girl's mother and father might not be able to leave with it on Saturday after all. But that was a risk she would have to take.

The telephone rang. Finally, the call she had been expecting. 'Margaret Challinor speaking.'

A posh southern voice. 'Rupert Vansittart, here, Mrs Challinor, calling from the Chief Coroner's Office. I'm sorry to have to inform you we have had two more complaints today regarding your conduct of the inquest into the death in custody of Ms Chen...'

The hounds had chased her down, were they now going to rip open her throat?

Chapter 66

Ridpath stood outside the house in Handforth with Claire Trent. She was on the phone again. From her body language he had the feeling it was somebody even more senior than she was. An Assistant Chief Constable perhaps.

He had told her of his discoveries in the upstairs bedroom. As soon as the forensics team arrived, she briefed them and asked them to check out the room first.

The crime scene manager was Helen Charles. 'No worries, Claire, and we'll go over the rest of the house with a fine-tooth comb. If our perp has left even a single flake of skin, we'll find it.'

Dr Schofield was still in the house, performing his initial examination of the body.

Claire Trent clicked off her phone. 'We've got a pissed-off sixth floor, Ridpath. It's almost as if I had purposely committed these murders to embarrass them at a difficult time in their lives. If I ever get like that, you have permission to shoot me.'

Ridpath stayed quiet.

She checked her watch. 'When's the bloody doctor coming out? He's been in there for nearly an hour.'

'He's thorough.'

'I need speed now.'

Just as she finished speaking, the doctor came out of the front door, slipping off his mask and the hood from his Tyvek overalls.

He walked towards them, chatting to the crime scene manager. As he got closer, he stopped and said. 'Well, in my eyes it looks like a carbon copy of the murder in the Removal Centre and in Chinatown.'

'So this is our third victim?'

He nodded. 'Twin marks from a Taser on the chest. In my opinion, it's the same as was used on the other victims, a Raysun X1. Same cut marks in the throat.' Once again, he mimed getting a person in a headlock, stabbing the knife under the left ear and dragging the knife across the Adam's apple. 'No defensive marks across the hands. Looks like the victim was unconscious or comatose when he was killed.'

'Alan Butcher is certain all the doors were closed when he was here. Looks like Tony Osborne knew his killer,' said Claire Trent.

Ridpath stepped forward. 'My bet is the killer knew all three of his victims.'

'So who was it, Ridpath? Who knew all three people?'

'That's what we need to find out, boss.'

'One more thing,' interrupted the pathologist, 'I use an ultraviolet light to check for marks and stains on the clothes or body I can't see with a naked eye...'

'And?'

'The ultraviolet picked out a mark on the wrist.' He passed Ridpath a piece of paper. 'I drew a copy of it because I know you want to get working straight away.'

Ridpath stared at the round drawing. It looked like a stylised elephant.

'What is it?' asked Claire Trent.

'If I'm not mistaken, it's an entry stamp from a night-club. It may mean nothing, but our victim was out clubbing last night.'

Chapter 67

Back at the station, Chrissy had already added a picture of Tony Osborne to the board in the situation room. Ridpath was at the front explaining his recent finding to the assembled detectives.

'We now have three linked deaths. Wendy Chen was the first on August 20th. Next came Liang Xiao Wen, who had the room next to hers in the Centre and was either involved in her death or may have heard what happened. Finally, just three hours ago, the murder of Tony Osborne, a custody officer at the Centre was discovered in his home in Handforth.'

'Anything on him?' asked Emily Parkinson.

'I made a preliminary search of his bedroom. It was obvious Tony Osborne was planning to do a runner to Thailand tomorrow. He had a new passport, a ticket and, according to an estate agent, had recently contracted with them to let out the home. We checked his bank details and 5000 pounds was paid into his account six weeks ago, followed by another payment of 5000 pounds three weeks ago.' A close-up of a bank statement appeared on the screen behind his head.

'Where did it come from?' asked Emily Parkinson.

'He paid it in himself, in cash, so untraceable. We've also checked through his phone records.' Another image on screen. 'Most of his calls were to a couple of bookies and his ex-wife. There are six calls to this number.' The image cut to a number circled in red. 'Guess what?'

'It's a burner phone, pay as you go.'

'Right first time, Emily.'

'And it's also the same number Liang Xiao Wen called from the IRC.' The screen changed again to show a close-up of the call sheet with the number underlined.

'We also found two sets of keys in the bedroom. We showed these to David Carlton, the Centre Manager and he says they look like the keys for his facility.'

'Were the custody officers allowed to take them home?'

'No, it was against standard operating procedure for keys to leave the Centre. All sets were counted and locked in a cupboard in Carlton's office.'

'Where did these come from?'

'It looks like Tony Osborne had them made. We're checking out locksmiths at the moment. Any luck Chrissy?'

'Nothing so far, Ridpath.'

'What's your conclusion?' asked Claire Trent.

Ridpath paused for a moment. 'There are two possibilities. Tony Osborne gave the keys to an outside person to allow them to gain entry to the Centre. He may have also been involved in rendering the CCTV cameras unusable to give that person an unobserved route to Wendy Chen's room. The man locked all the doors behind him until Joe Cummings came along and discovered the body at 4 a.m.'

'But why didn't he lock the door of the victim's room? She wouldn't have been discovered until much later when they opened all the doors,' said DS Parkinson.

'I don't know the answer. Perhaps the murderer wanted the victim to be discovered by Joe Cummings. It immediately gave Tony Osborne an alibi.'

'What's the other possibility, Ridpath?'

'Tony Osborne released Liang Xiao Wen when he did his rounds at 3 a.m. so he could commit the murders, and then locked the man in his room afterwards.'

'Pretty cold blooded...' said Parkinson.

'I agree, if it were true. But Osborne didn't strike me as the type. He would have wanted as little to do with the actual crime as possible.'

Claire Trent stood and walked over to Ridpath. 'If all three of these people are dead, it means our killer is still at large.'

'What's the motive for the deaths?' asked Parkinson.

Ridpath knew it was a good question, he just wished she hadn't asked it at that moment. Everybody was staring at him. 'The truth is we don't know. From my perspective, it all started with her death.' He tapped the picture of Wendy Chen. 'There's something we don't know about her. Her death was the catalyst for everything that followed.'

'Or could she simply be the first victim?'

'Explain what you mean, Emily?' said the detective superintendent.

'Well, we know Wendy Chen was trafficked into this country. Could she have come in illegally through one of the ports? Could we be dealing with a group of Chinese people traffickers like those involved in the deaths of 58 people in a container truck in Dover in 2001?'

'Remind me again, Emily?'

'In June 2000, a Dutch container lorry came on a from Zeebrugge in Belgium. Inside were 60 Chinese, 56 men and four women, and only two survived. It was determined that the deceased were illegal immigrants, and likely died of asphyxiation, though carbon monoxide poisoning was not ruled out. The 60 people were trapped in the container for more than 18 hours when the outside temperature reached 32 °C (90 °F). The survivors were found closest to the doors.'

'It's a possibility, Ridpath. These murders are a cover up of people trafficking. Was Liang part of the gang and that's why he was killed? It would also explain why he could afford an expensive lawyer.'

'Possibly... Emily, have we arrested Lam Tai Kong yet?'

'Not yet, the local plod said he managed to get away from them,' she answered.

'Bloody idiots, can't they do anything right? We also need to talk to the Immigration Enforcement.'

Claire Trent put up her hand. 'I'll get on it. I know Jeremy personally. Sorry, should have done it before.'

'And Chrissy, have we found out which club uses that stamp?'

'Working on it, Ridpath.'

'Work quicker.'

'We still have Joe Cummings and David Carlton in the interview rooms,' Emily Parkinson interrupted.

'They've been stewing for over three hours now. Apparently, the Centre Manager is fuming. Threatening blue murder, he is,' replied Chrissy.

'Let's have a chat with Joe Cummings first. I have a feeling once he knows Tony Osborne is dead, he'll start singing like Katy Perry.'

Chapter 68

'Dead? What do you mean he's dead?'

Ridpath looked across at Emily Parkinson. On the left, Claire Trent was watching through the one-way glass in another room.

'Exactly what I said, Mr Cummings. Tony Osborne was found in his home with his throat slashed at 3 p.m. this afternoon.'

'B-b-but it can't be, I just saw him this morning.'

'I'm afraid it's true, Mr Cummings.'

The custody officer shook his head. 'Like the girl?'

'You mean Wendy Chen?'

Cummings nodded.

'Exactly like her.'

Cummings went pale and gagged. Ridpath grabbed the waste bin and stuck it under his face. Cummings panted heavily, his face getting whiter. A few times he retched, but nothing came up.

Emily Parkinson took the envelope full of keys and dropped it on the middle of the table where it landed with a thud. 'We found these keys for the Removal Centre in his bedroom. What do you know about them?'

Cummings eyed the keys and immediately returned to the bin to dry retch again.

'What do you know about the keys?' repeated Ridpath.

'Tony is dead?'

'I saw his body lying in his living room.'

Cummings was silent for a long while, his eyes moving from side to side like a mouse cornered by a cat.

'We know you knew about the keys,' Ridpath said softly, 'how Tony had them made at the locksmiths.'

Cummings nodded slowly. 'He showed them to me once, said they helped him move around the Centre.'

'Why? Why did he want them?'

'He told me he was nicking stuff. Nothing major – things they didn't use from the storerooms. DVD players, bedroom stuff, towels, that sort of stuff. It was to get those bastards back for being so cheap all the time.'

'Which bastards?'

'New Hampshire and Tiny Bloody Tim.'

'You mean David Carlton?'

Joe Cummings nodded. 'He was forever docking our pay for demerit points and just being a cheapskate. It was all about how much profit they could make. Tony said he was getting his own back.'

'You didn't make your own set of keys?' asked Emily Parkinson.

Cummings shook his head. 'I wanted nothing to do with nicking stuff. Tony offered but I said no.'

'And the night Wendy Chen died, what happened?'

'It was like I said but...'

'But what?'

'Tony wasn't in the control room at 3 a.m., he was moving stuff out to his car. That's why he was late starting his rounds.'

'What stuff?'

'I dunno. Stuff he'd nicked. There were only two of us on, so he thought it was a good time.'

'Is that why he disabled the CCTV cameras?'

'Yeah, it was easy. Simply put a bit of silver foil across the contacts at the back and it shorts the fuse. There used to be a camera in the rest room until the management got bored fixing it.'

'What if I told you Tony wasn't putting stuff in his car, but letting the killer of Wendy Chen into the Centre? What would you say?'

Joe Cummings stared straight ahead, his eyes glassing over and his face becoming paler and paler. Then he grabbed the bin and held it next to his face.

This time, he wasn't dry retching.

Chapter 69

Ridpath reached home just past midnight. The house was quiet and, for a moment, a strange feeling of emptiness enveloped him. He saw a note on the mantlepiece with the message, 'Don't stay up too late,' followed by a series of cartoon characters describing the process of getting undressed and going to bed. The last picture showed a stick man with ZZZZZZZ coming out of an open mouth.

He fixed himself a large snifter of Glenmorangie and sat in the armchair.

Today had been a tough day but they were finally making progress. He thought of the three people who had died so far.

Wendy Chen.

Liang Xiao Wen.

Tony Osborne.

What linked all of them?

Wilmslow Immigration Removal Centre was one obvious link. All had either been detainees or worked there. Tony Osborne had been involved in some way in the death of Wendy Chen. Did he make copies of the keys and disable the CCTV cameras to allow the killer into the centre? Or was he even more involved? Letting the killer in and guiding them to the right room.

He paused for a moment, thinking of the Custody Officer, remembering his testimony from the morning in the Coroner's Court. Did he do the killing himself?

Ridpath shook his head. This killer was cold-blooded and ruthless. A man who would let nothing stand in his way. Osborne didn't strike him as that sort of man. And besides, the MO of his death was exactly the same as the other two.

This was one killer, one man, who had committed three murders.

But why?

What made him kill three people so brutally?

Was it the people traffickers preventing any possibility of their crimes being discovered? They had shown a casual brutality to their victims in the past. Leaving them to die of hypothermia in a refrigerated container. Abandoning them at sea in a sinking boat. Or simply leading them out onto the sands at Morecambe to pick cockles and allowing them to drown.

But this seemed to be such personal killings. Always one on one and always slashing the throat of the victim. The first may have been an attempt at faking a suicide, but the last two? They were just brutal murders.

He took another sip of the whisky. He always marvelled at the purity of the colour as it swirled in the crystal glass.

And then it occurred to him: the last two killings only happened after Ridpath started investigating the death of Wendy Chen.

Was the killer covering his tracks, removing all witnesses to something he'd done?

But what had he done?

Chapter 70

Mrs Challinor was also at home, but she was still reading her case notes and studying the files.

What had she missed?

Today had gone badly. Even though they now knew Wendy Chen had been murdered, the Removal Centre was still maintaining its stance of 'we followed our standard operating procedures as laid down by government statutory rules' line.

Bugger statutory rules. Bugger standard operating procedures. A woman had died and their one concern was they should not be seen as responsible.

And there was the arrival of the Chief Coroner's clerk to 'observe,' as he euphemistically put it. They too were more concerned with how this was going to play in the tabloids than if a grieving family had been treated correctly by the British government.

She ran her fingers through her curly grey hair. Do I need this crap at my age? Haven't I worked long and hard enough?

Perhaps Ridpath was right: she should have waited for the investigation to be complete before holding the inquest. MIT was now investigating, and with their resources they would find out the truth. Hadn't they already made more progress in two days than Barnes had made in a month?

She put her pen down and reminded herself her job was not to find a killer but to represent the family of the deceased.

How did Wendy Chen die?

Had Wilmslow Immigrant Removal Centre done all in its power to prevent her death?

Could Greater Manchester Police have investigated the death with more rigour and professionalism?

Who did it was less important to her than why it happened, when it happened, where it happened and how it could be prevented from happening again.

She stopped for a moment and stared at the pictures of her own daughter on top of the piano. They hadn't spoken in weeks. No real reason, just the pressures of business and life and time.

Tomorrow, when this case was over, she would call her, arrange a place to meet for lunch, just spend time together, two women talking about nothing and everything.

She picked up her case files and started reading the Head of Security's statement again, its bland generalisations and clichés annoying her.

At the back of her mind, a little devil was whispering. 'You've let this family down. They trusted you and you've let them down.'

However hard she tried, the voice wouldn't go away.

Chapter 71

Yang May Feng was lying on the bed, panting with exhaustion. She had tried to struggle against the handcuffs but all she had succeeded in doing was exhausting herself and reducing her wrists to a mess of blood, cuts and bruises. The gag around her mouth had bitten deep into the skin. She'd tried to shout, to let the woman next door know what was happening, but all that had come out was a few unintelligible grunts.

What was she going to do?

Wendy was dead and she would be the next to go.

A shadow appeared in the doorway. She strained her neck to look over in that direction but couldn't see who it was.

Then she heard his voice.

'I told you not to struggle but you wouldn't listen, May Feng. Now look at your beautiful arms.'

He stepped into the light. She could see he was carrying something in his hand. What was it?

'I've been busy since I last saw you…' a smile crossed his face, '…tidying loose ends. That's a good way to put it. And now you are the last one. The last little loose end.'

He sat on the bed beside her and stroked her face. She struggled to escape his touch, but he held her jaw between his strong fingers.

'Listen. If you want to stay alive, listen to me. I'm busy today but I'll come back this evening. If you want, you can come to the flat, take Wendy's place. What a shame about her. I did love her, you know. In my own way. She was a beautiful little sparrow to own and possess. But she wanted more. They always do. When she started talking, I didn't know if she would ever stop, so she had to be quietened. You do see that, don't you?'

He stared at her, examining her face and her body.

'Yes, you could take her place. Be my little sparrow. Would you like that?'

She nodded, her eyes wide with fear.

'Did I tell you her last words before she died? She said, "You?"' He chuckled at the memory. 'Innocent until the end, right until the time I tasered her.'

Yang May Feng struggled, then lay still on the bed. Perhaps if she humoured him, played along with his fantasy, she would have a chance to escape.

'Don't hurt your wrists, little one. And here, I brought you some water and some fried rice.'

He revealed a bottle of water and a take-away box of food.

'Did you think Daddy was going to kill you today? Oh, you are sweet. Not yet, little one. Not quite yet.'

FRIDAY
SEPTEMBER 20

Chapter 72

The phone rang at 4.30 in the morning.

Ridpath reached out to look for his mobile phone, knocking over a glass of water he had placed on the bedside table.

'Yeah… what is it?'

'It's Emily Parkinson, Ridpath. The local plod have located Lam Tai Kong. He's in a second floor flat. They want to go in now.'

Ridpath was instantly awake. 'Message me the address and wait till I get there. Only move if he attempts to escape. I don't want any more cock-ups.'

He got out of bed, looking back at Polly. Her hair was mussed and her hand was holding her ear, but she hadn't woken up.

He grabbed his clothes and crept out of the bedroom.

'Ridpath, you can't keep doing this… your health…' A voice came from the bed.

'Don't worry, Poll, not for long, nearly over.'

He crept out of the bedroom and started to dress in the landing. He ran into the bathroom and checked himself. He'd shave in the drive over to meet the local plod.

His phone pinged. Emily had sent him the address. Not far from Chinatown. He guessed Lam wouldn't live far from his work area.

He rushed downstairs, grabbing a leather jacket hanging in the hall and opened the door.

Outside, it was still dark with just a nip in the air to make him pull his jacket around his body. The car was covered in a glistening sheen of what looked like sweat.

He sat behind the wheel, plugged his phone into the hands free and rang Parkinson. 'Get on to dispatch and have a Police Tactical Unit on standby, I want to go in just before dawn at 6.00 a.m. Clear?'

'Clear, Ridpath.'

'Also call the guv'nor, let her know what's going on?'

'Will do.'

'And Emily, good work.'

'Thanks Ridpath. What time will you get here?'

He checked the car's clock. 'In about fifteen minutes. 4.55. Tell everyone no sirens or lights. I want this one sleeping soundly when we knock on his door.'

'Right, boss.'

Ridpath ended the call and started the car. He drove out of his road and headed for the A56 into the centre of Manchester. The city was quiet at this time in the morning. Only a few lonely souls wandered beneath the harsh orange of the streetlights, either coming home from a late night out in the clubs or off to work to start an early shift.

It was a time he loved, when the city seemed more like a sleeping bear than a vibrant, modern town.

He accelerated along Chester Road, past the two Old Traffords, one on his right and the other on his left.

He could feel the energy beginning to build in his body. That sense of anticipation before every raid. A feeling every actor must enjoy just before the curtains rise and he steps out onto the stage.

This morning it was all his performance.

He stopped at a red light and entered the address on the satnav. Not far away now.

'Go straight ahead and turn left in 200 meters.' The voice in his Audi had a slightly Germanic tinge to it.

He turned left and then right again as instructed. Up ahead, he could see Emily Parkinson standing at the side of the road next to a squad car with its lights off.

It was time to begin.

Chapter 73

The team were all briefed and in position ready to go, just waiting for Ridpath's signal.

He clicked his Airwave to give the order when, at the bottom of the street, an old milk float appeared. A milkman got out, and carrying a tray full of bottles, rattled over to a house, leaving two bottles beside the door.

He gestured to one of the uniforms standing beside him to stop the man coming closer.

The plod ran down the street, shouting, 'Oi, you...'

'Bloody idiot, he'll wake the whole neighbourhood,' Ridpath shouted, 'Go, go, go,' into his Airwave.

In front of him, a police tactical unit ran forward with a large door enforcer, known as the Big Red Key, and brought it down hard against the lock.

The copper with the enforcer stepped back and four armed police entered the house.

Ridpath listened to his Airwave. 'Ground floor clear. Going up to the second floor.'

The sounds of pounding on a door. 'Police. Open the door.'

No response.

'This is the police. Open the door immediately.'

Still nothing.

A crash, the crunch of wood splintering, followed by shouts of 'In. In.'

Feet thumping on a wooden floor, doors crashing open. Shouts of 'Clear. Clear.'

Then silence.

'He's gone out of the window and into next door's garden,' a voice came on the Airwave.

Ridpath grabbed the arm of Emily Parkinson. 'You take the left, I'll go right.'

He ran along the street followed by one of the plods, past a startled milkman still holding three bottles of milk.

At the end, he checked left and right and then left again. A flash of blue going into an alley.

He ran after the man.

Ridpath could hear his heart beating in his chest, feel his shoes on the wet road. Taste the freshness of the morning breeze in his mouth. Beside him the young uniformed copper was hardly panting at all.

Bastard.

He rounded the corner into the alley. Up ahead, Lam was running between the houses, dressed in boxer shorts and a blue T-shirt.

'Get onto the others, tell them where he's headed,' Ridpath shouted to the young cop.

The man stopped and spoke into his Airwave.

Ridpath ran on, slipping once on the wet cobbles as he hurdled a suitcase of old clothes somebody had dumped, and nearly landing on his backside. He recovered his footing and carried on running.

Lam was nowhere to be seen.

The alley went in both directions, left and right.

Which way?

Ridpath chose right and ran on for fifty yards before he saw a branch on the left.

He could feel his breathing getting heavier and his heart pounding. If he ever caught this bastard, he promised himself he was going to get fit again. Time to lose the weight and get back into shape. Perhaps being a coroner's officer had made him soft.

He turned the corner and Lam was there, desperately trying to get over a dead-end wall.

Ridpath stopped, hearing the sirens behind him.

The dawn was just beginning to break on a beautifully clear sky. He inhaled deeply and said, 'Lam Tai Kong, I am arresting you on suspicion of murder. You do not have to say anything. But it may harm your defence if you do not mention when questioned something which you later rely on in court. Anything you do say may be given in evidence.'

Another deep intake of breath. 'You're nicked, matey.'

Chapter 74

'I didn't kill nobody. I didn't do nothing.'

The solicitor placed his hand on Lam's arm to calm him and stop him talking. It was Henry Miller, the same solicitor who had advised Liang Xiao Wen at Rowley Station before his death.

On the opposite side of the table were Ridpath and Emily Dickinson. They had booked Lam into the local nick where he had immediately requested a solicitor. Surprisingly, Henry Miller had turned up within thirty minutes and was shown into an interview room to talk with his client.

The two detectives started the formal interview at exactly 9.00 a.m. with Claire Trent watching and listening from the viewing room.

'Present are Mr Lam Tai Kong, his solicitor, Henry Miller, Detective Inspector Ridpath and DS Parkinson,' said Emily pressing the record button on the tape machine.

It was Ridpath who was leading the questioning. 'If you didn't do nothing, Mr Lam, why did you run?'

'I was scared, thought somebody was breaking into my flat.'

'The police identified themselves twice, Mr Lam.'

'Didn't hear them, I was asleep.'

'A deep sleeper, obviously, DS Parkinson. Let's move on, Mr Lam. Do you know a Mr Liang Xiao Wen?'

Lam shook his head. 'Never heard of him.'

'Really? A car owned by you, BM18 46G was seen outside Cheadle Heath Police Station when Mr Liang was inside.'

'For the record, the screen is showing picture S76, an image of a BMW belonging to Mr Lam.'

'That's one of my cars but somebody must have borrowed it. I have lots of cars.'

'And you don't know Liang Xiao Wen?'

He shook his head again but with less certainty this time.

'This is what he looked like the last time I saw him.'

'On screen is a picture from the crime scene of Mr Liang's body as it was discovered in his flat. It is picture M36.'

Lam turned away from the photo.

'Are you sure you don't know Mr Liang?'

Lam stayed silent.

'For the record… I think that's a no comment from Mr Lam,' added the solicitor.

Ridpath smiled. 'Does Mr Lam own a club called the Golden Elephant, located on Aytoun Street?'

'No comment,' said the solicitor.

'We performed a search of the company's register this morning and he is listed as an owner.'

'On screen is a printout of the company information for Golden Elephant Trading Ltd, who are described in the company's register as the beneficial owners of the nightclub. Mr Liang's name is third of four. This is document D235,' said DS Parkinson.

Lam whispered to his solicitor and turned to Ridpath. 'I am one of the owners.'

'Is it a place of prostitution, Mr Lam?'

'It is a gentleman's club, detective. We do have dancers and women to entertain our guests. We don't condone prostitution, but what consenting adults do in their own time is up to them and has nothing to do with us.'

'You do not employ illegal workers in your club?'

'Not that I am aware, no.'

'And is this the stamp used on guest's wrists as they enter? A stylised elephant like this one?'

'The witness is now looking at document D216, a drawing of the stamp used by Golden Elephant on the wrists of all entrants to the nightclub.'

Lam nodded.

'Here is a picture of the body of Mr Tony Osborne,' continued Emily Parkinson, 'taken at the crime scene yesterday afternoon at 5.15 p.m. And following it a close-up of the man's wrist with the stamp prominently displayed under ultraviolet light. These pictures are photographs S136 and S137.'

Ridpath took over. 'He was also found dead in his home, killed in exactly the same way as Mr Liang. Mr Osborne had a stamp from your club on his left wrist.'

Lam stared at the picture and flinched. 'I know this man.'

'Oh?'

'He was in my club the other night.'

'When?'

'Don't say any more, they are just fishing for information. They have nothing,' interrupted the solicitor.

Lam turned on the solicitor. 'I'm not going down for this, I had nothing to do with it.'

The solicitor threw up his hands and sat back.

Ridpath pushed on. 'When was he there?'

'Wednesday night. Came in about eleven and had a couple of drinks at the bar.'

'That's all?'

Lam glanced across at his solicitor.

'He didn't meet anyone or talk to them?'

Lam stared down, shaking his head.

The solicitor was by his side again. 'That's a no comment from my client.'

'Are you sure?'

Lam stared across the table at the two detectives. 'No comment.'

Ridpath was silent for a moment.

'If that's all you have, gentlemen, and lady, I think this interview is completed, don't you?'

'Just a minute, Mr Miller,' said Ridpath. 'There is one other murder we are investigating. The murder of a woman, Wendy Chen.'

DS Parkinson clicked her laptop and another picture appeared on the screen. 'This is picture number S23.'

Lam became pale.

'Mr Lam, do you know this woman?'

No answer.

Ridpath pressed on. 'She was murdered inside Wilmslow Immigration Removal Centre in the early hours of August 20th.'

'You're not pinning the death of Wendy Chen on me too.' He turned to his solicitor. 'You can't let them do this I didn't kill nobody.'

'So, Mr Lam, you knew this woman? You knew Wendy Chen? We have reason to believe she was illegally trafficked into this country sometime in the middle of June. Did she work in your club?'

Lam was still staring at the picture of Wendy Chen taken that summer in Shanghai.

He didn't respond.

'I think this would be a good time take a break and confer privately with my client. If you could give us ten minutes?'

Ridpath stared across the table. Should he press on now or allow the solicitor time? If he ignored the request, the courts could accuse him of bullying the witness, putting him under undue stress to force a confession.

'Detective Inspector Ridpath...'

'You have ten minutes, Mr Miller.'

Emily Parkinson said, 'interview terminated at 9.45 at the request of the suspect's solicitor.' She switched off the recording machine and the two detectives stood up.

'Three murders, that's what you are facing, Lam. It means they throw away the key. You're looking at thirty years minimum.'

Chapter 75

'We're not getting much,' said Claire Trent.

They were sitting in a small area next to an old, decrepit coffee machine. The walls around it were plastered with old police posters.

'Everything we have is circumstantial, boss. We can't put Lam at the locations of the murders, nor can we even tie him to the victims.' Ridpath took a sip of coffee and grimaced, placing the plastic cup on the table. 'The solicitor knows it and he knows we know it.'

'Anything we can hold him on? How's the search of his flat going?'

'Some fingerprints, boss. The techs said they would call me as soon as the IDENT1 makes a match,' said Emily Parkinson.

'We can hold him a bit longer, but knowing that solicitor, without something new he's going to have him out on his toes before lunchtime.'

'What about resisting arrest? He did a runner this morning.'

'You heard him, Emily, he says he didn't hear it was the police. And when I cornered him, he came as quietly as a naughty child. CPS would never accept such a charge.'

'We're stuffed,' said the detective sergeant.

All three stood up. 'We'd better go back in and listen to what the solicitor has to say. Afterwards, prepare to let him go, but keep digging. We must be able to find something on him,' said Claire Trent.

Parkinson's phone rang. She answered it, listening carefully to the message.

'It was the techs, boss. They found Lam's fingerprints in Liang Xiao Wen's apartment. All over the place.'

'Confirmed they are his?'

'Confirmed in IDENT1. He has priors for assault and living off the proceeds of prostitution.'

'Go get the bastard.'

Chapter 76

Margaret Challinor read through the witness statement from Collins one more time. There wasn't much to ask him about the death of Wendy Chen as he claimed he was in London at the time. Had Ridpath checked his alibi? Barnes, the first detective, certainly hadn't.

She checked the clock on her wall. 9.45 a.m. Just fifteen minutes to go before the inquest began. She hadn't heard from Ridpath or Claire Trent since yesterday evening. Had they discovered something new overnight? If they had, they hadn't told her.

Should she ring Ridpath now?

As she picked up her phone, there was a knock on the door. She shouted enter, expecting it to be Jenny reminding her of the time, but instead a tall man with a receding hairline popped his head round the door.

'I hope I'm not intruding?'

'And you are?'

'Anthony Scott from the Chief Coroner's Office.' He walked in and shook her hand. 'It's a pleasure to finally meet you. We don't usually come to the North and I've heard so much about you.'

'Most of it good, I hope,' said Mrs Challinor.

Scott didn't answer. 'Can I sit?'

The coroner gestured towards the chair in front of her desk.

The man placed his briefcase on the floor and sat down, taking extravagant care to ensure the trousers of his pinstriped suit were lifted slightly to prevent bagging, and his legs crossed correctly.

Mrs Challinor couldn't help but stare at the shininess of his brogues, the toecaps reflecting the light from her desk lamp.

The clerk to the Chief Coroner said nothing.

'I hope you had a good journey to the wilds of Manchester.'

'It was tolerable but first class isn't what it used to be,' he sniffed. 'The coffee was served in plastic cups.'

Mrs Challinor looked at the clock. 'How can I help you Mr Scott? As you know, I have an inquest beginning in ten minutes.'

'The inquest, that's exactly why I'm here, Mrs Challinor. As you know, my job is to keep a watching brief on the performance of coroners, especially in high profile trials...'

'I wasn't aware coroners "performed."'

'I'm using the term in the managerial sense rather than the theatrical. We have received numerous complaints about your *performance* in this inquest.'

Mrs Challinor raised her eyebrows. 'Numerous?'

'Three to be exact.'

'From where?'

'I'm not at liberty to say. As you know, it is important that reports to the Chief Coroner's Office remain confidential.'

'So I am to be accused of not performing, but not allowed to know the identities of my accusers nor the specifics of the accusations?'

'Please, Mrs Challinor, you must understand I am here to help you.'

'In what way, Mr Scott?'

The man smiled and licked his lips. 'To help you improve your performance and because you have an inquest restarting in... eight minutes time, let me explain as briefly as I can.'

He carried on before she could respond.

'It is in nobody's interest to pursue this case with a single-mindedness that has so far dogged the proceedings. The young woman was an illegal immigrant to this country. As you may or may not be aware, the government is currently in discussions with New Hampshire Detention Services to expand its portfolio of prisons and immigrant removals centres which could lead to immense savings to the Treasury. In addition, in these chaotic times, it is important we do not undermine respect in the work of our police force. Putting these two considerations at the top of your mind, I'm sure you'll understand the importance of a good performance in court today.'

Mrs Challinor took a deep breath before she spoke. 'Mr Scott, a young woman was murdered in Wilmslow Immigration Removal Centre. New Hampshire since then seems to be more concerned with protecting their reputation and upholding their "Standard operating procedures" rather than any concern for the welfare of the charges in its care. As for the police, the initial investigation was shoddy at best, and incompetent at worse. Because of this inquest, GMP are now re-investigating the incident.'

Anthony Scott stood, holding out his hand. Mrs Challinor ignored it. 'Thank you for your time, Coroner, I believe you have an inquest to run. Please consider my advice today. It's meant with the best of intentions.'

He turned to leave her office. Just before he opened the door, Mrs Challinor said, 'Mr Scott, who cares for those who have no voice?'

He stopped for a moment and then opened the door to leave her office.

Mrs Challinor stared at the clock. It was two minutes to ten.

Chapter 77

'My client has prepared a statement which I will read out.'

They were back in the interview room and Emily had already started the recording tape.

The solicitor coughed twice to clear his throat. 'My client wishes to state for the record he knew the woman identified as Ms Chen. She worked at his club as a waitress on a part-time basis in July and early August 2020 for which she was paid in cash. He realises as the owner of the club it is illegal to employ people without the correct papers. Furthermore, he is aware it is his duty to report such people to the Immigration Enforcement Office. He deeply regrets not doing so and will ensure he complies fully with the law in the future.'

Lam sat back in his chair with a suitably contrite look on his face.

'So that's the game, is it?'

'I don't know what you're talking about, Inspector.'

'Admit to a lesser charge, hoping we can't prove anything else.'

The solicitor smiled and shrugged his shoulders.

'Unfortunately, we have three murders and your client is a major suspect.'

'I'm afraid you have nothing on him, Inspector. Except employing an illegal immigrant.' Another smile. 'A slap on the wrist if he's lucky and a small fine if he's not.'

'We'll see, Mr Miller.' He turned back to Lam and focused on the man. 'You told us before you didn't know Mr Liang Xiao Wen?'

The solicitor checked his watch. 'My client has already answered the question, Inspector. Are we just going to go around in circles asking the same questions over and over again? It would be a terrible waste of police time and resources if we did.'

'I'll repeat the question. Did you know Liang Xiao Wen?'

Lam smiled. 'I'll repeat my answer. No.'

'Have you ever been to his apartment?'

Lam yawned theatrically. 'No.'

'Please explain to me how your fingerprints were found in the living room and bedroom of his apartment?'

'My client has already said he does not know Mr Liang.'

'Fingerprints were found at the scene. We put them through IDENT1, the police fingerprint database, and your name came up, Mr Lam. A positive match.'

'Where's your proof, detective?' said the solicitor.

'We'll be able to show you the printout, Mr Miller, in about...' Ridpath checked his watch, 'five minutes. it's just being faxed over from the crime lab.'

'I... I...'

Ridpath leant in closer to the suspect and spoke softly, almost whispering. 'You just said you didn't know him nor had you ever been in his house, yet your fingerprints have been found at a murder scene? We'll take our time but eventually we'll tie you to the other murders.' A long pause. 'You're going to spend the rest of your life inside, Mr Lam. I'll enjoy throwing away the key.'

'I didn't kill nobody, it was nothing to do with me. Im not a murderer.'

'Prove it,' said Ridpath.

'It is not up to my client to prove he is innocent, Inspector, it is for you to prove his guilt.'

Lam glanced across at his solicitor and then at Ridpath. His head went down and he whispered, 'I'll tell you what I know.'

The solicitor grabbed his arm. 'Shut up, you fool.'

'Listen, you don't represent me, you're paid by the syndicate. I'm not going down for life for something I didn't do.' He turned back to Ridpath. 'I'll tell you everything I know, but not while he's here.' He pointed to the solicitor.

Chapter 78

Mrs Challinor entered the courtroom and stared out over the sea of faces looking up at her.

The family was sat on the left with their interpreter. The barrister for New Hampshire Detention Services was in the centre with his solicitor. Anthony Scott was sat next to Archibald Sutton on the right. Further across, the seven members of the jury were already in their positions and waiting.

In the front row were the two remaining witnesses, Stuart Collins and DS Ronald Barnes, with the smirking face of Lucy Bagnall and David Carlton next to them.

The rest of the courtroom was packed with spectators. This inquest had obviously gained a big following through the press reports.

As she sat, the courtroom fell quiet and the journalists' pens hung over their notebooks.

'Ladies and gentleman,' Mrs Challinor began, 'I have the sad task of informing you of the death of one of the witnesses at this inquest. Mr Tony Osborne was murdered yesterday.'

A buzz went around the court, gradually increasing in volume.

Mrs Challinor raised her voice. 'There have been some calls to suggest I abandon this inquest. But I would like to remind everybody, and particularly the jury, our hearing is into the death of Ms Wendy Chen in Wilmslow Immigration Removal Centre. It is not to find out who killed her, that is a job for the police, but to discover how, when and where she died in order to make sure it never happens again. We will now begin the second day of our inquest. Ms Oldfield, please call the first witness. A Mr Stuart Collins.'

Chapter 79

'You know I'm a dead man?'

'We can put you in a witness protection scheme, Mr Lam, but only if you tell us everything you know.'

Lam Tai Kong snorted. 'They'll still find me, wherever I am.'

The solicitor had left the room but the tape was still running.

'We can't help you if you don't help us,' said Emily Parkinson.

Lam Tai Kong bit his bottom lip. 'I had nothing to do with any murders...'

'Convince us.'

'When Xiao Wen was being murdered, I was at Europa Industrial Estate...'

'The one close to Cheadle Heath Police Station?'

Lam nodded.

'For the tape, the witness has just agreed,' interrupted Emily Parkinson.

'What were you doing there?'

'We'd just brought in a container of Vietnamese and we were processing them. The boys and men to work in the cannabis farms, while the women work in our massage or nail parlours.'

'These people were trafficked into this country?'

'Yes, we brought them in via Folkestone on Monday.'

'And who is we?'

'Myself, Liang and two Albanians, I don't know their names. One was the driver of the lorry from Zeebrugge.'

'He's still in Manchester?'

'No, he left as soon as we finished unloading the cargo.'

'Cargo?'

'The Vietnamese.'

Ridpath stared at Lam. 'We need more details, Mr Lam. How often do you bring illegal immigrants into this country?'

'I don't bring them in, the Albanians import them. We just buy the debt from them and put the people to work for us.'

'Explain how it works to me.'

Lam became animated as if detailing a business plan rather than illegal trafficking. 'Once a month, a lorry load is delivered into Manchester from Vietnam or China. We don't deal in Romanians or Africans.'

'How many people?'

'Usually it's 40, but it can be a few more.'

'What happens then?'

'We buy the debt from the Albanians…'

'Sorry, I don't understand,' interrupted Parkinson.

'Most of these people don't pay up front. They are loaned the money to come here.'

'How much does it cost?'

'Around 30,000 pounds. We buy the debt from the Albanians for 15 grand and we put them to work in the clubs, massage parlours and nail shops until they pay off their debt.'

'Forty times 30,000 pounds. That's over one million quid.'

'And don't forget, they are working for us too,' Lam said proudly.

'Did Wendy Chen come in one of the containers?'

Lam nodded. 'She was smart, that one, so we put her to work in the club…'

'Golden Elephant?'

'Where else?'

'Was she with her friend, Yang May Feng?'

'Yeah, you could never split those two up.'

'Where is Yang May Feng now?'

Lam shrugged his shoulders. 'I don't know her address, but she was at the club a couple of nights ago, working. She left with someone, a businessman from Beijing. I'm sure he'll pay her well.'

'So they were both working as prostitutes for you?'

'No, only Yang. Wendy Chen didn't want to do any extras.'

'Extras?'

'Sleep with the customers.'

'Why?'

'She had a boyfriend, didn't she?'

'Did you ever meet him?'

'Nah, she always talked about him, though, how as soon as she had paid us off, they were going to get married and live together.'

'Why didn't the boyfriend pay her debt?'

'I dunno. My own guess: he was just playing her along. He looked married to me.'

'You saw him?'

'A couple of times. I watched as he picked Wendy up from the club. He didn't know I saw him.'

'Could you provide a description?'

'I dunno. White, older, not much hair. All you white guys look the same to me anyway.'

'See if you can get a few more details for a description, Emily. I'll be back in a minute.'

'DI Ridpath is leaving the room.'

Outside, Ridpath stopped for a moment to gather his thoughts before going into the viewing room.

Claire Trent stood as soon as he entered. 'Well done, Ridpath, we've got him on trafficking charges and the importation of illegal immigrants into the UK, not to mention living off immoral earnings and all the rest. He's looking at a five stretch minimum. Paul Dawson will be dead chuffed.'

'But he's not our killer, boss.'

'No, you're right, we need to go through all the evidence we've got. There must be something we're missing.'

'Will he get witness protection?'

'A decision far higher than my pay grade and yours, Ridpath.'

'What if he asks for it?'

'Keep telling him it's available and keep him talking. I want to get details of how the traffickers work.'

Despite the result on Lam Tai Kong, Ridpath felt strangely deflated. They were back to square one again. Who had killed Wendy Chen, Liang Xiao Wen and Tony Osborne? And if it wasn't to cover up the importation of illegal immigrants, why?

'We're going to have to start again at the beginning on the murders, boss. We've gone wrong somewhere.'

'It happens, Ridpath. Let's finish interviewing this man, get a full statement from him and I'll get onto CPS and Paul Dawson. I'm sure he'll want to find out more about the Albanians. Think about it, Ridpath, if they are delivering a lorry a month to Manchester, what about London? Or Birmingham? Or Leeds? Are they getting people to those cities too?'

'You heard him, it's big business, guv'nor, the people are just another cargo. I'll go back in and finish the statement. Mrs Challinor will be disappointed. The inquest finishes today and we have nothing new for her.'

'The coroner does her work and we do ours, Ridpath. Finish the statement.'

'Yes, boss.'

He turned to leave, passing the bulletin board and the poster of Manchester's most wanted criminals, their faces still as ugly as before.

An idea crept its way into Ridpath's head. 'I wonder if it would work?' he said out loud.

'If what would work?' asked Claire Trent.

But Ridpath was already out the door and racing down the corridor.

Chapter 80

'Mr Collins, you told the police you were in London at the time of Wendy Chen's murder, didn't you?'

The man leant forward to the microphone. 'I did.'

'What were you doing there?'

'I was at a meeting.'

'When did you leave for London?'

'On the Friday. I thought I would make a weekend of it.'

'So you weren't around on the morning of August 20th?'

'No.'

Mrs Challinor could feel how weak this line of questioning was. In the absence of any other information, she decided to change the subject. 'But you have heard a knife was found next to Ms Chen's body?'

'That's correct. The knife wasn't from the Centre.'

'How did it get it into Ms Chen's room?'

'I have no idea. Either she brought it in or somebody else did. Since the incident, we have tightened our processes for searching detainees on their entry into the Centre.'

'A bit like closing the stable door after the horse has bolted, Mr Collins?'

Stride was on his feet, glancing across at Anthony Scott. 'I object, Coroner. The aside was a spurious commentary on my client's evidence. Frankly, it continues your disturbing management of this inquest.' Another glance across at both the jury and Scott. 'An inquest whose conduct has come under the scrutiny of the Chief Coroner.'

'Mr Stride, if you do not like my conduct of this inquest, there are channels for you to complain, if you haven't already. However, this inquest is not one of those channels. If you would like to sit, Mr Stride, I will continue my questioning of your client.'

'But—'

'Sit down, Mr Stride.'

The barrister returned to his seat, but the coroner knew his complaint was for one person. The man wearing the pinstripe suit sat on the table on the left.

She decided to press on with the questions. 'There are how many CCTV cameras in the Centre?'

'Off the top of my mind, 36.'

'And how many were inoperative on the night of Ms Chen's death?'

'Six, I believe.'

'Is this normal?'

'It's not normal, but it does happen. New Hampshire Detention Services operates some of the most advanced security and surveillance systems in the country. Unfortunately, it is inevitable some elements of the machinery are not operative at any given moment.'

'But *six* cameras? Out of 36?'

'As I said, New Hampshire operates some of the most sophisticated...'

'I think we heard you the first time, Mr Collins. Does New Hampshire Detention Services spend enough time maintaining its equipment?'

'We have a budget for maintenance, but...'

'I asked you whether it spends enough on maintenance.'

Stuart Collins coughed. 'You can never spend enough on maintenance, particularly when the detainees of the centres actively disable the cameras.'

'So it's the detainees fault the cameras weren't working?'

'I didn't say that. I said you can never ensure all cameras in any of the centres are all working, all of the time.'

The coroner scanned her notes. 'You only had two guards on duty the night of August 19th and the morning of the 20th. Do you think that is enough?'

'Our staffing falls within the guidelines set by the government in its statutory rules governing short term removal centres.'

'Ah yes, the statutory rules.' Mrs Challinor held a sheaf of papers aloft. 'I re-read these last night, and yet I could find no guidelines on staffing rates within them.'

For the first time, Collins appeared flustered. 'That's correct, the government lays down no staffing numbers for short term removal centres. It is up to us what we consider an effective number of staff.'

'Effective or cost-effective, Mr Collins?'

'Effective, Coroner.'

'And I will ask the question again, do you think two guards is enough to look after 34 detainees?'

'I do, Coroner.'

The coroner spent a long time writing in her notebook, to let the jury know she considered this an important point, before she finally returned back to the witness. 'One final question, Mr Collins. As the head of security for New Hampshire Detention Services, how is it possible a detainee was murdered in your Centre?'

'I don't know.'

'Doesn't it worry you? The Centre is one of the most secure places in Manchester and yet somebody was murdered there?'

'Of course it worries me as Head of Security, but I have examined our standard operating procedures and can see no reason for them to be changed.'

'A woman is murdered and you are not responsible?'

'No Coroner, we are not. The only person responsible is the man, or woman, who was the murderer.'

Chapter 81

Ridpath burst into the interview room.

Emily Parkinson calmly announced, 'For the record, DI Ridpath has just returned to the room.'

He strode over to the table and laid the pictures he had taken from the situation room onto it one by one.

'What's this? Who are these people?' asked Lam.

'I want you to take a look at these pictures. Have any of these men been to the club and are any of them the man you saw with Wendy Chen?'

Lam focused on the pictures and smiled. 'About my witness protection...'

'It is available if you co-operate, but the decision rests with the Crown Prosecution Service and officers far more senior than me.'

'That's not good enough.'

'Listen, Mr Lam, you are currently facing three counts of murder, not to mention a whole raft of charges regarding the illegal importation of people into the UK. The only way you clear yourself of suspicion of murder is for us to catch the real killer. You understand? I'll ask you again. Which one of these people do you recognise?'

Lam's eyes moved rapidly from left to right as he weighed his options. 'The witness protection programme? The Albanians will kill me in prison if I talk.'

The door to the interview room opened again.

Emily Parkinson said, 'Detective Superintendent Claire Trent has just entered the room.'

'Mr Lam, if you answer Ridpath's questions, I personally will request witness protection for you.'

'This is my boss, the head of the Major Investigation Team,' said Ridpath.

'You will have helped us apprehend a murderer and stopped a major people-trafficking group from continuing their work. I believe the relevant authorities will support me.'

Lam stared at Claire Trent. 'What proof do I have you will keep your word?'

The detective superintendent pointed to the tape. 'It's still running. What I just said is now on the record. I will keep my promise, but I must emphasise there is no guarantee the authorities will accept my recommendation.'

The suspect thought for a long time. Finally, he reached forward and tapped one of the photographs. 'This man used to come to the club a lot. He liked the girls.'

It was Tony Osborne's picture. 'Was he in the club the night before last?'

'Yeah, he came in about eleven and sat at the bar. He met with the man I knew was Wendy's boyfriend.' He leant forward and tapped another photograph on the table. 'This man.'

Ridpath and Claire Trent stared at each other. The Detective Inspector grabbed the photograph off the table. 'He's at the inquest.'

Chapter 82

'Thank you for your evidence, Mr Collins. Are there any questions from the family?'

The interpreter talked to the mother and father of Wendy Chen and shook her head.

'And Mr Stride?'

The barrister was about to get up but seemed to change his mind and shook his head too.

'Thank you, Mr Collins, you are excused but please remain in the court until the inquest ends. The jury may have questions for you.' Mrs Challinor glanced over at Anthony Scott. He was scribbling furiously in his legal notepad and not looking at her. 'We will now call Detective Sergeant Ronald Barnes.'

The policeman stood and walked slowly to the dock. After he had been sworn in by Jenny Oldfield, he adjusted the microphone and settled in comfortably into the chair.

'You led the police investigation into the death of Wendy Chen in Wilmslow Immigration Removal Centre on the morning of August 20th, is that correct?'

'I did.'

'What time did you arrive at the scene, Detective Sergeant?'

Ron Barnes pulled his notebook out of his inside pocket and flipped it open. 'At 6.25 a.m., ma'am.'

'But the crime was reported by other police at 4.06. Why did it take so long for a detective to come to investigate?'

'As you are aware, Coroner, there have been severe cuts to the police budget in the last few years. All my colleagues were busy investigating a stabbing which had occurred in a pub in the early hours. Nobody was available. The death was reported to our call centre as a suicide and confirmed as such by the responding officers. I came on duty at six a.m. and was immediately dispatched to the scene.'

'Arriving two hours after the first report.'

'Correct, ma'am, for the reasons stated.'

The coroner sniffed once and pulled out a folder from the pile in front of her.

'This is your initial report on the death of Ms Chen, Detective Sergeant.' The report appeared on the screen. 'The only witness statements you took were from the officers of the Removal Centre. You didn't question any other witnesses. Why?'

'I was told the detainees in the rooms close to the death were being deported. It would have been impossible to get interpreters to the centre before the deportations happened.'

'But couldn't you have requested the deportations be halted as these were possible witnesses to a crime?'

'You have to understand, ma'am, at that moment I was supervising the forensics team and the pathologist who were also on the scene. I received no indications from them this was anything other than a suicide. This conclusion was later supported by Dr Ahmed in his forensic report to me.'

'But you are aware Dr Ahmed and Dr Schofield have now changed their view. They now believe Ms Chen was murdered.'

'Yes, ma'am, and I must accept the new pathologist's report. However, I will reiterate, at the time, this was considered a suicide.'

'Considered by whom, Detective Sergeant Barnes?'

'By the Centre's staff and management, by the pathologist and the crime scene manager and by my own examination of the scene. The victim was found with a knife on the floor next to her body.'

'Detective Barnes, I put it to you that your investigation was shoddy, bordering on incompetent. You didn't question any witnesses, you didn't investigate the background of the victim, you didn't even check on the witness, Liang Xiao Wen, who was still in the centre and not transferred until later that day.'

The government's solicitor rose wearily to his feet. 'I must object, Coroner. You are badgering this witness. I must remind you this is not a court of law. You are here to seek the truth, not to apportion blame.'

'It's OK, Mr Sutton, I'm happy to answer the question,' said Ronald Barnes softly. His folded his arms in front of him and he said, 'The coroner is correct. The investigation was not as thorough as it should have been. I made the assumption this was a suicide when I should have examined the evidence and interviewed more witnesses.' There was a long pause. 'I have been doing this job for nearly thirty years and it saddens me I didn't perform to the best of my abilities in this case. I apologise unreservedly to the family.'

Mr Sutton was on his feet again. 'I thank the detective for his apology, but I must say he speaks from a personal capacity rather than as a member of Greater Manchester Police. The force does not accept in any way the investigation was anything other than definitive and robust.'

'Thank you, Detective Barnes, for your honesty. I have no more questions. Would the family like to say anything?'

The interpreter shook her head.

'Mr Stride and Mr Sutton?'

Both barristers didn't want to ask anything.

'In that case, members of the jury, the witness portion of this inquest has finished. We will take a short break and then I will sum up and offer you the possible determinations you can consider for this case. We will return in ten minutes at 11.15 a.m.'

Chapter 83

Yang May Feng shifted position again. Her arms were numb now, the bruised and battered wrists beginning to swell up against the cold metal of the handcuffs.

Last night, he had taken off the gag and slowly, gently fed her the cold fried rice and let her drink from the bottle of water. It was almost as if he enjoyed looking after her, enjoyed feeding her.

She had treated him just like another client. If he wanted to her to play the pliant Oriental wallflower, well, she would oblige. Anything to find a chance to escape before he tired of this game.

Before he left, though, he had put the gag back around her mouth, tightening it even more than before. She struggled against his hands but he was too strong.

She had to stay calm now, plan her escape. Next time he came, she would ask him to release her from the hand-cuffs. Perhaps she could grab something in the house and hit him with it.

She imagined a club striking into his skull, smashing it to pulp.

Why had Wendy been his girlfriend? She was a strong woman, an independent woman. One who wouldn't take shit from nobody. And yet she had been with this man. This animal.

She moved her body again and stared at the ceiling. A fly was buzzing around the light, its solid frame banging against the paper of the shade.

Was she ever going to get out of here?

Chapter 84

The police car raced along Oldham Road, crossing over into the opposing lane, swerving around bollards in the middle of the street, crashing through red lights, the siren wailing and headlights flashing.

In the back, Ridpath was on the phone to Sophia, who wasn't picking up. 'Come on, answer, for God's sake.'

Next to him, Claire Trent was also working the phones. 'Dispatch, I want an armed Police Tactical Unit at East Manchester Coroner's Court immediately.'

Ridpath listened with one ear to the conversation, and the other to the ringing of Sophia's phone.

'ETA in twenty minutes? Not good enough, dispatch. I need them there now. This is a code red emergency, I repeat code red.'

'Hello, Ridpath, where are you? The coroner…'

'Sophia, thank God you answered. I need you to pass a note to Mrs Challinor.'

'But she's in court at the moment. They've just gone back in. She's summing up the inquest…'

Ridpath's body lurched against the car door as Alan Butcher took the corner at speed. Behind him, the tires of the following police car screeched in pain.

'Doesn't matter. Go in and pass her the following note. "Keep everyone there for ten more minutes." Got it?'

Ridpath could hear the sound of pen on paper.

'Got it. I'll go now, but she won't be happy.'

'Just do it.'

'When are you getting here?'

Ridpath peered out of the window. The houses on either side of Queensway were flashing past. 'About eight minutes. Go now, Sophia.'

Before she could answer, Ridpath had switched off the phone.

'PTU will be there in seven minutes. What's our timing, Alan?'

'Less,' was the one word answer.

Ahead, an old Morris Minor was hogging the outside lane. Alan swerved round it onto the opposite side of the road, forcing a minivan to slam on its brakes.

'I would like to arrive in one piece, Alan.'

'Yes, guv'nor.'

They raced through a roundabout without stopping, heading into Stockford Town Centre. A few pedestrians, mainly older women, stopped to look as the two police cars, lights flashing and sirens blaring, sped along the road.

Alan took a hard right against a red light and accelerated to a stop outside the Coroner's Court.

Coming from the opposite direction, three minivans of the Police Tactical Unit screeched to a stop, blocking the middle of the road. Armed officers poured out in a black clad line, rifles at the ready.

Claire Trent and Ridpath jumped out of the car. The commander of the PTU raced over to them.

'What are your orders, ma'am?'

'Surround the court, nobody to go in or out.'

'Yes, ma'am.'

'You and two officers with me. We're going in.'

Chapter 85

Mrs Challinor placed her notes on the desk and took her seat at the front of the court.

The family and the barristers were already seated. Anthony Scott returned late, accompanied by Carol Oates. He hurried to take his seat while she remained near the entrance.

In front of her, Mrs Challinor could see the officials from New Hampshire Detention Services, Lucy Bagnall and David Carlton. Both had broad smiles on their faces as if a long ordeal was finally over.

Next to them, Stuart Collins was sullen, his arms folded across his chest and on his left, Detective Sergeant Ronald Barnes looked down, staring at his hands.

The clock ticked over to 11.17.

'Ladies and gentlemen of the jury. I thank you for your patience and attentiveness during this inquest into the tragic death of Ms Wendy Chen. As I stated at the beginning of this process, this inquest is not about finding somebody guilty or innocent, it's not even about discovering who murdered Ms Chen in the early morning of August 20th 2019...'

At the mention of her daughter's death, Wendy Chen's mother sobbed quietly. Mrs Challinor gazed at the walls as the translator put her arms around the woman's shoulders.

Her husband stared into mid-air stoically, not looking at his wife.

'…we must leave that job to the police. Instead our sole concern in this inquest is to find out how this woman died, where she died, when she died and, if possible, to gather any learnings which would prevent such deaths happening again.'

The double doors at the back of the court banged open and, in the entrance, stood Sophia Rahman. All eyes turned as one to see where the noise was coming from.

She strode to Mrs Challinor's desk, her high heels clicking on the wooden boards of the floor. She reached up to the coroner's desk and placed a folded piece of paper on it, whispering loudly, 'It's from Ridpath.'

Mrs Challinor opened the note. On it was printed in big, bold, black capital letters:

KEEP EVERYONE THERE FOR TEN MORE MINUTES

The coroner closed the note and said, 'Thank you, Sophia.'

She gazed at Anthony Scott. He was furiously whispering in Sutton's ear.

At the back of the court, Carol Oates was smiling.

Mrs Challinor checked the clock.

11.20.

She coughed once and began again. 'As I was saying, ladies and gentlemen of the jury, your job is not to consider guilt or innocence, nor is it give a verdict in this inquest. On the contrary, it is to make a determination as to the cause of death…'

She paused for a moment, glancing at her summary notes. At this point, she was going to give the jury the possible determinations for their consideration when they retired. She thought they wouldn't be long in their deliberations, perhaps returning as early as this afternoon.

She checked the clock.

11.21.

Why ten more minutes, Ridpath, what were you hoping to achieve?

The clerk to the Chief Coroner was checking his watch. Everybody was staring at her. Carol Oates was smiling.

She decided to continue. They were probably going to sack her for this summing up, but she had to give Ridpath more time.

'Ladies and gentlemen of the jury, the facts of the case are not in dispute. The Detainee Custody Officer, Joseph Cummings, found Ms Chen dead in her room at 4.06 a.m. in the early hours of August 20th. According to him, he believed she committed suicide by cutting her throat as there was blood everywhere and a knife on the floor. This view was supported by a pathologist who missed a key injury in the post-mortem and a detective who, in his own words, did not "perform to the best of his abilities". She glanced over to Barnes and Ahmed sitting next to each other, pausing dramatically. 'However, the determination of suicide was undermined when a second post-mortem revealed the presence of Taser marks on the victim's chest and the impossibility of this being a self-inflicted wound.'

She peered at the clock on the wall.

11.23.

'It is not for this inquest to determine, or appear to determine, criminal or civil liability, to apportion guilt or attribute blame.'

She took a deep breath.

'However, in cases such as these, the inquest should set out as many of the facts as the public interest requires. Under the terms of Article 2 of the European Convention of Human Rights, governments are required to "establish a framework of laws, precautions, procedures and means of enforcement which will, to the greatest extent reasonably practicable, protect life". The European Court of Human Rights has interpreted this as mandating independent official investigation of any death where public servants may be implicated. Since the Human Rights Act 1998 came into force, in those cases alone, the inquest is now able to consider the broader question "by what means and in what circumstances" did the death occur.'

11.25.

She had to keep going for at least five more minutes. She gazed across at the seven stolid faces of the jury. They were watching her placidly, listening to every word she said.

She took a deep breath and talked slowly, enunciating her words, the voice of the interpreter in Mandarin a whisper in the background.

'Ladies and gentlemen of the jury, until we leave the European Union, the articles of the European Court of Human Rights still apply. This inevitably leads us to an examination of the actions of New Hampshire Detention Services. It pains me to suggest this, but I believe this company has been more concerned about their corporate reputation and the possibility of further lucrative contracts from the government, than in caring about a young woman who was in their jurisdiction.'

The smiles had vanished from David Carlton and Lucy Bagnall. Anthony Scott threw the pencil he was holding onto the desk.

11.26.

'Indeed, you may want to ask yourselves, ladies and gentlemen of the jury, whether two custody officers is the correct staffing to look after 34 vulnerable detainees? In addition, the constant malfunction of indispensable equipment, in this case CCTV cameras, and the almost slave-like adherence to "standard operating procedures" at the cost of detainee welfare and health, may force you to question whether New Hampshire Detention Services is a company that should be allowed to operate Immigrant Removal Centres in the first place.'

11.27.

'I would like to say one more thing…'

As the coroner spoke, the doors to the court burst open. Claire Trent and Ridpath strode into the room, accompanied by three armed police officers, Heckler & Koch rifles at their shoulders as they fanned out through the court.

Claire Trent marched up to the front row with Ridpath by her side. She stood in front of one man and said, 'Ronald Barnes, I am arresting you on suspicion of the murder of Wendy Chen, Liang Xiao Wen and Tony Osborne. You do not have to say anything, but it may harm your defence if you do not mention when questioned something you later rely on in court. Anything you do say may be given in evidence.'

Chapter 86

Barnes jumped up and with an agility belying his age and weight, grabbed hold of Stuart Collins around the neck, pressing a Taser to the man's head.

Claire Trent stopped in her tracks.

The policemen continued to circle around the court, their rifles pointing directly at Barnes.

David Carlton and Lucy Bagnall scrambled away to the left, knocking over chairs in the rush to get away. The group of reporters panicked and fought to get out of the court, pushing and shoving each other out of the way. The barristers, Antony Scott and Archibald Sutton, ran to the door, fighting with the reporters over who would be first to escape.

Only Wendy Chen's family remained seated with the interpreter by their side, the old man's face as stoic as it had always been.

Mrs Challinor jumped up and shouted to Jenny Oldfield. 'The jury room at the back, take them in and lock the door.'

The officer manager herded the jurors towards the rear of the court, glancing over her shoulder continually at the action behind her.

Ridpath stayed near Claire Trent, his eyes on Ron Barnes and the Taser next to Collins' head.

'You can't get away, Ron,' she said softly.

Barnes was backing towards the witness box, his eyes darting left and right. 'Get out of my way. If you don't, he gets it.'

He jabbed the Taser harder into Stuart Collin's temple. The man yelped with pain.

Claire Trent walked forward slowly, her hands raised. 'You know we can't do that, Ron. Give up now, you're not going to get away.'

The detective sergeant continued to edge backwards, holding on to his hostage, his body turning this way and that as he tried to put Collins between himself and the rifles of the police tactical unit. 'You're going to let me out of here in thirty seconds or he gets it.'

He jabbed the Taser deep into Collins ear. The man yelped in pain, shouting 'Let him out, let him out.'

At the door, the reporters had all fought their way out with just two brave souls staying to film what happened.

Barnes continued to inch backwards. He didn't see the raised edge of the podium of the witness stand until it was too late. His foot caught it and his body jackknifed forward, arms letting go of the hostage for a split second.

Stuart Collins seized his chance and twisted free of Barnes' grasp. The Taser in the detective's hand was jolted sideways to point directly at Claire Trent. She flinched, throwing her hands up to protect her face.

Two loud bangs on the left and the strong, pungent smell of nitroglycerine wafted through the court.

Ron Barnes fell to the floor and didn't move, blood oozing from a wound to his chest and one to his temple.

'I thought he was going to shoot. I thought he had a gun,' shouted the policeman on the left, a thin vein of smoke still coming out of the end of the barrel of his rifle.

Ridpath kicked the Taser away from Barnes' hand and knelt down beside the body, placing his hand on Barnes' neck.

He was as dead as his victims.

Chapter 87

Three hours later and Ridpath, Claire Trent and the Mrs Challinor were sitting in the Coroner's Office.

Outside, the baying shouts of countless journalists all demanding the latest information drifted in through the half-open window.

They had finished giving their witness statements to the Deputy Chief Constable, the forensics team had taken their fingerprints and the body of Ronald Barnes had been removed from the court to a crescendo of flashing lights and whirring television cameras.

'We'll have to go out eventually,' said the coroner.

'Let's wait another ten minutes or so. I'll arrange and escort for you and make sure somebody is posted outside your house tonight.'

Ridpath's phone rang. It was Emily Parkinson. He covered his ear and moved to the far corner to take the call.

'How would they know my address?'

'It won't be difficult to find. For a case like this, "Policeman shot dead in courtroom", you may even have the foreign press and television there too.'

'Oh, God, no.'

'I wouldn't answer the phone tonight either. My bet is they'll be ringing you with offers of exclusives as soon as they discover your number.'

Ridpath switched off the phone and came back to rejoin the coroner and Claire Trent. 'That was Emily Parkinson. Since Lam Tai Kong heard about the death of Barnes, he's been singing like the proverbial canary. Apparently, Barnes was part of the Syndicate, taking a cut of every person smuggled into Manchester.'

'No wonder he could afford the place in Bramall,' said Claire Trent.

'His job was to let the Albanians and Lam Tai Kong know about police investigations into their activities and tip them off if any operation was planned against them. The Syndicate seem to have their fingers in a lot of the pies of organised crime. This bust has barely scratched the surface. I wonder how many other police they have corrupted?'

'Luckily, that's not our job, Ridpath.'

'I have a feeling it might be in the future, boss.'

'But how did Barnes get involved?' asked the coroner.

'The end of a career? Greed? Perhaps he was always corrupt...'

'No, I meant why did he get involved with these murders?'

'He was Wendy Chen's boyfriend...'

'So why did she go to him to report on their activities?'

Ridpath shrugged his shoulders. 'We can only guess she didn't know he was involved with the Syndicate who had smuggled her into the country. They are searching his house as we speak. They've found multiple passports, foreign currency and two other Tasers, each with ten wire pods ready to be fired.'

'He killed Wendy Chen?' asked Mrs Challinor.

'Probably, although now he's dead, we'll never know for certain. All we have is that he was seen talking to Tony Osborne the night before that man's death. With a bit of luck, the search of his house will uncover more evidence.'

'So that means...' the coroner tugged at the skin around her jaw, '...if he hadn't panicked in the court and seized Stuart Collins, he would still be alive and denying every-thing.'

'True,' answered Claire Trent.

'I still want to release Wendy Chen's body to her parents tomorrow.'

'I won't stand in your way,' answered Claire Trent.

'Thank you. It just leaves one outstanding matter. Have you decided yet, Ridpath?'

'Decided what, Coroner?'

'Whether you are staying with this court or moving back to work with Claire in MIT.'

Ridpath stared at his boss. 'You told her?'

'Four days ago, as soon as I made you the offer. It wouldn't have been right to keep it from Mrs Challinor.'

Ridpath's phone rang again. He checked the number displayed on the screen. It was Dr Morris from the hospital. What did he want? And then he remembered: the results from his blood test. The doctor was going to tell him today whether his myeloma had returned.

'Well, have you decided?' asked Claire Trent.

Ridpath ignored the question and answered the call.

'Hello, is that Detective Inspector Ridpath?'

'Speaking.'

'It's Dr Morris of Christie's. Regarding your blood test...'

Ridpath held his breath and crossed his fingers.

'...it's good news, your white blood cell count is normal. It's right in the middle of the standard range. The previous test must have been a rogue result.'

'Thank you, it's taken a load off my mind.'

'Good, I'll see you on... October 20th for your next blood test. Please make an appointment.'

'Thank you.'

He switched the phone off, looking across the table at the two women.

Claire Trent asked again., 'Well, Ridpath?'

'I am, actually. Very well. The truth is I haven't decided yet. I'm going to take the weekend off and take my family to the Lakes. I'll discuss it with Polly and give you both an answer when I get back.'

Ridpath smiled at both of them.

For the first time in a long while, he felt in total control of his life.

Epilogue

The body of Yang May Feng was found three weeks later when the Hong Kong businessman returned to his flat.

He noticed a strange smell as soon as he entered the apartment, finding Ms Yang still lying on the bed, her mouth gagged and her arms handcuffed to the headboard.

At the subsequent post-mortem, the pathologist, not Dr Schofield, found she had died from the collapse of her internal organs, caused by the combined effects of dehydration and starvation.

She was eventually declared the fourth victim of Detective Sergeant Ronald Barnes.

As no next of kin could be found, she was buried in an unmarked grave in Southern Cemetery.

Only one person went to the funeral.

Detective Inspector Thomas Ridpath.

DI Ridpath Crime Thriller

Where The Truth Lies
Where The Dead Fall
Where the Silence Calls
Where the Innocent Die